THE PILGRIM

THE PILGRIM

BOOK FOUR of the ALFORD SAGA

PAUL ALMOND

McArthur & Company
Toronto

First published in Canada in 2012 by
McArthur & Company
67 Mowat Ave., Suite 241
Toronto, ON
M6K 3E3
www.mcarthur-co.com

LIBRARY AND ARCHIVES CANADA CATALOGUING IN PUBLICATION
Almond, Paul, 1931-
The pilgrim / Paul Almond.

(The Alford saga ; bk. 4)
ISBN 978-1-77087-163-2

I. Title. II. Series: Almond, Paul, 1931- . Alfod saga ; bk. 4.

PS8601.L56P55 2012 C813'.6 C2012-900166-X

The publisher would like to acknowledge the financial support of the Government of Canada through the Canada Book Fund and the Canada Council for our publishing activities. The publisher further wishes to acknowledge the financial support of the Ontario Arts Council and the OMDC for our publishing program.

Canada
Canada Council for the Arts Conseil des Arts du Canada
Ontario Arts Council Conseil des Arts de l'Ontario
Ontario Ontario Media Development Corporation Société de développement de l'industrie des médias de l'Ontario

Cover design by Devon Pool
Cover photograph by Linda Rutenberg
Interior design by Tania Craan
Printed and bound in Canada by Trigraphik | LBF printing

10 9 8 7 6 5 4 3 2 1

To

my lovely wife

Joan

who makes everything possible

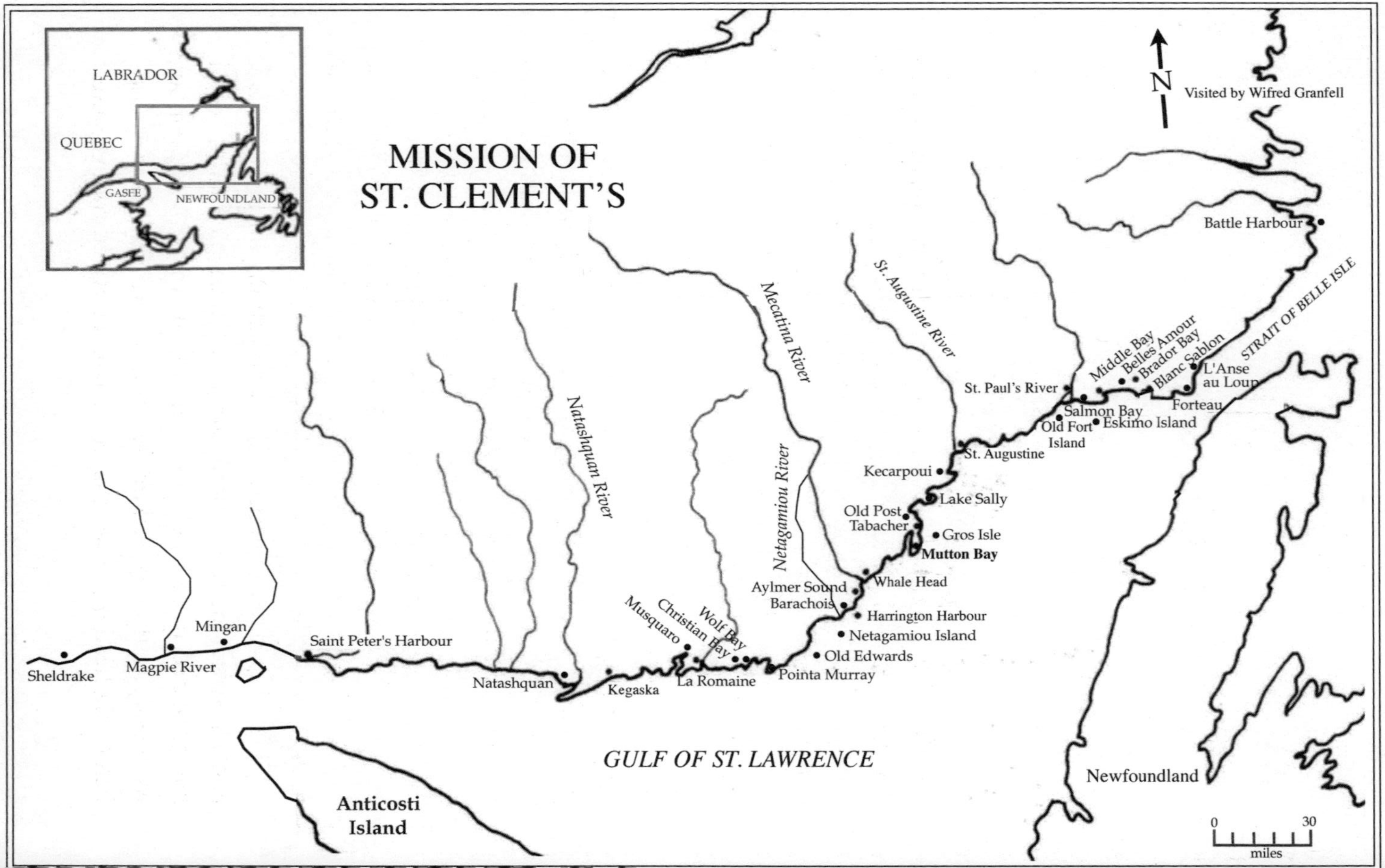
MISSION OF
ST. CLEMENT'S
LABRADOR
QUEBEC
GASFE
NEWFOUNDLAND
N
Visited by Wifred Granfell
Battle Harbour
STRAIT OF BELLE ISLE
L'Anse
au Loup
Forteau
Blanc Sablon
Brador Bay
Belles Amour
Middle Bay
St. Paul's River
Salmon Bay
Eskimo Island
Old Fort
Island
St. Augustine
St. Augustine River
Mecatina River
Kecarpoui
Lake Sally
Old Post
Tabacher
Gros Isle
Mutton Bay
Whale Head
Netagamiou River
Aylmer Sound
Barachois
Harrington Harbour
Netagamiou Island
Old Edwards
Pointa Murray
Wolf Bay
Christian Bay
Musquaro
La Romaine
Kegaska
Natashquan River
Natashquan
Saint Peter's Harbour
Mingan
Magpie River
Sheldrake
GULF OF ST. LAWRENCE
Anticosti
Island
Newfoundland
0
30
miles

Chapter One

September 1896

I just loved facing this east wind — my favourite spot on the schooner these past two days. Leaning in the prow against the wooden breast hook, I got time away from the passengers for a good think about my days ahead in the mission of St. Clement's, the largest church territory in all Quebec. My first posting: four hundred and fifty miles of barren coastline on the Canadian Labrador.

What had his Lordship the Bishop been thinking? Only a month ago, in August, I had been summoned to his office at the cathedral in Quebec City. Bishop Andrew Hunter Dunn had been selected from among the British clergy in London five years previously. A man who knew what he wanted, they all told me, not one to be argued with, not one who took his duties lightly, but a good, godly man. If I were lucky enough to get a parish, where would he assign me? Somewhere on the Gaspé, I expected. After all, only a few weeks before I had graduated from Bishop's University with my B.A. and then taken Holy Orders as deacon.

The ship gave a lurch as she went about on another tack and I grasped the breast hook firmly. Against the fearful cold I had wrapped myself well, for although it was only September, we were already several hundred miles northeast of the Gaspé Peninsula heading down the St. Lawrence River, though surely well beyond its mighty flow, sailing now through the rough salt currents of the Gulf of St. Lawrence.

I must've seemed a lonely figure in my dark coat, wrapped with my scarf and fur hat, every inch, I supposed, the lone clergyman going off into the unknown. I did see myself as rather heroic. Or perhaps I was thinking this way to quash the fears that kept washing over me. How on earth would I ever fulfill those enormous expectations? A parish so large! Settlements so scattered! And everyone so poor...

That final meeting with the bishop had given me heart, but also some solid misgivings: "Young man, I am sending you into one of the most inhospitable places on earth. Never have I been to the jungles of South America nor have I travelled in the deserts of the Sahara and the Gobi. But I have been to the Labrador, and I can tell you that nothing on earth compares to its hostile and forbidding environment. You will find almost no forests — nothing but barren rock on which their houses perch, haphazard, unprotected from the elements, with little affinity for their landscape.

"Their inhabitants are hard, tough, and unyielding like the very rocks on which they live. Mind you, they need to be, just to survive."

"My Lord Bishop —" I began, but Bishop Dunn dismissed my interjection with a wave of his hand. "I know what you will ask: why not send a more experienced clergyman? Well, I shall tell you. None but the fittest could survive in that largely forgotten land. I have been looking over your records at that fine university and have been corresponding with your able professors. They tell me you are of an athletic bent and that physical undertakings cause no hardship. So while I would agree that it is a daunting prospect for one so young, I have no doubt, from what I've heard, that you'll rise to the challenge magnificently."

I dropped my eyes. "If you say so, my Lord Bishop." I just hoped he would not be disappointed.

"I myself was there just a short time ago, last summer in fact, when I consecrated the tiny church in Mutton Bay, your future headquarters. I also selected a site for another church in Harrington Harbour. It was summer," he seemed to relax at the memory, "and the weather was kind, the people most generous of spirit." He paused and then looked at me with an almost sorrowful gaze. "But imagine those long winter nights of darkness! How that isolation must weigh upon their souls! It defies my imagination how any man cares for his family in such conditions, where few venture and even fewer survive."

Not a very encouraging send-off.

But now, as Julius Caesar said, the die had been cast. Here I was on the schooner *La Canadienne* heading for my first assignment, letting the wind tear fitfully at my face and its gusts threaten my footing on the pitching deck. I even felt certain that now, in this next year, I would finally achieve that long-hidden yearning to meet — in some curious way — actually meet, my Saviour. Walking beside me, or face to face in a vision, who knew? But I had nurtured this secret longing within myself for as long as I could remember (developed I suppose from some forgotten children's tale). I had often dismissed it as a foolish dream, but still it had grown in those crevices at the back of my mind. Indeed, a wild dream, possibly to be fulfilled on these granite shores.

How the past three years of university had flown! Coming home that first Christmas in 1983 after three months in university, arriving at Matapedia, I had been filled with foreboding. How would my family take my decision? Because I was the first from the Coast to go to university, it had been silently presumed I'd become a doctor and return to the Coast. We had left Montreal late in the afternoon, and my companion in the train carriage was still fast asleep; we had gossiped long into the night.

"Matapedia, next stop, five minutes." Matapedia was the junction point for all the Gaspé. There had been some talk of a railway branch line coming our way, and beyond, as far as Gaspé town, but so far nothing. After all, it was only fifteen years ago that they had completed this line from Montreal to Halifax.

The burly conductor stomped past and my travelling companion awakened. With freckles and sandy hair, Frank was three or four years younger than me. He had accompanied his father to Montreal to check into some shipping affiliations and now was going back to Halifax to continue his studies for a second mate's ticket. In the spring, he planned to sign onto one of his father's schooners sailing from Nova Scotia.

Not the life I would lead, I had told him: I wasn't at all keen on the bounding main. But what kind of a life did I expect? Had my decision about the future been taken rather too hastily? Had I just been bamboozled by my companions? Carried away by youthful exuberance?

"Getting off here, John, are ya?" Frank leaned close to the window and cupped his hand around his eyes to see out. "Pretty heavy snowfall."

I mumbled an affirmative to disguise my nervousness. If Old Poppa came with Lively, our fine but now rather aged horse, how would we make it all the way home, a good hundred miles? Out the window, those big fluffy flakes seemed likely to continue all this day.

I felt the train slowing down. Not a bad ride, I thought: nice spacious carriage, red leather seats, and rather attractive lighting under the curved cream-coloured ceiling. When I had left that first September in '83, all the family had gathered: six brothers and sisters, from Mac and Molly down to little Earle, two years old, and of course my dear mother. As I had looked down out of the buggy, ready to set off, I could see her blue eyes bright with tears. She rarely showed any emotion, understandably, having raised seven children. Of medium height but thin to the point of being skinny, she had always worked hard from morning till night, as do most mothers hereabouts. Old Poppa too, even though he must have been sixty, had the wiry frame of a young worker, though his long drooping mustache, turning grey, made him seem more of a paterfamilias. Still bounding with energy though, no doubt about that.

When the train had jolted to a stop, I wrapped round the wool scarf Momma had knitted me, tugged on my hat, and put my hand out to shake Frank's vigorously. "I've sure enjoyed talking with you, Frank. I expect we'll meet again, you travelling on that schooner and such."

"Oh for sure. If we call in at Paspébiac or somewheres near, I'll make sure to find you. Have a good Christmas, now. And good luck with them studies."

"You too." I had grabbed my leather suitcase and joined the other three or four travellers descending from our carriage.

Lord, that snow was coming down! I got off at the far end of the platform and, without pausing, made straight for the huddle of men stamping their feet by the naked lantern underneath the station overhang.

I was so pleased to see my father, I don't know what came over me. My initial impulse was to give him a big hug, though of course we never did that. So when he hauled off his mitt and stretched out his hand, I hauled off mine and grabbed his in both my hands. We stood for a moment looking at each other in a silent moment. Then we turned and headed over to the sleigh where Lively stood waiting.

A couple of older men said they thought I looked like Old Poppa when he was a young man, but I just don't see that. Except, perhaps, for my bushy eyebrows. But whereas he was fairly tall, certainly thin and wiry, I myself am more chunky, more solidly built, and by no means could I be considered fearsome. My sturdy build, and the fact that I'm pretty fit, did allow me to make the first rugby team at Bishop's. I'm pretty proud of that. And I might even do well in the spring, I had thought, when we got to racing. But my hair is thin and my head set squarely and firmly on my body. And I'm even a bit short.

"You came alone, Poppa? Not sure I like the look of all this!" I hurried to throw my bag in the back and pull a covering over to keep it dry. I climbed up, but we couldn't see more than a few yards ahead.

"She's been coming down terble," Old Poppa said. "We had a job to find our way these last few miles. Decided to come the whole way last night afore it got too bad. Slep' in the station. But Lively's done this twice, so I reckon he'll know his way back. If it don't turn too cold and freeze up, like they been saying at the station." He leapt up next to me, spry as ever, and grabbed the reins. "Giddap," he called and off we went.

Dawn seemed to be lifting. Across our knees, the sheepskin blanket that we call a "buffalo" was covered in snow, and Lively had slowed to a crawl. "Why not try the bay?" I asked. "Might be fewer snowdrifts." I don't know what possessed me, but I felt a little panic creeping in.

"That ice, she's not solid enough. Last night I saw a lot of slush. Lively's had a long hard run the last two days. I don't blame him for tiring none."

"Time we got a new horse," I mumbled through my scarf.

What a time to find myself on the road home with Old Poppa frozen to death!

"Been thinking that way myself. But he's a terble fine stud. Hardly a farmer don't ask for him to service their mares in the fall of the year when I pass with the mail." Poppa delivered the mail from New Richmond down to Shigawake and then beyond to Pabos, where it was taken by another fella on to Gaspé.

In the silence that ensued, I turned my thoughts from these approaching dangers to my big career decision. How would I ever break the news?

After a couple of hours of heavy slogging through snowy woods, in which I despaired of ever making it, I noticed Lively take on a bit of speed. The next village of Restigouche, I wondered? No, instead, a sturdy, square, stone building. Poppa gave an exclamation of satisfaction. "Never thought he'd find it. Trust Lively to know where there's a house!"

Lively turned in: he'd had enough. Poppa got down, walked over and banged on the door.

It was opened by a young man in his thirties who looked at us with some suspicion. "Lost your way?"

"No, but… Ah... Is Mr. Robert Busteed in?"

The man shook his head. "We lost my uncle last summer."

"Oh, I'm so sorry." Poppa seemed nonplussed. "Well, I'd sure appreciate it if we could stop in for a few minutes while my horse gets his breath."

Almost grudgingly, I thought, the man opened the door and we stepped through into the hall. Poppa stuck out his hand. "I'm Jim Alford, and this here is my son John, a student up at Bishop's University."

"Thomas Busteed. I'm Robert's nephew." They shook hands and Thomas reached for Poppa's coat. "You knew him?"

"Yes, but one whale of a long time ago. When I was nineteen,

I came through here heading to Montreal. In the 1850s." We began to shed our snowy garments.

From upstairs came a woman's voice. "What is it, Thomas?"

"Two travellers, one b'the name of Jim Alford."

I happened to be looking up the stairs and saw the woman, probably in her seventies or eighties, drop the towel she was carrying and hold onto the banister.

"Are you all right, Aunt Elizabeth?" Thomas asked

"Yes, yes. I'll get Helen, and we'll be right down." She turned, and hurried off.

Well, I thought, this indeed meant something. But what?

This old stone house had fine furniture, no doubt, and a separate dining room. On the thick walls hung pictures, some portraits, indicating a refined taste. Over a hundred years old, I was told, to which I replied, so's ours! But ours had been built onto, rooms added, and was made of wood, with little to speak of on the walls. During our nourishing breakfast, I kept watching my father and Elizabeth. Even at her age, probably in her seventies or eighties, she seemed unusually shy in his presence, and almost, if I may use the word for an elderly lady, coquettish. My father, for his part, seemed to be disguising an emotion that lurked just beneath the surface. What was it between the two of them?

The answer was not easily forthcoming.

While trying to figure out this curious relationship, I was prodded for details of my first three months at Bishop's University. "It's such a fine place," I waxed enthusiastically, "with all that red brick, some ivy starting to climb up, those pointed towers like really old buildings; they say it's neo-Gothic. Our comfortable dormitory, you just really feel like studying, like reading everything you can get your hands on."

"And they keep you at it?" Helen asked. She was shrunken, but clearly had been graceful and ladylike, but was now struggling against the onslaught of age.

"They sure do, Miss Busteed, though it's not necessary. We're all doing our best to learn as much as we can, and as quickly. This opportunity my family has given me will not be wasted, I can assure you."

I noticed a look of appreciation in Poppa's eye. "He's sure gonna be the best doctor in all Canada."

That took me aback! "A doctor, Poppa? We've never discussed —"

"Of course we did. You said many times —"

"Well, I admit you mentioned it, but surely there was no definite thought of me pursuing that career."

"Why else did we send you? Why, it was here in this very house I met Daniel Busteed, who was, I presume," Poppa said, turning to Thomas, "your uncle?" Thomas nodded, and Poppa went on, "He was good enough to take me for a drive to show me his hospital across the bay in Campbellton."

"It was hardly his hospital, Mr. Alford," Thomas said. "But it is true that he brought back what little knowledge — and I'm afraid I must emphasize little — that he had acquired on his one trip to London. He worked here with it all his life, caring for his good neighbour."

"Yep, told me all that. We drove in his fine sleigh, I remember, and his horse really impressed me." I hadn't often heard Poppa being quite so fulsome. But he was young at the time and the recollection must have been important to him. "When I got home a year later, first thing I did was persuade my own father to get us a horse like that." He turned to me. "Our first Lively. I was about your age, John, in fact, younger."

With that he glanced at Elizabeth, who I swear seemed to

blush. A light shone in her eyes, though her gnarled fingers, crippled with arthritis, were hard to ignore as she tried to grip her spoon and raise the porridge to her mouth.

I hoped this discussion of my future would not go any further. I hadn't realized how important my being a doctor was to Poppa. I had decided upon a career that was quite contrary to his wishes, but one that focussed all my thinking and drove me even more conscientiously to books and learning. I changed the subject. "So, Poppa, you stayed here overnight?"

"Three days, I think. On the way to Montreal."

Montreal? I'd never heard him mention that. "Really? You went to Montreal?"

"Yes, but we aren't going into all that now. It's long gone. The only thing I learned was, nothing is nowheres as good as our old homestead. I've stayed ever since."

He'd closed that line of questioning, but it certainly opened another avenue of thought. I adjudged from their present ages that Elizabeth had been older than father, and the two sisters had remained spinsters. When their brother had died earlier this year, they had written to this nephew, Thomas, who had left here at nineteen, crossed the continent, adventured down the Columbia River, and then lived in Spokane. They had offered to leave him this house if he were to return. And return he had, three months ago.

"Well," Poppa said, "I thank you ladies for the finest breakfast I've had for a long time." He rose. "And Elizabeth," he paused, seeming to control some hidden feelings, "it's real good to see you again, looking so very fine."

She smiled and dropped a little curtsey in his direction. As well she might: I didn't find her looking quite that fine.

"Lots of time, lots of time," Thomas said.

"Not lots of time," my father answered. "Long drive ahead of us. I doubt we'll even make it to New Richmond in this heavy blizzard. Not a lot of markers between here and Cross Point, neither. But Lively will find his way."

I was not so sure. But much as I dreaded the trip to come, I was worried even more about what might happen when I made the announcement of my newly chosen path.

Chapter Two

The day broke with a smile over the Gulf of St. Lawrence. I came right up on deck as dawn was lifting and a low sun was rising over the eastern waters, the wind crisp and cold. There ahead of me, in answer to all my anticipation, lay Sheldrake, on the shores of the Labrador and the extreme western end of St. Clement's mission, or perhaps beyond its limits, for all I knew. I had received a curious message in Quebec City that the local clergyman, Reverend Charles Eugene Bishop, would meet me here, although I knew our mission boat was anchored down by Natashquan — he used it to visit all the outports. I was not sure how Mr. Bishop intended us to get to our mission boat, but I presumed he had it all worked out. We'd then head for Mutton Bay, our headquarters.

I fingered my starched white collar, put on especially for the reception committee on the dock even though I was just a deacon, having been ordained such on August thirtieth in Holy Trinity Cathedral before leaving. My heart was full of anticipation and my head churned with thoughts. I rejoiced that the Lord had brought me to such an enormous task and hoped that He would not have done so had He not known me capable. But as a mere mortal, oh yes, I did have my own doubts. Mr. Bishop had himself been admitted into the full priesthood only this summer and therefore was nominally priest-in-charge. But with a diocese this large, I presumed that we would be sharing duties, myself taking some minor portion of the wide-ranging area.

As I looked more closely, I was surprised to see nothing of the barren grey granite Bishop Dunn had described. Here was a well-forested shore so far as I could see from this distance. Had he made it all up to prepare me for the worst? Well, I would soon know a good deal more. Down I went for breakfast.

The meal on the schooner was ample and I breakfasted well, partaking of more than I should, perhaps, but then again, I knew not what the day would bring. Sailing before a bright wind we had passed one or two moored schooners and on the dock, which I could soon see plainly, men were unloading a couple of fishing boats, codfish of course, though the season was coming to an end. But certainly, no delegation had gathered to greet my arrival. Doubtless they'd be seeking shelter from the wind in the small building at the shore end of the dock.

Our schooner soon dropped anchor and I and another passenger were helped into a dory lowered to take us ashore. I had arranged with the captain to have my main trunk dropped off at Natashquan where our mission boat was moored, so that I could travel these many miles lightly, not knowing whether we would be walking, or going, as I suspected, in a horse and buggy. So in my grip I carried a few clothes, my Bible, and my copy of *Pilgrim's Progress* to sustain me through these first exciting days of my new posting.

Two sturdy sailors rowed us ashore and helped us up onto the dock or — as it is called here — the stagehead, that portion of a wharf stretching out over the water from the shed, itself called a stage. I pulled up my suitcase and turned to make the acquaintance of my parishioners.

Not one had appeared.

Gracious! Had I made a mistake? Should I quickly go back

to the schooner and sail on to Magpie River? No, the captain had told me he was making straight for Natashquan where his next passengers and freight would be put ashore; he'd not be too pleased to make a detour, especially as I had paid my ticket only to Sheldrake. Well, this was just the sort of situation that I should get used to: unforeseen circumstances. And deal with it I must.

The fishermen, mostly French-speaking, were nonetheless accommodating. No sign of any clergyman here certainly, though several had heard of Mr. Bishop. While I was deciding on the best course of action, one fisherman told me in broken English that when he had left Magpie River, a clergyman had been seen going from house to house. I presumed therefore that Magpie was where I should have met Mr. Bishop. I inquired about a horse and buggy, but the men laughed: no horses hereabouts, that's for sure. Skiffs, dories, rowboats, and in the winter, komatiks, that curious wooden sled pulled by teams of huskies, that was how one got around on this far northern shore of the St. Lawrence River. So shank's mare, just plain ol' walking, it had to be. With a thong that I managed to acquire, thanks to my clerical collar, I lifted my suitcase on my back and carried it by means of this improvised tumpline round my forehead, as my father had demonstrated from his own early pioneer days. I set off walking as vigorously as possible, for Magpie was a good twenty-five miles distant.

How far all this was from my little Shigawake. Back at the Old Homestead, my announcement that I would become a clergyman had been met with consternation, incredulity, and also, I'm pleased to say, much delight. Old Poppa, who had spent many evenings in our youth reading us the Bible, admitted the church to be a worthy calling. One day, I might even be going back there as clergyman. Would I actually enjoy that? I had seen how various factions there approved or disapproved of things the clergy did or didn't do over the years. Of course, as long as I can remember, Mother took me to church with Molly, and later Mac, while Poppa stayed outside with the other men to gossip and exchange manly talk. The church itself had only just been built five years before I was born, largely due, Poppa told us, to him getting a few neighbours together, for it had been my grandfather's dying wish. I do remember when I was four or five they erected the steeple. And then, before building the church, my grandfather with his youngest son, my father, had organized getting our school constructed in the Skenes's lower field — the one that I went to. Against some opposition, apparently, which I now find hard to believe. In fact, when Poppa was young, he himself, with our team of oxen, hauled the timbers for those foundations.

I hiked without a stop all morning, but made myself sit and take a short break at lunchtime. I was doubly pleased at having eaten my large breakfast, for though I had felt pangs of hunger, I was able to vanquish them. Of course, *Pilgrim's Progress* came into play, for there I was, the protagonist, Christian, striding down the road of life, along a well-worn trail through fairly heavy woods — much the kind of forest I was accustomed to in the Gaspé, though here the spruce were shorter, and on the whole the birch and alder had not attained any great size. Not a lot of maple either, which grew in profusion in the Gaspé. I only passed one traveller, moving slowly with his wife, who did indeed confirm that this was the way to Magpie. I looked up as I heard over my head the familiar calling of a skein of Canada geese, flying south. And lo, before the afternoon was half over, I beheld a man coming toward me who must be none other than the good Reverend Mr. Eugene Bishop.

In no time at all, we were chatting like old friends. Gene

was tall, quite thin, clean shaven, with sadly prominent ears and large, almost effeminate lips. But a dear man, with a good sense of fun. For some reason, which we both dismissed as quickly as the subject was brought up, we had each been mistaken in our destination: Sheldrake, I found out, was not even a part of St. Clement's Parish. So we had each, in our own fashion, set out to rectify the mistake. And thus had met on the path to Magpie.

"Now in a few hundred yards, I know of a turning I would like us to take," Gene said. "A fine family have set up home here, and we should call in on them for they receive a clergy visit rarely, I'm afraid."

I readily agreed, and in due course we found ourselves knocking on the door of the Foremans. It was little more than a log cabin, built recently of modest proportions, but quite sufficient until the owner acquired more substance.

What a look of delight on the young man's face! He could not have been more than twenty, at the most. "The Good Lord has sent you, Mr. Gene! Welcome, welcome."

"Thank you, Ralph," Gene said, and in we went. From the table arose a young and exceedingly pregnant lady, obviously his wife, whom he introduced as Esther.

Gene presented me as the new deacon assigned to our parish and I shook Ralph's hand, and Esther's. She only seemed about seventeen, with lovely brown eyes, now lit by a warm smile. "We've been hoping you'd come, Mr. Gene, because I'm not well enough to travel to Natashquan —"

"And never sure when you'd be here," Ralph interjected.

"Well, Mrs. Foreman," I said, "this is a delight for me. I've just been assigned to this lovely —"

Ralph held up his hand. "Oh, she's not 'Mrs.' yet. That's what we want you gentlemen to do now."

Well! I confess I was struck dumb. Here this young couple

had been living in sin for Lord knows how long, and had not been joined in Holy Matrimony! What on earth would Gene do? They seemed so happy to see us that the stern admonishments on the tip of my tongue about their vile deed might not be so appropriate. I was in an agony of indecision.

"Well well well," Gene said, "I expect we can arrange that this very afternoon, if that would please you?"

"Oh, it pleases us the very best," Ralph applied. "Now Esther, you get these fellas a cup of tea and something to eat and I'll run to our neighbours, only half a mile away, and there's another couple beyond — I'll invite them all. We'll have a real wedding party!" He seemed indeed happy, and once I thought about Gene's selection of words, the wind was quite taken from my sails. There would always be time to condemn this practice, but again, with no clergyman anywhere near for months at a time, perhaps the Church's view on the matter should be revisited. And how indeed could one publish the banns in this forsaken place? So here I was, my first day in my parish, about to marry a couple who had lived in sin for months, and with our apparent blessing? I did have some adapting to do, I could see that.

That night, I don't know where they all came from, but a good dozen or more villagers were dancing around the cozy room to the tune of a fiddle that some old fellow had produced. Rum flowed like water and everyone seemed to be enjoying themselves, so that this time, I even imbibed some myself. Why not? As their new deacon, I had no idea, really, how to behave, although I knew I must retain my sense of decorum. Rev. Mr. Bishop had taken a couple of tots with evident pleasure and was now dancing with an older woman who was having the time of her life. Next to the fiddler, an even older man was beating his feet and a third was working a pair of spoons on his knee like a professional. Well, I thought, what an enjoyable opening to a new career!

Just then, across the room one of three girls detached herself and approached me. Plain rather than pretty, heavily built but with sparkling eyes and an obvious sense of fun, she said boldly, "Come along, Mr. John, no good you standing alone in the corner with all us girls wanting to dance." She reached out her arms.

I had been to dances, of course, on the Gaspé, but not after I'd taken Holy Orders. No book on the priesthood instructed me what to do next. Well, I thought, follow the leader, Mr. Bishop. I joined in and she proved full of fun, easily following the calls of the fiddler as we threaded our lively way around in a circle.

The reel ended with us all sweating and the door thrown open to let in fresh air. Several couples streamed outside, myself towed by the firm grip of my dancing partner, whose name was Susannah. Our host, Ralph, came out with a flagon of rum and filled the mugs retrieved from the table outside. I availed myself of a large jug of water first, to quench my thirst. I wasn't going to quench it with the demon rum.

After a healthy slug, Susannah grabbed me by the hand and tugged me down the trail. I dug in my heels. "Susannah, are you not up for dancing the next reel?"

"Of course we'll dance, Mr. John. But I got something to show you first."

I was not sure I wanted to see what she had to show me.

"You're one of the finest-looking fellas we've had here for a long time," she said. "Most of our men is just jackasses, far as I can see. And they look like that, too."

"Susannah! You should speak more charitably of your neighbours." She was clearly the local rule breaker — a deacon's garb would keep most girls on their decorum but obviously it had not impressed her.

"Oh, I give as much charity as I can to any neighbour that asks. But I know one person is not gonna speak up, and that's you, Mr. John! So I's gotta take whatever I can get."

Temptation was rearing its ugly head. In the flash that followed, I felt covered with indecision. I had as a young man known several young ladies rather more intimately than any gentleman of the cloth should — but again, well before my ordination as deacon. So I was acquainted with the ways of the flesh, and moreover not one bit averse to their pleasures. However, I now had to pay attention to the Commandments as laid down in the Holy Book. These canons had become firmly lodged in my consciousness.

So I shook my head. "Sorry, Susannah, I've got to go back in."

She turned, came up, threw her big arms around me and planted a big, warm kiss on my lips before I could object or rebel.

She stood back and looked. "Can't you do any better'n that?"

I rapidly collected myself. "I can, but as your deacon, I'm not sure that the present circumstances would permit such goings on," I said sternly. Then to soften it, I went on, "I confess I'm sorely tempted, Susannah, but let's just go back in, and enjoy our dancing."

As we did so, I reflected that, surprisingly, I had been rather adept at deflecting this burst of temptation. Yes, so far, I appeared to be weathering whatever circumstances threw at me. And thus found myself even looking forward to the next challenge.

Chapter Three

On Gene and I walked from Magpie to Mingan, a shorter distance than from Sheldrake. There we picked up a packet boat to Natashquan, where we found our little mission boat, the skiff *Evangeline*, still being repaired by the able Owen Cheveller (actually *Chevalier*), our skipper from St. Paul's River. We were delayed for a week, putting us into October, but we spent the time making the acquaintance of our parishioners there, teaching local children, and generally keeping busy to ward off the irritation we both felt at being so delayed.

I found Owen a gruff but learned individual who knew not only all the capes and bays and inlets along the shore, but taught school occasionally in Aylmer Sound as well. The boat was comfortable in its way, two sturdy masts and a tiny cabin, with enough room between two narrow bunks for a wood stove and table. Practical rather than aesthetically pleasing, the *Evangeline* had been named, Owen told me, after the Acadian legend. This mystified me: Longfellow's poem, a great hit some fifty years ago, had nothing whatever to do with the Labrador. Anyway, the boat seemed sufficient for running around the parish in the autumn before freeze-up, and again in summer once the ice had broken.

So off we went to sail the length of St. Clement's mission, four hundred and fifty miles to Blanc Sablon, and perhaps beyond to L'Anse au Loup, *Wolf Cove* in English. As we sailed, Gene roughed out the duties expected of us, which I was surprised to learn included writing letters for many who couldn't read or write. But mostly we talked theology and compared notes about our studies and backgrounds. A fine companion, Gene sat gossiping with Owen and me around our campfires on the shore. For suppers we ate the odd fish Owen caught, or a chance sea duck or plump murre if he'd been lucky enough to shoot one.

One of the things Gene and I talked about was how each of us had gotten our "call." Coming from Montreal, he'd had a very different upbringing, not nearly as lucky as mine, for I was taught very early on the value of hard work. Even my sisters knew it: they also did men's work when they got time off from doing the dishes, washing clothes, and helping Momma with manifold other chores.

I remember I was lying in bed where I roomed in Old Lodge with four other undergraduates. We had spent the previous day in lectures, of course, and in watching the Bishop's team practise football, a sport which I would soon join with vigour. The Old Testament lecture disturbed me: what a wicked lot they were! All those massacres, wars, slavery, King David taking his officer's wife and then sending him to his death — it made for dreadful reading. In fact, I discussed it all with my roommate, Victor, who was hoping to become an English teacher. Schools were in dire need of teachers, he told me: if I took that up, I'd be almost guaranteed getting a school of my choice. So I began to think that I might like to do that.

Another of my roommates, Harris, an excellent football player, had decided to go into history, perhaps getting an advance degree and becoming a professor. I hadn't learned enough about history in our Academy in New Carlisle; in fact, I hated the whole school thing — being away from home and coming back only on weekends. How I would look forward then to taking over the barn work from Mac and Poppa! Of course, we never worked on Sundays, save to milk cows, feed pigs and chickens, and do those mandatory tasks that keeping animals required. Mind you, being away in Carlisle school had been good — how else would I have survived Bishop's so handily? So history was an option, too. I was definitely focussing on a future occupation.

That night, when we turned off the lights, I found I couldn't sleep. My mind kept churning: how was the harvesting going and those wonderful threshing parties, and those jolly "fulling" parties around vats of wool after shearing. How much I missed all that! Did I really want to go live in some big city? Lennoxville, the local village, was about as big as I could take. The city of Sherbrooke, three or four miles away, I did visit and what I saw I didn't much like. I even made a short trip to Montreal on the train, and found it much too overwhelming.

Was I dozing off? My eyes flew open with a very real sense of a presence in the room — as though the space became dense with an overwhelming weight; I even had trouble breathing, so intense was this feeling. I believe I actually sat up. And then I felt it: the grip of what I can only describe as a giant hand, but also feminine, the touch being so soothing and gentle, although at the same time, possessed of some superhuman strength. I just couldn't move.

And then, I heard a soft but omnipresent voice: "John. John."

I answered, "Here I am." I wanted to say, who are you, but further words strangled in my throat.

The voice said simply, "You are mine forever, John."

Mine forever? What on earth? And then of course, I knew. I would never be so bold as to suggest it was the Lord himself, although now that I know more about Him, it would have been entirely possible. And that reinforced this desire for a more substantial contact.

Then the heaviness, the stifling weight, left the room and I saw out the window across the quadrangle, the shapes of buildings appearing in the dawn. I drifted on a cloud of peacefulness. Really. Such a comforting feeling, at last, firmly and completely, to KNOW. For I was aware then that I had been chosen. No more restless nights wondering what my life would be. I would become a clergyman.

Soon after we left Natashquan, the trees, mostly spruce, grew smaller, stunted, and finally disappeared altogether, save for the odd cove or "drake." These long low stretches of smooth granite, pocked with inlets and capes, were covered only by multicoloured lichens and occasional tiny, late-blooming flowers. Lots of berries everywhere, which we stopped to pick: especially redberries, which I didn't know from the Gaspé, but a delicious supplement to our rather plain meals.

We intended to reach every family that Gene remembered visiting, and some he'd only heard about, especially on islands where parishioners had not yet moved back to the mainland. "Fishermen here," Gene explained, "move out with their families into their summer places, mostly on islands, where fish are close and plentiful. They only return to the permanent homes in the autumn."

Each time we were welcomed and given a meal, after which we would invoke the Lord with prayers, psalms, and occasional hymn singing. These people I found relied a good deal more on their faith than we did on the Gaspé. No wonder, for here, more than anywhere, I felt close to the Almighty, there being so little in the way of distraction.

As we progressed along the coast eastward toward the Atlantic, the fall foliage on the banks diminished, their leaves making patchwork coverings on their granite pallets. In some coves, and around streams that tumbled into this turbulent gulf, a few brave trees still bore the dark reds or yellow-brown leaves with a kind of persistent pride.

As we went further, the absence of spruce and birch revealed great naked capes and achingly denuded shorelines. Some had thrown across their shoulders shawls of autumn lichens and ripened berries whose russet coverings kept them safe from the harsh frosts that bit savagely into every living thing after Christmas. Once November drew to a close and "slob" ice began to spread outward from the many coves, navigation would be shut down until teams of dogs and their komatiks could be placed in service. I'd been told repeatedly about the severity of the winters and I did wonder how I'd survive them — and manage a dog team, our only means of transportation. Well, I would soon find out.

Our plan called for us to go as far east as Blanc Sablon, near St. Paul's River, where I would drop Gene before returning to Mutton Bay, my own centre of some thirty or forty families. Gene had married and was anxious to return to his wife, Anna Bell, who was teaching school at this eastern base of ours. They would winter there, while from Mutton Bay I would travel by komatik to the rest of the outlying communities. The thought filled me with some nervousness, because I had grown accustomed to Gene's comforting presence, though he'd only had a year of ministry here and was indeed only a few years older.

A heavy fog bank began to move in on our third day of travel. Owen found a convenient inlet to wait out this navigational hazard. Both Owen and Gene were quick to point out how instantly changeable and often dangerous this weather could be. Having visited La Romaine, and the various islanders preparing to move back to the mainland, we now hoped to make Sunday service at Christian Bay, near Kegaska, where Gene said a few

English families, the Bucklands, Stubberts, and so on, eked out a living. But the next morning, fog still kept us prisoner.

Our first night aboard the *Evangeline*, Owen made himself comfortable with pillows on the tiny floor space in spite of my protestations: being the youngest, I felt that I should be using that makeshift bed, but Owen insisted. Thus we clergymen slept comfortably, if a bit guiltily, on the two bunks.

During a second night of being fogbound, I awoke to feel the ship rocking. Ah, that heavy wind would mean the end of fog, so I went back to sleep, pleased that we'd soon be off. But in the morning Gene and I crawled out onto the deck to find it covered in snow. Heavy wet flakes were falling everywhere, with visibility almost negligible again. The glass began to drop, fast, meaning lowered pressure and thus bad weather. We were in no danger, but Owen would not weigh anchor, much as both Gene and I chafed at our inactivity: so many families to be visited, and winter coming on, witness the falling snow, about which I questioned them.

"Like as not, we have one good snowfall in October," Owen affirmed. "But then it clears up until November, and that's when you never know what you're going to face."

Until November — what about now? How could one plan anything on this coast? And all travel was of course shut down in spring and fall, when komatiks and boats would not serve. At any rate, Gene and I passed the day in reading *Pilgrim's Progress* and discussing passages with each other, and toward nightfall the snow stopped. But the temperature had dropped and even our enclosed space on the boat seemed so awfully chilly I had to throw my overcoat over the blankets.

At dawn, Owen got us up and we were soon under way. A light wind moved us along at a good clip, and in the afternoon, we called in at three houses on a bluff, where one family remained. They had been preparing to row to the mainland the previous week, but the fog and snow had kept them here.

"Good supply of cod," the husband told us, "these last three weeks, no idea why. I wanted to stay while they lasted, but the wife kept saying, we'll all freeze or drown. So we're taking off in the morning."

We anchored the night by the little outpost, soon to be empty of occupants until next summer. The next morning we got up and found they had already departed. We ate a good breakfast and sailed on to Wolf Bay where we had prayers with the Jones family, Gilbert and Louisa, and their twelve children, still at their summer home on the island. We kept winding our way along the shore inside the outer islands, to be sure we did not miss a soul. Gene thought these Joneses would be the last of the island families, but this was given the lie late afternoon when I caught out of the corner of my eye some movement.

"Gene, look."

At the tiller, Owen shaded his eyes and Gene stood up. Yes indeed: someone wildly signalling.

Gene turned the tiller and we tacked in toward the lone group. But there were no houses nearby. What would they be doing here, all alone? As we came closer, we saw two children lying together under a coat, while another little boy clutched his mother who still waved frantically, even though she could see we were heading right for them.

We came close and dropped anchor. The three of us leapt overboard and waded ashore. The mother, a tall lean woman who looked fifty but was surely younger, dropped to her knees, clasped her hands in prayer: "Praise the Lord, we're saved, but too late, too late!"

The little boy ran to us through the water and leapt into the arms of Gene, who hugged him. "My little son, you're freezing.

Here, come on the boat. Owen, get the stove started. Get this child warm."

I hurried onto the shore and quickly went over to the mother who knelt, bent over, crying her heart out. Then I came upon a sight that battered my heart: two small children, wrapped in each other's arms, lay beside her, but now so very still.

When I helped her up, she clutched me with such fierce strength. Her icy fingers enwrapped my neck as she continued sobbing. I saw I must get her onto the boat, so I disengaged her arms and tugged her out into the freezing water. But she seemed unwilling to leave the dead children. Firmly, I got her into the strong arms of Gene and Owen, who hefted her into the boat and safety.

"Don't leave 'em, don't leave 'em," she wailed. "I cannot, I cannot go, I must stay."

Gene and I exchanged looks. What was there to say?

Gene, the more experienced, spoke gently. "We won't leave them, ma'am, never you mind, we shall bring them with us. Now you get warm, ye hear. Go below, please, our stove is hot, start warming yourself and take care of your little son. John and I will go get the boys."

Gene motioned to Owen and whispered, "Got any canvas?" Canvas here comes in three weavings: a heavy one for sails, one for winter garments, and a third for general coverings. Owen produced a couple of fragments, enough for one child, I thought, and then we looked at each other. I had no idea what to do next.

Below, I saw the mother and son shivering by our wood stove with our blankets round their shoulders, sipping their hot tea. Owen crawled over the deck and from a rear compartment pulled out a rather unclean sack. I shuddered: could we really consign a dear little boy to this? On the coast I had often seen open coffins with their corpses carefully prepared by local women for burial.

But this was my first time dealing with dead bodies, frozen stiff in fact. Well, I told myself, better get used to it.

"You stay 'ere, Mr. Gene," Owen suggested and we both leapt into the icy water, leaving Gene to deal with the mother and her son. We splashed ashore and somehow managed to gather up the stiffened bodies of the two children, so deathly white, but by the same token, so angelic. We carried them back to the boat, trying to keep the sight from their mother, and stored them under a covering in the stern.

With Owen at the tiller we set off for Harrington Harbour, the nearest settlement. Gene had heated our saucepan of soup from the night before and once the woman fed her son and herself, she was able in broken sentences to recount her tale of woe. "We just come — me and the little ones, m'husband bein' off up the coast on the last fishing trip. We come over 'ere to Netagamiou Island t'get our winter's supply of redberries. The place is full of 'em." I confess, with the grisly sight that greeted me, I had not noticed the profusion of berries. "We spent the morning picking, and then, with the fog rolling in, we started back to our boat only to find it had drifted away."

Gene nodded. "Yes, the fog stopped us dead, too." Then quickly he went on to say, "We moored in an inlet, and waited it out — in the safety of our boat, of course."

"We had no such safety," the woman went on. "We just huddled together as best we could. No protection, we tried to nestle in among the lichen and berries, but it was some cold. In the morning, you couldn't see your hand before your face in the fog. If my husband 'ad come back, 'e'd a been off lookin' fer us fer sure, but he must'a still been away." With that, she began once more to sob quietly, trying not to disturb her son, who also took up crying.

I reached out and touched her. My heart had broken along with hers.

"Well, we had our berries to eat, but that's all. No spring water on the island, we was some thirsty. The berries helped, but awful bitter, raw like 'at. And then, you seen it, the snow started up."

I nodded. "That snow... How anyone could've survived..."

"I don't know how, we all just clung together for warmth. But after a bit, first Danny, and then Jack, they both... they faded, just faded away. When I felt they was colder than cold, I let them drop." With that she began to cry once again.

Now events began to move rather quickly. Before we had gone an hour tacking into the wind, two boats came sailing toward us: parishioners from the Barachois, having been alerted by the husband to the family's absence.

What a heart-rending encounter! The husband leapt aboard and was soon hugging his wife. When he heard from her of the tragedy, he bent over and, already exhausted and battered, sobbed horribly. We left him and his wife and child alone in the cabin as we tacked our way home.

We arrived at Harrington Harbour before suppertime and unloaded our unhappy cargo. Such a welcome sight, that squiggly line of homes scattered along a twisting shoreline of granite, heavily indented with narrow creeks that gave access to the waters for the residents, all with their stageheads and tethered fishing boats. At each side, headlands reached out to shelter the harbour.

We set the funeral for the morrow and Gene introduced me around, though the occasion was hardly the arrival that I had anticipated, this being one of the main centres of my parish. The devastation brought on by the deaths of the two children was palpable; they had been a well-liked family and the next day most everyone in the village turned out for the moving and memorable service. I found myself, as I read the lesson, close to losing my self-control in the midst of all this terrible sadness.

The night before, Gene had proudly shown me the skeleton of the church sited by the Bishop the year before, to which many energies were now being applied. I marvelled at the proportions and how enterprising these good folk were. They had even constructed a sawing platform, for instead of digging a deep trench as we do on the Gaspé, they'd built a rough scaffold for a man to grip the saw at the upper end, while his partner stood on the ground. This way, the two could cut boards from the logs brought from the inland forests. Already the foundations had been laid and a few uprights lay about for lifting into walls. Mr. John Bobbitt, our lay reader here, had been instrumental in organizing it all, with Levi Wright as the actual builder, a good Anglican in spite of his first name.

This funeral was not how the day ended, however. I had left Gene at the graveside with the family when, coming down the path, I was met by a fisherman. He told me someone from the large schooner unloading autumn supplies had asked for me. The crew member had gone into the old shed at the back of the wharf, or rather, stagehead.

I wondered what on earth could be the trouble? Was the man in fear of his immortal soul? Did he require absolution for a dreadful deed, or just some special solace? Or perhaps there had been a mutiny on board? As I strode down the path behind the fisherman, my mind roiled with many wild imaginings. I was not used to this position of responsibility.

The fisherman walked across and stopped at the stage. He gestured inside. I thanked him and, after he went off, I hesitated, and then not knowing what to expect, opened the door.

A lantern hanging from the ceiling threw its glow across the old nets, new killicks, fishing gear, and other oddments. Was this to be a dangerous meeting? When a figure came forward out of the gloom, I tensed up.

Then I recognized my freckled, red-haired companion from the train ride to Matapedia three years earlier. We had talked long into the night about his plans for becoming a mate on one of his father's schooners. His face broke into a happy smile when he saw me. "John! What a lucky happening!"

"Indeed it is! Wonderful to see you." We immediately fell to talking about the intervening three years, me having taken Holy Orders, and him having shipped on a different schooner each year, learning a great deal thereby.

Through all this, I could see something was bothering him. "So tell me, Frank, what caused you to seek out a clergyman? Not done something wicked, have you?"

"No, John. Maybe I should call yez Mister John? God luv me, I wish it were that simple. It's not me, fer sure." He hesitated, and gestured apologetically. "See, I had t'meet ya hidden away, like, because if anyone found out 'twas me what told on them, I'd be in fer it." He looked around, rather nervously I thought, and then stepped forward and leaning close, whispered into my ear.

His news was so shocking that it took me time to fully comprehend the implications. He stepped back. "So you got to rescue her!"

"Me? But how?" I asked. "Is she the only cook on your schooner?" He nodded. "So what shall I do? Bring a party of villagers to attack the ship?" I was at quite a loss.

"Of course not. You're a man of the cloth. The captain will listen to you. I found none other at any of the last ports o' call: nor magistrates, justices of the peace, no police in fact."

He was right. "Nor even a mayor," I agreed. "These folk hereabouts have developed no formal organizations like Shigawake's village council. I guess they work by a sort of consensus."

"So no other authority for me to appeal to." He fell silent, and looked at me. My thoughts tumbled about, seeking any escape.

He grasped me by the arm, and his eyes gleamed. "Now look, if they find out it's me spilling the beans, one day, I'd be just 'swep' overboard.' I got no wish to end my life like that. But I want justice done." After a pause, he said, "Her name's Lorna Maclean, but you better not say that at all at all... they'll know how ya found out."

Not one of the duties Gene had outlined, for sure! I doubted if he'd even met this situation. So should I pass it over to him? No, it could be dangerous. So how could I, in all conscience, step away? "You think I should go on board alone?"

"No other way." Frank looked at me with a hopeful intensity. "But gimme time to get back so's no one'll suspect. I made up some story about seeing a relative. I gotta be back and out of harm's way when you come."

"So you want me to get out to your schooner, confront the captain, and convince him to let the only cook for twenty hungry crewmen come back on shore with me and leave his ship forever?"

He nodded. "I been pressin' my father to stop this business of women cooks on schooners. I heard o' other such goings on last year, too."

Good lord, I had no idea such things were sanctioned on these passing ships. Frank crossed quickly to the high window, peeked out, waited a few moments, then shook my hand quickly and, looking in my eyes, wished me well. He prayed our paths might cross again in the not too distant future and, with apologies for his hasty withdrawal, was gone.

I remained behind for a while in the dim light of the lantern, which I then extinguished. I needed time to plan how I should go about this. But alas, not a plan entered my head. What a devilish task — coming hard upon the emotional trauma of burying the two dear little children. Well, nothing for it but find a fisherman to row me out, and do my best, no matter how bizarre the task and how inadequate I felt.

Chapter Four

I climbed the rope ladder onto the schooner deck with such trepidation and misgivings. What if Frank had been wrong? No, I trusted him. But then, how should I deal with the captain? What could I ever say to release this poor girl from her plight? Imagine, those sailors just having their way with her every night. If she had fought them off, she'd be in fear of her life. Especially if she went with her story to the captain. At the very thought, my ire rose and my resolution thickened into anger.

I had dressed for the funeral in my black cassock and tippet with my heavy coat thrown over so now I could clearly be seen as a man of God. I still felt nervous, nay terrified, for these schooner-men were a rough lot, and although a good many of the crew were churchgoers, many more were not. The few deckhands unloading freight into a rowboat seemed surprised as I clambered over the rail. One of them went off to get the captain while I waited, balanced between apprehension and determination.

Soon someone in a captain's hat limped forward, a heavy black beard hiding his youth for he could have been under thirty some, though he wore the grizzled look of a sailor who had seen a good deal and suffered more. When he saw my clerical garb, he paused momentarily, and then came forward.

"Captain Clifford, at your service," he said.

I introduced myself as a deacon and extended my hand. We shook perfunctorily.

"So you've probably come to ask my men to your church tomorrow. Well, I'm sorry, Deacon, but I have a schedule to keep and much as the crew will miss the great benefits bestowed upon them by a church service, I must obey my owners. I'm sorry, sir," he finished, implying the interview was at an end.

As he half turned, I blurted out, "I haven't come about the service tomorrow, Captain. Another matter, rather more grave, and certainly private." He looked at me askance. "Is there somewhere we could talk out of earshot?"

The captain stiffened as if he knew what was coming. "Not sure we have time, good sir," he growled. "We must be under way shortly."

"I'm afraid I must insist," my voice grew firmer, "or the consequences may be more dire than you anticipate."

He eyed me with a new appreciation and, I would say, distaste. "Very well," he jerked his hand and led me to the afterdeck behind the wheel, his open precinct. He turned and eyed me. We were both silent while I tried to form the right words. Then I came right out: "It concerns the young lady cook you have on board. I'm afraid —"

The captain cut me off. "Oh good sir, that's a lot of rubbish. Of course I heard the rumours, nasty ones indeed, but only gossip. I myself questioned the maid a few days ago, and she put my mind at rest. So I let the matter drop."

I eyed him. Now what? Obviously, Lorna was much too afraid to spill any beans while on board.

"So if that's all you've come about, Deacon, I thank you for your trouble, and I'll see you back to your fishing boat."

"Sir, the only way you'll see me back to my boat is with that lady." I dared not speak her name.

He stopped, his face hardening. He was about to spit something out as he might at one of his men, but he thought better of it and collected himself. "That maid is my only cook for twenty hungry men." He shrugged. "What can I do? My duty is to my men, and my cargo. I just cannot let her go."

So there it was. Head-on confrontation.

Was I going to leave the maid to those nightly indignities, nay, vile tortures, and back off like some coward, though that course of action was the most simple? My hackles rose. "If that maid stays on the boat, captain, you will be placing your immortal soul in danger!"

"My immortal soul, sir, can take care of itself. Now please, do me the favour of leaving my ship. As captain in charge of the vessel, I demand you disembark forthwith!"

I softened. "I shall be happy to leave the ship sir, but only with the maid. And before you object, let me —"

"Object? I do object, and strongly. My crew comes first, no matter what rumours you may have heard. Gossip or no gossip, she stays here, she fulfills her signed obligations under which we took her on, she cooks, and you will kindly have nothing more to say on the subject! The ship is under my charge. I am the one completely responsible, and I —"

My turn to interrupt: "Exactly! As captain, you are completely responsible for what happens on your ship?"

"I am, sir. You know the law of the sea."

"I do indeed." I paused and leaned toward him. "What you have just said puts every wrong done to that woman squarely upon your head!" I let that sit, and then in a burst of anger went on, "If she has been violated," he quickened as if slapped, "that, sir, will be your doing!"

His chin jutted out and I noticed his hand curl into a fist. "What are you daring to say, sir?"

I tensed. "I'm saying that at your next large port of call, I shall see to it that an officer of the law is waiting. I myself, as a gentleman of the cloth, will testify at the court hearing certain to follow. And then you, sir, may well spend the next ten years in jail!"

The captain held himself still, breathing heavily, staring at the floor. After some time, he spoke. "What proof have you got that she has been tampered with?"

I almost blurted out Frank's name, but stopped myself. I took a gamble. "The maid herself. Once safe in custody, she will tell all. And if she does not arrive safely at that first port of call, you, sir, will then be tried for murder!" My ire was getting the better of me and I found myself shouting.

The captain paused, clearly thinking fast. Not often, I imagine, had he been so challenged.

"All right," he said slowly, "I shall have a guard posted at her room and shall see that no harm comes to her for the rest of the trip."

"I'm sorry, Captain, that is not good enough. I repeat: she is coming with me. Now please, let us not prolong this difficult conversation any further, or my parishioners in Harrington will be rowing out to support my demand."

He stood for a long time, motionless. Then he nodded. "If there were any truth to these rumours, then you might have a point. I think you are wrong. But some doubt may exist, so you can take the maid and be damned!"

The good Lord must have nudged me, for I found myself saying angrily, "I shall never depart with that slur ringing in my ears. You will retract it, captain."

He sighed, already bored with this interchange, his mind by now working perhaps, as a good master, on how to feed his crew. "Very well, I retract it." He went out, summoned one of his men, gave orders, and headed off.

I walked to the railing, composing myself as best I could,

waiting for what seemed an eternity while groups of crewmen stood around, muttering. Was I about to witness a mutiny?

In the doorway to the lower quarters, a really tall woman appeared, Lorna Maclean as I knew, but bent as if in pain, wrapped up in a shawl so as to hide her face. Carrying a meagre cloth bag, she limped forward like a cripple, climbed over and onto the rope ladder, and mutely descended, with me following.

I was not able to see her face until we arrived at the home of our lay reader, John Bobbitt, owner of one of the larger houses in Harrington Harbour. He had kindly agreed to put up clergy when they came through, for he had lost his wife three years ago in '93. He was out at the moment, reputedly "seeing" someone, but his relative, Sarah, had come in to prepare our beds and arrange our last cup of tea before we retired. She looked up in alarm as our newfound charge was ushered in. Lorna, who still had not spoken, was by no means slight, being tall or even taller by inches than I was, with long stringy hair and a bold, rather gaunt, haunted face. As she dropped her shawl momentarily, I saw welts on one side of her face and a cut lip. Sarah immediately took charge and brought her into a bedroom where she bathed her face and got her into bed.

I quickly outlined the situation to Gene and recommended that Lorna see the local nurse. But as Gene reminded me, no doctor or nurse served in the Canadian Labrador. "We rely here on midwives, although there is Bill Ransom, who is handy with a pair of blacksmith's tongs. For a dipper of bakeapple, he will pull your tooth." He smiled, but this quickly vanished as he agreed we should send for the midwife. If such nameless goings-on had taken place, the young woman should be examined and evidence gathered, if we ever wished to press charges.

I was of course anxious to know from the poor girl's own lips her account, but we both saw that she should first avail herself of this safe haven and rest here for several days, before she would be in any condition to divulge what sufferings she had undergone.

In the morning, Gene and I offered the Lord's Supper in a fully attended Communion service in the school building. Gene gave special prayers for the new church to be built by the combined efforts of the parish.

After our dinner at noon, we discussed what should be done with our new charge. Gene felt it was asking too much for John Bobbitt to take her on, so we agreed to bring her with us in the mission boat to Mutton Bay, the winter headquarters where I was to stay. "Aunt Minnie, being a widow in her seventies, would probably welcome a helping hand this year. In any case it would only be until spring, when she can return to her relatives in Nova Scotia."

"Now you've mentioned several other aunts and uncles," I interrupted Gene. "Don't tell me you're related to everyone?"

He laughed. "No, older people hereabouts are never called mister or missus. As a term of respect, you always say uncle or aunt." And I fell right into the practice, for it was a charming one of which I heartily approved.

But early the next morning when we were due to leave, our charge lay dead asleep. After a quick discussion, it was decided we should leave her here, and give Mr. Bobbitt money to send her on the packet to Mutton Bay, whither I would return after our eastern voyage.

So off we went with Owen on the *Evangeline*, trusting the weather would hold. After a long and rather trying sail, we reached Mutton Bay that night and I met "Aunt" Minnie, where we stayed. We alerted her as to the new guest due shortly. I was tickled to learn that Mutton Bay was so-named because the

French name, Baie des Moutons, which when applied to water actually meant *Bay of White Caps* had been mistranslated into *Bay of Sheep*, and this became Mutton Bay. I was reminded of our own Cape Despair, on the Gaspé, which comes from Cap d'Espoir, *Cape of Hope*!

The next day I walked over to the charming little church: above the central door, the front wall narrowed to form the beginnings of a steeple, which began in a curious triangle centred by a round window, on top of which sat the attractive bell tower: all in all a delight, for here I was entering my very own church. And the next morning, after this first service in my new parish, which included parishioners from the adjacent community of Tabacher (or *La Tabatière*) we took off again in the *Evangeline*, calling in at every inhabited outpost. By now most of the island fishing camps had been emptied — even the herring was pretty well over — and the inhabitants safely installed in their permanent quarters on the mainland.

We made it as far as Kecarpoui (pronounced here as *Ke-cark-way*) calling in to render prayers at the grouping of houses in Lake Sally (from the French: Lac Salé, *Salt Lake*). As we left, the sky began to darken, but we thought it better to keep going — we had so little time left before the weather would get even colder and slob ice begin appearing by the shores. We still had some days sailing to St. Paul's River, but Owen knew of the occasional cove in this deeply indented shore where we could seek shelter, or even spend the night if we did not find an actual settlement.

Toward evening when we were looking for a safe harbour, the wind rose rather suddenly and with it, the sea. Soon Owen had trouble controlling the boat. Ahead, we could see a threatening cloud and below it, dark wafting curtains heralding rain.

"There's a fine cove about a mile down," Owen told us. "Let's make a run for it." Gene put on his raincoat and I went below to snaffle mine, with my scarf and hat. Not a happy situation!

The storm bore down on us more quickly than anyone imagined. I looked back. The inlet behind us was over a mile away. Worse, the whole mainland consisted of smooth granite across which the wind swept unimpeded. I heard Owen say, "I don't think we're going to make it. That wind is swinging. I'm going to turn about and try to make the lee of the island there, behind us."

"You think that will do?"

"Never used it before, but as they say, any port in a storm."

I could see he was trying to keep concern from sounding in his voice, but I was apprehensive. I confess, I don't enjoy the sea. I was never attracted by fishing nor have I ever hankered after sailoring. I put up with the *Evangeline* as being the only means of travel here when there's no snow, and I had made up my mind to make the best of it. But now as the boat started corkscrewing and diving into troughs of waves that had so quickly begun to build as seas began breaking over us, I was truly distressed. We were being driven onto island shoals at one side that were jagged and threatening.

"Close the hatches," Owen ordered grimly. I helped Gene grab the companionway's loose front cover as the wind tried to snatch it from us. We slid it down the vertical slots. Owen yelled over the building wind, "Any ropes, tie 'em down!" We both leapt to his command, grabbing any in sight, Gene doing the tying and me throwing loose ropes into the cockpit. After that, I slid the hatch covering into place over the companionway.

That cloud and its squall was bearing down on us so swiftly that I heard Owen's frightened cry, "Sails, we've gotta get them sails down. She's going to hit!"

Up ahead, the sky was black as night.

Gene tore at the sails and dropped the aft one, but the foresail stuck. The gale had not hit yet, but still Gene hollered, "Use a knife! Cut 'er away, she's worse than I thought!"

"Where, where?" No knife in sight. Owen held out his. Frantically, Gene snatched it while I watched helplessly.

Just as we got the sails down, the storm struck us in all its fury — like being walloped by a sleighload of logs careening down a hill. The howling wind and horizontal driving rain made the waves buck like a frenzied horse. Spray lashed at us — and the boat tipped right over, almost on its side. I thought we were goners. But somehow, it righted itself. Gene kept gathering the sail in frantically and I helped lash it safe, falling as I did, then rising onto my battered knees.

With no sails, we drifted helplessly and the wind began heaving us directly at the rocky point of the island. I knew Owen could not swim, but although Gene and I could, five minutes in this icy water would finish us off. We just had to save the boat. But how?

I spied the oars and tried to unbind one, hoping to right the rocking vessel. Gene bent to help, but once the oar got free, a mighty gust tore it from my hands. Off it went into the waves.

Just as we were being surely driven right onto the jagged reef, Owen shouted, "The jib! Get some of the jib up, about four feet! Quick!"

We tumbled over each other as we clambered onto the deckhouse, the rain stinging our faces and making our eyes water, clinging to whatever we could find. We were blown sideways, down, and heeled over, but if we could just pull the jib up a bit...

Most of it was either loose on deck flapping about, or beating us about the legs, but we did need some hoisted — we were losing the boat and our lives.

Somehow, I'll never know how, we managed to clear a bit of

that jib and haul it up enough — just the size of a tablecloth. With that to steady us, Owen managed to right the boat. Instead of drifting, we drew slowly ahead.

When we started to go before the wind, my heart in my mouth, I could see we had only narrowly missed the rocky reef. While the storm continued to harass us with its frenetic rain and blinding wind, we tore along before the gale into open water. Finally, I saw we were free, though with battered sails and tangled rigging, thoroughly wet and uncomfortable.

That night, as I lay on the tiny bunk with the rain still beating hard and the wind ravaging the waves, I said special prayers to the Lord for having saved us and our boat. And my mind turned, as it had several times on the voyage, to the tall young woman whom I had rescued. How was she faring? In a curious way, she seemed to have taken hold of my heart, her helplessness drawing me to her even more firmly. I hoped she was recovering nicely.

Chapter Five

We continued through autumn storms up past Eskimo Island to Blanc Sablon, and even beyond to L'Anse au Loup, our easternmost port of call. Here we turned around, close to the Strait of Belle Isle, that "ice-berg alley" lashed by Atlantic storms between the vast and frigid Labrador to the north and the British colony of Newfoundland to the south. I was pleased that my large parish went no further. By now I had an inkling of what lay in store for the next two years, or however long the Bishop decided.

This strung-out mission was by no means well off: subsistence living, I would be tempted to call it. On the Gaspé we do have rich years and lean years too, but here everything depended upon cod, and seals. When the cod did not run abundantly, no one cured enough fish to barter for winter provisions. And if the seal run was down, the dogs went hungry, the lack of pelts and oil made for a very hard winter. But the many close relationships meant that no one perished of starvation, though some years I gather they came perilously close. This year I prayed that the seal run would be good; I had enough on my hands without coping with mass starvation.

On the way back, we dropped Gene at Old Fort Island, from which he would be taken by a fisherman into the settlement of St. Paul's River and rejoin his wife and baby. His one hope, as he had told me, was to get a church built there, but we both feared that might be several years off. A brave man, a wonderful companion, but how on earth had he been able to leave his family for so long?

So indeed, two long weeks after I had rescued that willowy, bedraggled Lorna, Owen and I sailed into the stagehead at Mutton Bay, my headquarters for the winter, where presumably she had ended up. As we unloaded the boat, I confess I was delighted not to have to get on board again — at least, not until next spring's breakup.

I set off across the snow-covered village toward Aunt Minnie's, with Owen helping carry my belongings. My mind had often been focussed on the well-being of Lorna Maclean and I wondered if she would still be here, or had she caught a last sail back to Nova Scotia?

As I trudged along, I couldn't help but wonder why those first inhabitants here, some half-century ago, had chosen such barren promontories for their year-round home. So little to recommend it — by no means an accommodating environment, it seemed to me. Attractive, oh no doubt, with its looping inlets dividing the village. Unified now with a dusting of autumn snow, it still seemed so very inhospitable: square, boxy houses with red or tarred roofs perched unnaturally on the uneven granite shore. Their positioning arose from no careful selection of building sites but rather, from having been seemingly scattered haphazardly like toys across the brittle landscape by a careless child. The whole community comprised not more than a couple of dozen families, making fifty or sixty parishioners in all. Most of the houses sat only a few feet back from the water on granite arms that looped around, each family getting thereby an individual wharf or stagehead, and at its back a stage for preparing and storing fish.

We reached the top of a slight rise and started over toward the house of Aunt Minnie on a footbridge across an inlet. As we were walking rapidly, I glanced again at the square white house and stopped short. Walking behind, Owen almost bumped into me. There, in the light wind, stood a tall figure in a dark skirt, but what was she doing? Splitting wood? A man's job! I shook my head and glanced at Owen, who grinned. "Seems like they put 'er to work!"

We hurried on, not talking, and then as I drew closer, I was to get my second shock of the day.

She tossed a couple of split logs aside and turned. When she saw me coming, she stood as if struck, and then dropped her axe and ran lightly down the slope and straight into my arms, clutching me with all her might, shaking slightly. I confess I was taken aback. She buried her face in my shoulder, and then I could feel her sobbing. I allowed my arms to go around her, although I felt embarrassed. Then a wave of empathy washed over me and I began to hold her as tightly as she held me. Owen, seeing this meeting, hurried by and went to drop my bag at the door of the house, after which he turned and, with a broad grin, waved and set off to his relatives where he would spend the night.

Slowly, she disentangled herself and then, shaking her head, turned to wipe her eyes and went back to her chopping.

I followed. "Well," I felt somewhat at a loss for words, "I see they've got you working, Lorna!"

She nodded, managing a brief smile. Then she gestured to the door and got another log of birch, while I went inside to make myself known to Aunt Minnie.

I greeted her, certainly more formally than that emotional meeting outside, and I asked her how Lorna had been doing.

"Took 'er about a week, I'd say." Aunt Minnie helped me off with my coat and then went over to the stove to prepare the obligatory cup of tea. "And then, one morning by the time I'd made myself breakfast, I looked around, and the house was spic and span. Lorna had gotten up early and was cleaning like the best of them." She smiled, and I reacted with surprise. "All that day it went on, till I made 'er stop and sit while I gave 'er a bowl of soup. She seemed so anxious to please, and so happy to be 'ere."

"Has she spoken to you?"

Aunt Minnie shook her head. "Not a word since she arrived, poor dear. I 'spect she's been through so much on that awful schooner. We just 'ave to give 'er time."

I nodded. I knew she would come out of it, but when? Well, I too would give her time.

So that was the story. As we talked, I recounted my journey to Aunt Minnie, telling her of our narrow escapes, how we had nearly lost the boat and our lives, and how other storms kept plaguing us so that we found ourselves seriously at risk twice more.

"But you are sure you don't mind Lorna staying here for the time being?" I asked Aunt Minnie.

"Mind? My dear, I couldn't do without 'er. Do you know, whenever I was short of water, she'd go and bring me buckets down from the pond."

So at least my mind was put to rest in this regard. I would now have no worries about her and could continue pursuing my duties as priest. Gene had warned me I'd have to begin teaching school while we were held captive by the slob ice. Once enough snow fell and the land froze up solid, I could begin using the dogs and komatiks, and get off ministering to other villages. But not for at least another month or more.

The next morning I awakened early as was my habit, but I found myself enormously tired. I went downstairs to a good breakfast which both Aunt Minnie and Lorna had prepared. Apparently the latter had gotten up early to make a fire before the rest of us, a chore she had adopted and a welcome one at that. I was introduced to brewis (pronounced *brews*) which is hardtack and salt fish, both soaked overnight, and brewed up to be served with scrunchions (small cubes of fat pork, fried to a golden brown). These make it palatable, to my taste, although it all sounds dreadful. Much admired along the coast here, it was a traditional Sunday breakfast. I soon got used to it, and began to look forward to it before church.

After chatting with Aunt Minnie and swapping the latest news, I retired to my room to read over the lessons for this Sunday, for I had my sermon to prepare. But before I had even finished the Gospel, I found myself falling asleep, and indeed did not wake until I heard someone knock at my door.

I sat up, astonished. Already noon! The door opened and in came Lorna with a tray. She stood looking down at me, motionless; was she taking me in for the first time? At the same time, I looked at her: she had already lost that gaunt look and was beginning to get colour in her cheeks. Her once stringy hair was now a lustrous black, beautifully combed and tied into a bun. In fact, I found her more striking and much younger than I had first imagined. Her size had given her a maturity that her age did not support. But no doubt, a quiet dignity permeated her youthful presence. Her black eyes stared, apparently unaware of my returning look, and then she collected herself and set the tray down on the table beside my bed. She lifted a hand as though to touch me, thought better of it, and left the room, glancing back at me with a wondering look as she closed the door.

I suppose she and Aunt Minnie had realized how tired I was and had decided to keep me quiet. Very welcome. So I had my fish soup, which tasted fine, and some homemade bread with molasses, finishing with a dish of bakeapple preserve. Then I lay back once more to read over Sunday's lessons and, believe it or not, fell asleep again.

Another knock awakened me about midafternoon and Lorna came in, gesturing downstairs. I nodded and sat up, and she retired quickly. I put on my boots and went downstairs to find my two churchwardens: Thomas Buffett, nice and young with a moustache, the people's warden, at whose wedding I later officiated, and his companion, Thomas Bobbitt, heavy-set, patriarchal, bearded, the warden here for eleven years. We proceeded to discuss the arrangements for the Sunday services, and they offered to bring me the next day over to Tabacher, another community, more densely populated, only five miles away.

Perhaps because I had slept so much during the day, my night was uneasy. I tossed and turned, and then had nightmares invaded by wolves. They were about to ravage me when I woke up, and then I distinctly heard what seemed to be long howls echoing over the granite outcropping. Other howls answered, after which a chorus of barks rang out. I went to the window, and looked across the snow-covered land upon which a harsh full moon was flinging its ominous glare. All was still, no light in any window... no four-footed demons that could I see. I shivered and crept back across my cold, wood floor to snuggle under the blankets and try to get back to sleep.

The next day I found myself striding with Thomas Bobbitt over hilly and quite wooded country on our way to Tabacher. "Funny, you know, I thought I heard wolves in the night, but then this morning, I realized it might just have been huskies."

"Could be a bit of wolf in them dogs," my warden said. "We've been bringing 'em back from the islands the last while, getting their pens ready to hold 'em good."

"I have to admit I've never driven a dog team. On the Gaspé where I came from, we use horses, of course, and in the old days, oxen."

"No horses here, dogs only. They're fast and steady, if you train 'em good."

I wondered if I'd ever get them "trained good."

"Have you any idea why your ancestors came to settle on Mutton Bay for their permanent home?"

"Smart fellas, them folk were," Thomas said. "Plenty o' flat rock to dry the cod, and plenty of waterfront for 'em to land it. Best place around," was Thomas's considered opinion. "Now over there in Tabacher where we're goin', it's got the biggest seal fishery on the coast. Old Sammy Robertson got it off the Labrador Company, maybe seventy-five year ago, when 'e first come. Now 'is grandson Sammy John runs it."

I'd heard about the seal fishing and was pleased we'd be seeing the foundry. Gene had warned me not to forget that, every year round about now, we had a Sunday service devoted to prayers and supplications for the seal harvest.

We entered Tabacher on foot by the inlet known as Red Bay, by Pointe de Gros Mecantina, full of English Catholics ministered by a priest, Father Poudrier. I determined to meet him as soon as I could. A bit further on, we crossed an isthmus and walked past another inlet to Tabacher Cove where my warden introduced me to a bewhiskered and dignified Sammy John Robertson. It seemed the Robertsons pretty well owned Tabacher: certainly they were related to everyone. We walked past his house and found him supervising a couple of men who were repairing platforms a dozen feet above the flat rock shelf.

"Just fixing our seal scaffolds," Sammy John told me, after we'd been introduced. A heavy-set man with an honest look in his eyes and, like all the men here, a rock hard body, though not tall. "We put the seal carcasses up there once they're sculped to keep 'em frozen till spring, when we render down the fat. Keeps 'em safe from dogs and other animals. Pelts, we hold 'em in sheds till spring."

"Any wolves?"

"Way inland where we go hunting. None out here."

"And what are the chances of a good seal hunt this fall?" I asked.

He shook his head. "You never know, you never know." The village's livelihood depended upon it flourishing, and some years it didn't.

"You sell the pelts?"

"Yep, there's a fella comes round to buy 'em in the spring. The meat feeds the dogs. We eat it too, specially the flippers — ever had one?"

I shook my head. "And that's all you live off?"

He nodded. "Cod too, o' course. But you'll see it all when we start in a couple of weeks. Then we'll be able to get going on our komatiks."

"The dogs like seal meat?"

"Best thing for them, along with cornmeal, and sometimes we get a whale."

I was anxious to see this seal hunting, for we did none on the Gaspé.

"You gonna teach our children?" he asked.

On the way over we had discussed the matter. More children lived here than in Mutton Bay, and although the Tabacher folk often made the trek over for their church service, I knew it was too much to ask the children to do.

"Might be able to." I turned to Thomas. "Could I teach maybe mornings in Mutton Bay and afternoons in Tabacher?"

"None of 'em other clergy folk ever took that much on, Mr. John," said Thomas Bobbitt. "But if you likes, you could start. When it gets too much, we can leave it to one school till ya start your rounds on the komatik."

On the way back, Thomas broached the subject again. "I

been asking around for someone to start helping you, going on a few test trips with the dogs. Pretty hard to find someone though. There's a team Mr. Gene used last year, and they might do. But I don't know how we'd feed 'em, and get someone to drive you."

"Food for the dogs, it's a problem?"

"You see, pretty much everyone who works on the seals gets their share of meat. So I'm not quite sure 'ow we should arrange that this year. I been talking to Thomas here, asking 'im what we should do."

"Why wouldn't I work on the seals along with everyone else?"

"You, Mr. John? Clergy don't do that kind o' work around 'ere."

"Well, I was brought up on a farm, I do like dogs, and I would prefer mine to be well fed, and so if that's what it takes..."

"Dogs, Mr. John." Thomas stopped walking and looked at me. "You gotta be careful. They're not pets 'ere. They're workin' animals. You go soft on 'em and they'll run all over you. Only two year ago, one old fella was killed by 'is dogs. He must've given 'em some fresh rabbit, or fresh meat, and the smell of blood drove 'em crazy. When 'e went into the pen, they tore 'im to pieces."

I reacted with horror. "You don't mean that's actually true?"

"It's the truth all right. And five years afore that, one of the children over in Whale Head just missed being kilt by dogs what escaped their pen. So ya see, no laughing matter."

I realized I had more on my plate than I had bargained for. "What about my working along with the men in the seal hunting?"

"Hard work," was all Thomas said.

"Well, let me give it a try."

He nodded, and we spoke of it no more.

We were walking back quite quickly, which impressed me. "You always walk this fast?" I asked.

"It's bath night. I got four kids. We all gonna take our baths afore supper. So I can't be late."

Bath night! I certainly had forgotten. Time for me to get good and clean, at last.

Another surprise awaited me when I arrived. When I opened the front door, Lorna rushed forward and indicated I should go straight upstairs and not look into the main room, where I saw something was hidden behind a makeshift curtain, a blanket strung between chairs. Frowning but curious, I went up and heard Aunt Minnie's voice call after me, "Bath night."

"Don't I know it," I called back. Saturday, everything got scrubbed, I discovered: floors (on hands and knees) chairs, tables, everything. And at the end of that, we scrubbed ourselves.

"Come down in ten minutes. We'll have a surprise." She sounded tickled pink.

I got out of my heavy clothes and put on a pair of sealskin slippers I had received as a present on one of my visitations. Ten minutes later, her voice called, "We're ready!"

Wearing only underwear with my long coat as covering, I went down, feeling the heat at once; the stove had been well fired. Lorna stood beside Aunt Minnie, and they both looked well pleased.

When I peeked behind the blanket strung between the chairs, I saw a large puncheon tub, a wooden vat really, used for fish. This one had been well scrubbed and was watertight. Large enough to get into, as well. "Wherever did you find that?"

"Only bath like this in Mutton Bay, that's fer sure," Aunt Minnie said proudly. "Seems your friend 'ere seen the like in

Halifax and she went out and found one on some stage. She 'ad to work for three days cleaning their place in return for it. It's all 'er doing."

I looked at Lorna. She hid her face behind her hand, so obviously pleased with herself, but at the same time shy.

And what was more to the point, the water in it — a considerable amount — was steaming hot.

"She 'ad to make three more trips to the pond to get enough water fer ya. I must say none o' my other clergymen been treated so good! You're a lucky fella, Mr. John, to 'ave rescued such a prize. I reckon there's nothin' Lorna can't do."

"Oh thank you," I said. "I just wish you'd be able, soon, to talk to me..."

A hurt look flitted across her face. Then she took Minnie by the hand and they hurried out. On the chair hung a fresh towel above a big bar of homemade soap.

Once they had left, I wasted no time stepping into the tub and tried curling down to get under the lovely warm water. No doubt, I hadn't felt so royally treated since I left home. Yes, my confrontation with that captain was bringing rewards I never expected.

I sat soaping myself, completely relaxed and dreaming of my service tomorrow. I'd start with simple morning prayer — that would be best. And who knows, I might even start having two services, one here in our little mission house, and one over in Tabacher at the one-room mission. I felt quite prepared for the future, because cleanliness, as my mother often said, is next to godliness. How lucky to have this bath. Yes, I reflected, Lorna is indeed a prize!

Chapter Six

The seal fishing had been going on for two weeks when on Saturday I arranged for Lorna to wake me before dawn. The winter was definitely upon us, though without enough snow for long-distance travel. I had settled in pretty well, teaching school now for four weeks and taking on my share of daily chores, including daily trudges up the hill with my still-mute Lorna to get water from Vincent's brook behind the village; a big enough supply had not been laid in for Aunt Minnie during the summer. Lorna was getting healthier every day, and once when I tripped and spilt my buckets, she broke into the most delightful peals of laughter.

But early this morning, when I felt a gentle shaking and opened my eyes to see my dark-haired companion bending over me, lamp in hand, I found it hard to make myself rise. I thanked her, she put down the lamp and withdrew, and I forced myself out of bed.

I don't know when I have ever felt so tired. As I dressed, I reflected that teaching school, a job I had not subscribed to nor trained for, was taking far more out of me than I ever imagined. Instructing a dozen children in Mutton Bay in the one-room mission house all morning, and then walking some five miles over to Tabacher Cove's mission while eating lunch, then having to find lessons and keep interested another two dozen children of all ages, was almost more than I could handle. I also had pastoral calls to make and sermons to prepare for two services on Sunday and another one during the week. Now it was already the season of Advent, with three more weeks to Christmas.

I went downstairs and gulped the bowl of porridge with molasses that Lorna had gotten up earlier to provide. Thanking her and putting on my coat, I went out to join the others for the day's seal fishery.

My legs felt wooden and my heart wasn't in it. I needed my Saturdays for rest. We rode over the snow to Tabacher, five of us, my first time on a komatik with some ten dogs pulling us. No question, I reflected that the special events of this week had just caught up with me.

The previous Wednesday, Russell Hackey had left Tabacher to go round his trapline in the interior, but not enough snow had fallen to go by dog team. So he had gone on his rackets (from the French, *raquettes*) as snowshoes are called here. A terrific snowstorm had caught him on the way home, and in the ensuing whiteout, with no trees and few landmarks, he'd lost his way. Had he been with dogs, they'd have brought him safely home. When the storm abated the following afternoon and search parties went out, they found his frozen body not a quarter of a mile from safety. And that's where I came in.

His wife, Martha, had waited up all night with five young children. After they had found his body, she went completely mad, tearing her hair, screaming, racing around, striking herself, even attempting to batter one of the smaller children. So they sent for me.

Of course I had absolutely no experience handling such an event. When I arrived, she was restrained by two strong men who had a tight grip on her. But this situation could not last; she kept wrestling frantically. Fortunately, the terrified children had been taken by relatives to another house, in spite of the woman's protestations and wails. I learned all this from Thomas Buffett who had come to fetch me. No one knew what to do. And I confess that included me.

When her older sister ushered me in, although taken aback by the sight of those two men holding Martha, I made myself walk steadily forward, where I stood motionless before her as she howled and gritted her teeth at me. What should I do?

And then, I believe the Lord prodded me into speech. I raised my right hand above her and cried in a loud voice, "In the name of our Lord Jesus Christ — Satan, be gone from this good woman!"

I made the sign of the cross over her. Then I bent and, staring into her face, firmly pronounced the words a second time.

Bless my soul, didn't she relax? I stood up. The men slowly released their grip. She sat, head bowed, and began crying softly. Then she doubled over onto the floor and cried out to the Lord, wanting to know why he had abandoned her husband.

I knelt before her and took hold of her shoulders. "He has *not* abandoned your husband. He has taken him to a far safer place, where storms never rage, the sun always shines, and His light sheds unending love. Russell is safe in the arms of his Lord."

Her crying softened, though still she lay weeping on the hooked rug.

I knelt back. Her two guardians now looked at me with great interest. I lifted my hand to indicate they should remain seated.

Several minutes passed with none of us moving.

"She can't stay here alone tonight," I heard whispered in my ear. Her older sister had bent down and was clearly asking what to do next.

I nodded and held up my hand again. "And now, my dear Martha," I said to the woman, "I want you to go with your sister, and —"

"No no no no, don't leave me, Mr. John, you can't — I won't let you leave me, please, don't leave!"

Now what? I was quite foxed. But then I heard myself say, "I won't. Don't worry, dear Martha, no one will ever leave you alone again, for the Lord himself —"

"Stay with me, stay with me please," she cried broken-heartedly, and I must say my heart strings were mightily tugged.

"All right, Martha, come, you shall accompany me to Aunt Minnie's where, in our prayers, we shall approach the throne of the Heavenly Grace, and there ponder on the wonders of His doing."

I rose.

Opposite me, her two guardians rose also. I turned to her sister. "Get her warm clothes and her night things, and bring her over. We have a spare room. I shall sit and pray with her through the night."

One of the men looked worried and murmured, "I'll be right ready should you need me, Mr. John."

I thanked him and they helped her into her coat. She tugged on a heavy hat and boots and the little entourage made their way to Aunt Minnie's, where her sister got her into bed.

Well, I spent the night sitting by her bedside, reading some psalms, the twenty-third, of course, which she knew by heart, and also my favourite, the forty-sixth: "God is our refuge and our strength; a very present help in trouble." We prayed out loud, and sometimes I alone while she listened. Finally toward morning she fell into a deep sleep. I grabbed a pillow and lay on the mat beside the bed; I did not want to let her out of my sight. But then, when morning came, I had to go off to teach school, and so I left her in the hands of my youthful charge, who then summoned Martha's older sister.

But now on the jolting komatik, I could not get the sight of her five children out of my mind. How would she care for them this winter? How would she feed them with her husband gone? That image had been gnawing at me since the episode and contributed, with lack of sleep, to my present sense of exhaustion.

We reached the flat ice covering this inlet. Beyond it in the low sun, I could see open water. I was about to get into the boat when one of the fisherman, Alfred Robertson, a cousin of Sammy John, looked at me. "You're not goin' fishing in that gear, Mr. John? Better come with me."

His house was not far away, and I followed him to it where, once inside, he got his father's trousers, arm wrappers, and the white canvas jacket everyone wore at this time of winter. I reminded myself that I should have bought one, so perhaps now I would give myself a present at Christmas. I had a warm hat from the Gaspé and he lent me some heavy woollen mitts. His father had passed away the year previously and he had kept his clothing.

"Won't these wool mitts get wet in the water?"

"Sure do. The water round your hands warms up, and they keep yer fingers from freezing."

Back we went to the boat and the five of us dragged it over the ice and launched it into the icy water littered with rocking ice pans.

These seal boats were propelled by two men pulling hard on two oars at one side and one man opposite, toward the back, who manoeuvred a large oar, the "blaine" oar, like a sculling oar. This passed through a whiff, a rope loop, which is how he steered and balanced the boat.

The wind began streaming across the ice as the sun rose; it bit into my cheeks with teeth of steel and I wrapped my scarf tighter.

On the way over, my attention had been drawn to an open

patch of black water. Heads rather like black dogs were rising above the surface and looking about: seals, playing like children, splashed and dove. They would hold still and stare at the boat, and then kerplunk! Disappear into the icy depths. Closer at hand, one little seal lifted his round, shiny head, whiskers twitching, probably a one year old. Then he turned and dove with a splatter back to join his school.

"Cute little fellas, eh?" said Alfred as we rowed on.

My heart sank. I knew the seals would migrate in great herds from Greenland down to and along the Labrador coast, turning and migrating through the Strait of Belle Isle and along the Canadian Labrador heading to their whelping grounds off the Mags and PEI. So these seals still hadn't pupped yet: it was the "teenagers" I was seeing.

We rowed out to a white buoy that indicated one end of the sixty-fathom net stretched the previous day from one island across the whole channel. Shaped like a seine net with a kind of V at the centre, it caught seals heading through the channel at night which then found themselves with no outlet and eventually got tangled up and drowned.

We began pulling the net up, four of us abreast, the man at the rear on the blaine oar still manoeuvering the boat.

I found it heavy work and began panting even after the first couple of minutes. We hauled and hauled at the net without any sign of a seal. We just kept pulling and then after a bit, when I was about done in, the scutters (tail flippers) of a seal appeared. The fisherman next to me, Alfred, hauled off his mitts and in those freezing waters began to disentangle the seal with his bare hands. He had to unhook the net around the flippers while the other men pulled it sideways, until finally, the whole seal, all five hundred pounds, shiny, black, plump, was rolling around next to the boat as we kept pulling at the net. I was shouldered aside as Ivan Green, the fisherman on my left, bent over with Alfred and grabbed the flippers. They bounced the seal a couple times, dousing it deep in the water and lifting it up again, until they got enough purchase to haul it over the gunnel and tip it into the boat.

"Any of them ever alive? " I asked rather fearfully.

Ivan shook his head. "Always dead." He began hauling again and the four of us went at it, pulling up the net until another seal surfaced, dead as well.

After a few seals had been landed in the boat, I took my place to pull one in, grabbing hold of a flipper on one side with Alfred on the other. We practised bouncing it — but I nearly took a header into the water as it went down, and then as we pulled it up I fell backwards into the boat on top of the other seal carcasses. The men laughed good-naturedly and I got up, embarrassed, and we began pulling the net in again.

This went on until we had gotten a goodly load of seals into the boat. I thought it dangerous to haul in any more for the waters were up to the boat's gunnels. Nervously, I watched another one hauled in, but then by mutual consent we turned the boat round and headed for shore. The wind was fierce, and we who were not rowing stood and beat our arms about our bodies to warm our fingers.

Another boat had made it before us. With its added weight of seals, it had broken through the not-so-thin ice. We headed for this opening and once in the narrow channel, everyone piled out and, slipping along the snowy ice, pulled the boat up the waterway to the shore.

I saw a couple of teams of dogs trotting toward the sealing station. One team had already begun dragging the dead seals along the ice behind the komatik toward the granite cape where they'd be processed.

Once we landed, our fishermen got out seal-dogs, similar to the sharp pulp-hooks we used in the Gaspé, curved like a question mark with a round loop at one end as a handle. Alfred brought his dog down hard to spear the head of one of the dead seals and, with the help of a couple others on the slippery ice, hauled the heavy carcass out of the boat. They proceeded in such fashion until all the seals lay in a row: black, humped islands on a sea of flat white ice.

Hollis Reed drove up on his komatik, keeping his team well clear of the others. The dogs had been setting up a chorus of barks, growls, snarls, and yelps. As I stood watching, Hollis winked at me. "One o' mine is terble fierce. So I got to keep 'im clear o' the others."

Then Hollis drove his hook with its cord into the head of the nearest seal, tied this to the komatik, jumped on, and shouted at his dogs. Off they stormed, all six of them, hauling the slippery seal over the ice a hundred yards to where the scaffold stood like an impending crucifixion against the grey sky. A couple of others had gathered there to sculp (butcher) the seals, or raise them onto the scaffolding.

"What now?"

"Once our seals are drug up, we go back for more," Alfred assured me with a smile. "Some of these we sculp now, others we leave whole for the spring. That's when we get the foundry working to render down the fat."

I was utterly beat, ready to drop, but I didn't want to let on — the last thing I wanted was for the village to think their clergyman a weakling. So off we went in the boat and repeated the whole exercise a second time, until well into the afternoon. We had hardly taken a break for our dinners, stopping only for hot tea and some bread and molasses. I don't know when I've been so tired.

While Alfred's team was unloading what was to be his last lot, the rest of us gathered about a fire someone had built to heat a kettle. I saw one of the dogs start tearing at a seal. The owner went over to beat it off with a whip. Another fisherman got down on his hands and knees to chisel up a patch of seal blood that had frozen itself into a wide red pancake on the ice. He took the chips and threw them to the team, so that the dogs had a little something to go on with. They tore at it, fighting among themselves. Ravenous, I thought, and I said so.

"Naw, they's always that way, eh? Unless you give 'em a real big feed. And they know that's what's coming tonight, big feed o' seal."

I drifted away with my hot mug of tea, sensing the air and hoping there would not be yet another trip out on that black water today, for I just could not manage it. A boy, probably six or seven, came trotting over the cape toward us carrying a hot can of soup for his father. As he came closer, he tripped on the shiny ice and began to tumble down the hill. One of the dogs ran across to sniff at him and before we knew it, the rest of the dogs had followed and then they actually began to nip and tear at the fallen child.

His father let out a yell; the men leapt up and ran for the child, screaming at the dogs.

I was closest and awkwardly slithered as fast as I could toward the dogs that were now biting at the child with bared teeth and pulling off actual flesh. As I reached them, I tumbled into their feeding frenzy, but once under the welter of legs and snapping insanity, I thrashed at them with my mittened hands, one arm over my face to protect it, trying ineffectually to beat them off the boy. The men arrived with whips and poles and freed the child, and I got to my feet.

But the child lay motionless.

The father grabbed him up in his arms, shouting to another who marshalled his dog team. We ran for his komatik, fell on it, and off we tore to Old Post at the far end of Tabacher, to find Aunt Alice, the middah, as midwives are called.

I couldn't stop replaying in my mind the menace and utter madness of that horrible scene while the father kept calling out, "James, James, don't worry, we're taking you, you'll be all right, you'll be fine." But as I looked behind, I saw a distinct trail of blood.

We arrived at the middah's and rushed inside. The father laid his child gently on the table while Aunt Alice hurried to bring hot water from her stove. I sat numbly in one corner.

I've no idea why I had jumped on the komatik with the father: I must have felt a clergyman's place was with anyone needing help.

Aunt Alice worked at the boy, cleaning him, using a sewing needle to stitch the many cuts, while his father held his thumb on an artery as instructed. Would the lad be saved? I didn't dare think. I just sat staring at the floor, my heart beating, my whole body exhausted, shaken, indeed tormented to my core, by this experience. What a cap to a horrendous week, with Wednesday's tragedy, awful beyond all thoughts.

Finally, after all that Aunt Alice could do, the little fellow just gave up the ghost.

After saying a prayer over him, I walked home to Aunt Minnie's, my head sunk on my chest.

When I opened the door, Lorna's face lit up but then frowned as she saw my distress. She and Aunt Minnie stood silently beside the tub they had been preparing for my Saturday bath. I shook my head and mounted the steep staircase, unable to speak.

At the top, I turned into my room and closed the door. I took off my shoes and sat on the edge of the bed. What was all this for?

Why had the good Lord brought me here? I had not been able to stop the death of the little lad. I had seen the results of Russell Hackey freezing to death. Doing my best, working so hard all day, I had only ended up with feelings of helplessness, no good to anybody. Why come here if I had no effect upon the course of these good people's destiny? I felt broken, covered in despair.

Where are you, Lord, when I need you, I asked. This is just the perfect time to appear to me. I need you so badly.

Silently the door opened. But I did not hear it. I leaned down, pressed my face into the bed, bereft, my eyes filling with tears. Stop it, you coward, I growled, sit up, be a man! Get yourself together! But I could no more move than fly. I just wanted to die. I had failed, failed myself, failed the lad, failed the village, failed everywhere and everyone. I wished I were a child again, with no worries or responsibilities.

I felt someone come and sit close. Lorna lifted my shoulders and placed my head against her shoulder. And I heard the words, "Don't cry, Mr. John. Please don't cry."

And then I did exactly that, I did let the tears come. I found myself clutching her as though she were my mother. All the weariness, the emptiness and, especially, the frustration at not having had any effect on anything, had proved too much. My exhausted soul could no longer bear the strain. I let myself cry like a baby, while Lorna rocked me, whispering soothing words in my ear.

And then after a moment, I lifted my tear-stained eyes and looked at her. "You spoke!"

Lorna smiled, and then frowned. "I spoke..."

Pretty momentous. I needed time to absorb that.

She seemed to brighten as she realized that her speech had been restored.

But I didn't move. It felt so good, like being in a mother's arms that I had not felt since I was ten years old. I needed to be held, to be loved, because with all the love that I had tried to give in the village, and with all the love I had seen reflected back in their eyes, there was nothing, just nothing like the touch of a woman, the embrace of her warm arms enfolding me as when I was little.

Finally, I managed to collect myself and sat up straight. I reached my hand over and clutched hers without looking at her. "You must think me such a wretched coward. A spoilt child. Incapable of carrying out anything worthwhile as a clergyman."

"No, John. I have been through it and understand. You are by no means weak, but brave to admit such helplessness."

Yes indeed, of all people, she was the one to know what I'd gone through, for she had gone through so much worse. And I knew I could rely on her not to spread the news of these moments of utter weakness to the rest of the village.

"Now, John," she said in firm tones as she might use to a child, "you sit here for a while. Aunt Minnie and I have a hot bath for you. You take it, and come back up to bed. In the morning, you'll feel like a new man." She paused, and stroked my arm, reassuringly. "This brush with the dark forces, it'll clean your spirit and build your hopes again. Done you good, I'm sure, though maybe it's hard for you to see that. I knew somehow it might be coming."

No doubt, some modicum of truth in what she said. How wise she was! She went on, "And now, tomorrow, you'll take that funeral like any ordinary clergyman. I know these depths of despair better than you might imagine, and I also know that one can emerge, with God's grace."

"Lorna, Lorna..." I wanted to thank her, to explain how important she had become to me now. But all I said was, "You may be right. Although, for the life of me, I can't see any worth in myself." I sat straighter. "No, no, despair is a sin. With prayers, I'm sure I shall be able to put it all behind me."

She got up, quietly closed the door, and left me to myself.

But was I so sure? Not really. In fact, was this the beginning of a doubt about the great compassion I had always believed Our Lord to bestow upon His race? No, I told myself, do not let that in: it could run riot with everything I was doing. I must persevere somehow. I tried to sustain myself by remembering from college that first, or was it the second, proof for God we learned in our first year of Theology: that God, in order to be truly loved, had to give us, His people, our free will. That meant we were, of course, free to make mistakes. And free to turn our backs on Him. So now again, my mind churned, oh yes. Would these setbacks become real obstacles to my belief? I hoped not. I just hoped they would not continue to weigh me down too heavily.

Chapter Seven

At last, Christmas morning arrived. I woke bright and early, for I was taking an early service here in Mutton Bay and then going by komatik to Tabacher, where I was taking a later service. This last while, one of my oldest students in his late teens, Clayton Green, Ivan's son, had been helping me by driving my dogs and instructing me in the proper manner of doing so. I had changed my pattern. To conserve energy, I taught the first half of the week here and the second half there, so on each trip to and from Tabacher I had been receiving lessons. You shout "ak ak" for right and "radda radda" for left. The team assigned to me seemed more pliable, and certainly less ferocious, than the dogs of Fred's team which had been put down, the invariable rule once animals had tasted human blood. I confess I didn't feel sorry for them. I had often visited the father of the lad they had killed, as well as Martha Hackey, the widow whose husband had frozen to death. She seemed to have recovered and was bearing up: her children were at home, but relatives had rallied round to make sure she'd weather the winter.

I got to church early because I wanted to make sure all the decorations were in order. My ladies had done a wonderful job of sprucing up the church, even having made a tiny crêche. The smallish Christmas tree stood in one corner, fetched by our lay reader, Mr. Organ, and his team. Fine wreaths of greenery decorated the ends of the pews, some were even tied with red ribbons carefully saved from year to year.

Everyone turned out on a sunny but cold Christmas morning. A mood of optimism and cheerfulness ran through the congregation as they gathered. The seal hunt was still going well. I had begged off any further involvement, saying I just could no longer deal with so many duties.

Finally, the service began with a rousing Christmas hymn: "We Three Kings." It was going to be, of course, a Communion service: the wine and bread had been consecrated by Gene. I had begun reading the first lesson when my eye caught a tall figure kneeling in the back row. I looked closer, for it seemed as though a new parishioner had appeared from nowhere. In a community such as ours, not only did we know everyone, but also the last detail of everyone else's business, as well as all comings and goings. But the figure seemed familiar, and then all at once, it struck me: Lorna! She had come to church.

I got such a surprise that I faltered in my reading and it didn't help that I noticed her smother a smile as she bowed her head to hide what might be seen as any delight at my discomfort.

Since that night when I had revealed myself rather too openly and she had finally begun to speak, her recovery had been rapid. She had become more involved in village affairs, often going out to help the elderly in return for little favours or exchanges of food that relatives would give to her and that she would bring home. Of course, for me, it was wonderful to have a companion I could talk with, over my hurried breakfasts and in the evenings. When Aunt Minnie retired, Lorna and I would stay up, sometimes quite late, discussing matters that were close to my heart: theology and the teachings of Our Lord. It was particularly enjoyable because my favourite, St. Paul, the travelling saint, had begun to intrigue her as much as me. Together we explored his writings. So it was only natural that she should start coming to church, I reflected, as I kept on with the service.

But when she came to the altar rail for Communion, she appeared so very striking, dressed in an outfit she had not previously worn. Such a transformation! Her appearance set my head spinning, I confess, though I sternly brought my thoughts back to the Lord's Supper, which I was administering.

Aunt Minnie had been lucky enough to have some of her relatives visit from Harrington Harbour. This Christmas season her niece and husband had sledded in from Wolf Bay as soon as the channel between Harrington and the mainland had frozen over. Her son, Will, whose wife had died soon after the birth of their second child, had also brought his children to visit their grandmother. So we had a housefull. Lorna willingly took on the challenge of caring for them all, making meals from our diminishing store of provisions, and doing a marvellous job, as Aunt Minnie kept saying.

After the service we settled into a fine dinner prepared by Lorna and Aunt Minnie with her niece. The grandchildren loved opening their presents from their father. I had given Lorna a pair of sealskin boots gotten after my seal-fishing trip and Aunt Minnie a crocheted shawl from Shigawake that my mother had given me, as a present for any future landlady. Aunt Minnie professed herself delighted, as did Lorna. Aunt Minnie presented me with a heavy sweater she had knitted while I had been out teaching school. Lorna had been working at Captain Joseph Blais's simple store, much in need of care when the captain returned from sailing after the freeze up, and he had traded her a wonderful, lined canvas coat for me for my winter's travelling. It fitted perfectly and I felt rather grand wearing it.

It was painfully obvious to me that Will, Aunt Minnie's son, had eyes only for Lorna, almost to the point of ignoring his own children. Ridiculous though it may sound, I even felt some stirrings of jealousy. It was clear that he wanted, and what is more, needed, a wife. And I suspected that Aunt Minnie had sent word for him to come and meet Lorna this holiday, though nothing was ever said.

A couple of days after Christmas, we were sitting around the table, gossiping by the light of a coal-oil lamp. It gets dark this season before four in the afternoon, so the evenings are long and by no means as cheery as in the summer. Will was leaning across the table, staring most provokingly I thought into Lorna's face, who was sitting back demurely, glancing from him to me. Was she aware of what was going on? I was trying not to watch and, glancing out the dark window, I saw without warning, I swear it, some kind of old-fashioned ghost. It disappeared, and then reappeared. But was it a ghost? It was all white with two big black sockets for eyes. Then a second figure appeared — could that be a witch? I was so startled that I almost spilt my tea. The others whirled round and the two apparitions ducked below the windowsill. I looked at my companions in consternation. And then we heard two sharp raps on the door.

What on earth? My anxiety was by no means vanquished by a burst of laughter from Aunt Minnie. An odd sound like a frog croaking formed the words: "Let the mummers in!"

"Took 'em 'nough time to get 'ere," was all Aunt Minnie said as she rose and bustled to the door, myself and Lorna remaining at the table, looking at each other and wondering what was going on. Will, of course, had risen with his mother and now welcomed an assortment of what I presume were demented human beings. None but the insane would dress themselves like that.

Men were dressed as women, women as men, old clothes mingled with oilskins, sou'westers, white canvas, and all manner of bizarre garments. Several layers of clothing went to make up these homegrown costumes: dresses over outerwear, skirts over pants, bulges in odd parts of bodies contrived by the mischievous to reshape themselves. Fur hats worn backwards, cloth caps, sacks on which features had been stenciled, with holes cut for the eyes. Some wore higher heels to make them look taller, others came in stout slippers. I detected padding in legs and bellies to make the slender fatter, and loose hanging tunics of sheets to hide those already overweight. One had managed a wig of tousled red wool and had made a fake nose out of cork, outlining thin lips outrageously in red berry juice.

Aunt Minnie quickly explained that between Christmas and the Feast of the Epiphany, Twelfth Night, mummering was all the rage. Our first task now was to guess who these mummers were. We tried to get them to talk by various ruses, but borrowed clothes and cleverly placed padding prolonged the uncertainty for a while. Aunt Minnie and her niece brought out the cakes and jams and goodies which she had been preparing the last couple of days for just this occasion. There was much laughter and fun, though the mummers all kept their voices disguised.

Lorna had the idea of going up to one who looked like a man, and trying to tickle him so that she could tell by his laughter. A couple of women had built themselves out with the use of pillows, large and small. One of Will's lads grabbed a thread from a corner and pulled on it, unravelling the pillow to spill the feathers all over. They covered the room, causing some merriment.

One of the older men, who later turned out to be John Chubbs, produced a fiddle from under his cavernous uniform and sat down on a chair to strike up a jig. Almost at once, the entire company was frolicking around the room, smearing bits of jam on their faces as they tried to eat under their hoods while someone else's hat fell on the floor, revealing a mass of red hair. "Aggie Green!" we cried, recognizing the teenager. Her father, Thomas Green, took Sunday School for me, and Clayton, her cousin, was my driver. We went on dancing, and I saw Will go over to try to spill out more feathers from the chest of one of the mummers.

"Ouch!" the mummer cried. "You can't unravel these!"

We all laughed heartily and in spite of myself, I joined in, grabbing hold of one of the mummers and whirling round in the square dance. Cups of tea were handed out, and sweetened juice. Finally everyone flopped on chairs, tired from the dancing.

"C'mon now," a gruff and still disguised voice called out. "Come, Mr. John, come, Lorna and Will, you gotta join us. We 'ave another house to go to — one that's serving something stronger than Aunt Minnie's juice!"

I glanced at Lorna, who leapt up happily and went across to the pegs by the door, where she grabbed a coat.

"Just a minute," I called out and tore up the narrow staircase to get her some men's clothes, even though she was taller, but certainly no heavier, than I was. When I came down, she had gotten me an apron, a shawl and a bonnet, and I proceeded to dress myself as a serving woman. Will had found some fishing gear, put on a heavy sou'wester backwards and fitted an oversize pair of sealskin boots. The niece and her husband elected to stay home with Aunt Minnie.

In our crazy disguises, Will, Lorna, and I joined the others to troop out into the snow and over the bridge to the Hockeys, where the rum would "flow like water." I was a bit hesitant, not knowing quite how to take this occasion when the devil alcohol would rear its ugly head. But of course, this one-and-only season of mummering was all very much part of tradition. Dancing, drinking, making jokes, cutting up, having fun — I might as well get into the swing of it.

Someone rapped smartly on the door with a stick and the cry went out, "Let the mummers in."

Uncle Willie Reid threw open his door, and we janneys, as mummers are called, all trooped in.

It so happened there was another group already there, for Willie was known for his generosity with a keg of rum and a barrel of homemade beer. Another fiddler, who had stopped his music when we arrived, struck up "St. John's Reel" and our fiddler joined him. Willie went around filling up the cups with rum or homemade beer. I allowed myself to take some and when I glanced, I saw that Lorna too was enjoying a tot.

What a marvellous evening! Willie's place was big enough for us all to dance two separate circles, and one young woman had brought over some salt pork from her mother's, so the food and drink flowed and we danced ourselves merry.

The party seemed to be winding down. The last reel had ended up in a frenzy of spinning, after which a couple of the men found themselves sitting on the floor, having fallen over. The fiddlers and feet beaters stopped and helped themselves liberally to jugs of beer, while the rest of us, knowing by now who each other was, began to collect our wits.

Three or four of the older folk began putting on their coats to leave. Will had poured himself another cup of rum, and I followed him as he crossed to where Lorna was talking to a couple of the ladies. She was still dressed as a man but had taken off the sheet over her face so that she could breathe more easily while dancing. She was flushed and I must say looked extremely pretty.

"So, Will," I said, "I think it's my bedtime. I'm heading back to your mother's." I glanced at Lorna. "Perhaps you're ready to go, too?"

"Oh no." Will took her by the arm. "She's staying, there's still a lot of life in the old fiddler yet. We're gonna dance a couple more, eh Lorna?"

Lorna shook her head. "I'm sorry, Will, I do think it's my bedtime. You forget I get up early to prepare everything. I'll come with you now, Mr. John."

Will frowned. "No, no, no, Lorna stay a bit. You gotta stay a bit." He pulled her to him and put an arm around her waist. I cringed inwardly but tried to show nothing. She gently disengaged his arm and then, quickly dodging his other attempt to grab her, hurried across the room to get her coat. I followed her and out the door we went.

She shook her head as we went down the steps and headed up the path. "My head feels light," she said. "Time we left for sure."

I saw her tottering and hurried close, whereupon she seized hold of my waist to steady herself. "Hang on to me, Mr. John. I don't feel so well."

Fortunately, I had stopped at two good swigs of rum myself and so felt confident on my feet, but she was distinctly tipsy, through no fault of her own, I was quite sure. No matter what man she was dancing with, and I danced with her too, each tried to pour more rum into her in spite of her protestations.

So the two of us, clutching each other, struggled home over the icy bridge — I would almost say staggered, but that would apply more to her than to me. At the end of the bridge she had to stop and lean against the rail. But she didn't let go of my waist.

We stood together and then her head fell against mine, so that her hair, which by now had fallen loose, surrounded me. I breathed in its essence in the night air. We looked out into the moonlight falling on the hills of Mutton Bay.

The sounds of a fiddle from another house drifted across the white spaces. A few dogs barked. Otherwise, all was silent. Although cold, it was not bitterly so. I found it impossible not to wonder at the still beauty of the night. We remained silent, close, for I still kept hold of her, afraid she might fall.

She turned to me, and looked into my eyes with unspoken, innocent longing. Our faces were only inches apart. "Time we got back," I said firmly, and moved her off from the bridge across the snow-covered rocks toward Aunt Minnie's.

"I've gotten to know you pretty well, Mr. John."

"Oh dear," was all I could reply.

"No, Mr. John, you're such a good and fine man. Even if you had not rescued me, I know that my feelings for you would have —" and she slipped and almost fell.

I grabbed hold of her and although she was a couple of inches taller, briskly manoeuvred her the rest of the way, up the three stairs to Aunt Minnie's, and inside. We divested ourselves of our heavy coats and she flopped on a chair, shaking her head.

"I don't think I can navigate those stairs," she said in a small voice.

"That's no trouble. I shall help you."

She looked up at me with such big dark eyes, almost as a child might look up at her father. Or was that possibly a different kind of affection?

I helped her climb, step by step, quietly so as not to wake Aunt Minnie and the children. We gained the upper landing and she leaned against the wall. "My head is spinning."

If I let her go, I knew she'd fall, so with my arm still around her waist and her arm over my shoulder I moved her forward, turned left, and opened her bedroom door. I couldn't just push her into the room, so indeed I went in with her and walked her over to her bed.

She flopped on it and sat there, and then shook her head and passed her hand over her brow.

I turned to go, but I realized that would be callous. "Now, Lorna dear, it's time you got into bed and had a good sleep."

She nodded. But I could see she had no idea what to do next.

I guided her head back onto the pillow. And then I lifted her long legs in their trousers onto the feather bed, covered them with the patchwork quilt and stood back.

Almost as soon as her head touched the pillow, it seemed that she had fallen asleep. She lay, her dark hair flowing over the pillow, the moonlight framing her superbly formed features, now relaxed completely.

I couldn't move. I just stood looking down at her face and her dark hair awry but still glossy in soft waves. I realized that this was a very privileged view, that none but her future husband would ever see.

Then her eyes opened and they seemed to focus on me. "Kiss me good night, Mr. John," she said in the voice of a little girl.

After what she had done to help me in the past, I could do nothing else. I knelt beside her bed and bent to kiss her on her cheek. But as I did, she turned her face up so that her lips met mine.

The touch of those lips, so unexpected, so astonishing, filled every ounce of my being with glorious elation. Never before had I been a party to such a simple but meaningful kiss. I raised my head, breathing heavily, and rose.

I heard her murmur, "Thank you, Johnny."

I stood for a moment, drinking in this sight of her stretched out on her bed under the quilt, face relaxed and so well framed by those black locks. Then I turned, went out, and softly closed her door.

Chapter Eight

January 1897

The Sunday after Christmas, I got my first nasty shock.

Outside on our church stoop, I was greeting the parishioners before they went home, when out of the corner of my eye I saw the somewhat robust head of the Women's Altar Guild hovering, her husband Archie waiting further down the snowy path. The last couple of parishioners went on their way, but she didn't come up, so I turned and went in to hurry out of my vestments.

In sailed Bessie Yarn, closing the door behind her.

I smiled, but saw she had something on her mind. Her face was a mask, under which I detected a determination coupled with nervousness.

"Lovely turnout for New Year's," I said pleasantly, as a way of beginning the conversation.

"Oh yis yis yis. But a lot lovelier if a certain person didn't take it as 'er right now to join us every Sunday. Don't do our church justice."

Whatever did she mean? I went over to hang up my surplice and take off my cassock. "A certain person?" I had no idea in the world what she was talking about.

She paused and stared. Then, as if she had taken a deep breath, she launched out, "Mr. John, I 'ave enough charity to know that at Christmas, we allow everyone to come and worship. But now it looks as if she's coming back every Sunday – a person not fit to set foot on 'oly Ground."

Lorna? Was she talking about her? I had no idea what she was getting at. I felt my jaw tighten as I repressed an urge to lash out. "Mrs. Yarn, are you suggesting that we close our church doors to anyone we happen to consider unworthy?"

"Oh no, Mr. John. But somewheres, a line 'as got to be drawn. That girl, the likes of 'er, dallying with all them sailors one after another, well, do we really want that kind of woman coming 'ere to contaminate our menfolk?"

Contaminate? "Of course, anyone with a contagious disease should be prevented from infecting the rest of our congregation. But, if I divine your reasoning, you're not speaking about that."

"I certainly am not. I'm speaking about 'women of easy virtue.' And you know very well who, bein' the one what rescued 'er."

Women of easy virtue — what a dreadful tag to assign to our lovely Lorna, who had now, for the second time, graced my service.

As I had walked down the aisle during the opening hymn, I had spotted Lorna — taller than the other women, modest, well dressed, even demure, and oh yes, pretty, I just could not believe anyone ever assigned this vision the label "woman of the streets."

"Bessie," I said sternly, "she was a cook on a schooner. Those tribulations she met there caused her a disturbance so severe that she lost her ability to speak — surely none of her own doing!"

"The menfolk 'ereabouts are all 'appy to mind their own business. It's just when someone comes along looking like 'er, men's 'eads turn. The same on that schooner, I can bet you. Don't tell me she didn't invite what she got!"

I held my tongue, because my angry retort would have brought me much anguish. I took a breath, as we clergy had been taught to do. "Bessie," I said gently, "she will come to my church whenever she wants and as long as I am in charge."

I let her absorb that, and went on, "No one would ever believe a word of your accusations. That girl's mind is as pure as the whitest snow."

Bessie Yarn gave a snort.

I knew her to be a mainstay of our congregation. Not only did she run the Altar Guild with tireless efficiency, ironing my surplice, caring for the vestments, she also saw to it that the women of Mutton Bay kept our church spotless, well dusted, and always in order. She was, as a leader, someone to be reckoned with. So no angry defiance that I might throw in her face now would be at all constructive. I had somehow to win her over. But how?

"Dear Bessie, you yourself are quite above reproach. We all know you to be one of the pillars of this church, and indeed of this whole community. But without any shred of evidence to support your accusations —"

"No evidence? What about my husband? Every time she walks by, 'e stares at 'er like a lovesick puppy. He talked of nothing else when she first arrived, until I shut 'im up good and proper."

Aha! Now I saw whence came her concerns. Believe me, I had no idea that Lorna had caused such a stir among the menfolk, or hopefully, to only one of them. In any case, here was a conundrum more difficult than any I had hitherto approached. In a matter so personal, how could I get Archie Yarn to see Lorna in her true light, rather than this idealizing, this stoking of her image in his mind? How could I get him to know her as I did, a lovely, though partially damaged, human being trying to heal herself, to make her way in the world, and at the same time be as helpful to others as she could. My own interest in her, unless I was deceiving myself, was nothing more than as a clergyman who had rescued her, and as a friend who would guide her. I said as much to Mrs. Yarn.

"You see, Bessie, if you saw her as I do, and indeed as I hope most other women will, once they get to know her, all will concede that she is absolutely no challenge whatsoever. She will be going back home to Nova Scotia in the summer," I noticed she relaxed a little, "and she has no designs on anyone here. She, like a child rescued from drowning, is just trying to stay afloat — and even, I might add, hoping to make a few friends while she does it. You have my assurance on that."

I was watching her as I talked, and I saw her features soften. Perhaps the clarity of my voice, combined with the fact that I was still her clergyman, had a calming effect. She knew me as a friend of Lorna, and so would know whereof I spoke.

"So you intend to allow that hussy to keep on as part of our congregation? Kneel at our church's rail, and partake of the Lord's Supper, along with the rest of us?"

That phrase somehow sounded as if she had used it before, hopefully only to her husband and not the Women's Guild. But her voice had lost its earlier tension.

"The past is past, Bessie. As you know, our Lord said, I came not to call the righteous, but the sinners to repentance. If you are unable to accept my dictum, that she is absolutely innocent and by no means to blame for those tribulations on that schooner, then at least remember our Lord who hung on that cross in propitiation for all our sins. You must try to do likewise. Forgive her. Welcome her, as He would have done."

"Well, one thing I just can't understand," Bessie Yarn said, after a significant pause while she digested my remarks, "why did she take that job in the first place? There's rumours about schooners."

"You don't mean that on every schooner, the cook is being violated?"

"No, of course not, Mr. John. Most crew men, as I said before, are honourable, and their captains honest."

"So would you then agree that, in fact, she might have been thinking the same thing when she accepted the captain's offer?"

I had her there. She dropped her eyes, paused, and then nodded.

By now I had put on my coat, and retrieved my hat and mitts.

"Well," she declared, "I'll think about what you said, Mr. John. Lot of it makes sense. If only my husband..."

"He will get over it, Bessie, don't worry about that. If you are tender and loving, as I know you to be, how could he not? But if you continue to reprimand him and act suspicious, you will only drive him away. So your duty now is to your husband. You just make him feel loved and secure, as any good wife should."

As the words came out of my mouth, I had no idea where they came from, but they did contain a certain amount of understanding of relationships — which I confess I myself did not have.

Again she nodded, and then she actually smiled, as if relieved, and held out her hand. I took hers in mine, and then I blessed her, and she went out into the morning sunshine. I remained behind on a nearby pew to do some thinking. How widespread was her sentiment? Had I scotched it properly? Or would it continue to haunt me? And Lorna? I decided I had to remain vigilant.

As for the next couple of weeks, they came and went, I don't know where. I continued teaching five days, visiting the sick on Saturdays, preparing my sermon, holding services, and even one weekend made a foray back into the woods with Clayton Green, who had been teaching me how to handle the dog team and helping me to cut extra wood for Aunt Minnie. In the evenings, Lorna and I continued as before, discussing the Scriptures and exchanging a few gratifying words at breakfast. The altercation with Mrs. Yarn after church, and the events of the night of mummering, were not touched on, neither was my earlier breakdown after the seal hunt. But one morning she confessed that she was not looking forward to the time when I would have to leave. Once the waters had frozen thick enough to allow safe travelling with our dog team, I planned to make one trip East and one West, several hundred miles in all.

But here it was approaching the middle of January and I had to get ready. The last two days in Tabacher School were rather harried for I wanted to give them homework while I was away. It didn't help matters that the one room was so cold the ink froze in the pens. We were running out of wood, because I'd been piling it into the stove to keep the place warm. Although the parents should have seen that we needed a good supply, they thought I'd be leaving and had let it dwindle.

During the month, I wondered about taking off alone with the dogs. The last few trips to the school I had been driving the dog team myself, with Clayton sitting behind and offering helpful tips. Then he told me he wanted to come along on the trip with me, because he was determined to continue his lessons. He dreamed of becoming a teacher himself. Quite a bright youth, taller than me, thin, with a shock of black hair and dark eyes, he had an oddly boney face for one so young. He excelled at arithmetic so I knew he would do well in the sciences, of which I had little knowledge. Proper English he found difficult to write but I thought that would come.

On the one hand I looked forward to the adventure, calling in on the parts of my parish which were sorely in need by now of a pastoral visit; but on the other hand, I was not sure how I'd handle the long stretches alone, not really knowing the ropes. So it was decided that on my first trip eastward, he would accompany me, and that put my mind at rest.

Fortunately, the team had taken other clergy on such trips and our lead dog, Tuck, was well acquainted with the route. She was the oldest dog on the team and certainly the canniest. A good team depends upon a good leader. Of course with Tuck leading, there was bound to be a dog called Nip, with Snap, Grey, Dim, Blue, and finally Rob, the heaviest and pluckiest, nearest the komatik. They were all harnessed by individual traces made of sealskin, forty-feet-long, to Tuck, the shortest of eight feet to Rob, so they could travel Indian file on wooded trails. All these strands were attached to a stout bridle of seal hide called the pittuk, which goes around the two forward struts, fastened to them with a knot that in an emergency can be quickly released. Our komatik was red ochre, fourteen-feet-long, low-lying, with open slats lashed (no nails) across two runners, and a box in the middle for supplies on which we sat. Usually these boxes were covered in sealskin, or caribou hide. The runners slid on whalebone and in cold weather we glazed them with ice.

A heavy snowstorm forestalled my departure but gave me the extra two days needed to prepare everything. Aunt Minnie supervised the provisioning, with Lorna helping. My wardens turned up with more good advice, bringing extra seal fat for the dogs. In addition, they told us we'd need a good half a sack of cornmeal, about fifty pounds, a couple of seal carcasses and a goodly supply, about a gallon, of cod oil to pour onto their food. For ourselves, we brought mainly salt cod and fat salt pork, with of course tea and molasses. Aunt Minnie also baked quantities of beans with pork, but hardtack and dried codfish were our main staples, with Aunt Minnie's molasses-and-raisin bread for special treats.

I could see Lorna watching the preparations for my departure with some apprehension. "I don't like to see you go off with that lad." She was working on a rug hooked from burlap sacks that once held hardtack or potatoes. After cutting the sacks into strips, she'd put the strips into water with spruce or fir bark and other plants to add colour and then boil it all up along with "*cateau*" or resin till it got thicker, and the colour would set in the burlap.

"He's only a year or two younger than you, dear Lorna."

"He may be. I just worry about you, that's all." She dropped her eyes and went on with her "barking," as they called the process. I confess I was too excited at the prospect of this, my first major winter trip, that I did not adequately respond to her discomfort. But then again, I was leaving this group of parishioners and had carefully arranged the church services with my wardens and lay reader as to which lessons they should read and how they ought to proceed. I hoped to be back in about three weeks.

The morning for my leaving, January 20th, dawned with the sky still overcast, but the last of the snowstorm drifting away. Clayton turned up bright and early and Lorna fed the both of us, a fine meal of porridge with dollops of molasses. We wouldn't be getting porridge for a while, so I had a second helping.

I embraced Aunt Minnie, thanked her for everything, and asked her to keep a good eye on dear Lorna and look after her. Then I turned to Lorna, and she hugged me so hard I even felt her body shaking. She buried her head in my shoulder and whispered, "I don't want you to go, Jack."

This was the first time I'd heard my nickname mentioned. I had probably told her that my sisters and little Earle called me that.

As I held her tightly I said to her, "Now look, you take care of Aunt Minnie for me. And please, Lorna, take care of yourself."

And then, because I didn't want to prolong the parting, I hurried outside where Clayton had the komatik ready with the dogs hitched. I wanted him to drive the first leg so that I could hang on and just enjoy this beginning of what I hoped would be an exciting three or four weeks. I thought little of the dangers sure to ensue.

Before going far, we headed out onto the frozen strait among the islands, far enough from shore to avoid drifts built up near any headlands. This route to St. Augustine ran on the landward side of a chain of islands, so the ice had frozen hard under the dusting of snow.

We kept scanning for signs of habitation. The "livyers," as they called permanent residents, wintered in coves and at the mouths of rivers, to use the protection that occasional woods or rocky capes might provide and for easier access to interior forests for firewood, trapping, and hunting. The streams also provided feeds of trout.

Before leaving I had packed a few textbooks and found time to map out in my mind the topics that I would like to teach Clay. Later I determined I'd examine him to find out if he had indeed been absorbing my lessons. I was the most versed in biblical history and classics from my time at Bishop's. But I felt I should focus rather on his English, some history of North America, and indeed, a little geography, for I found the inhabitants of the Canadian Labrador woefully short on knowledge of the rest of the world, such as Russia, the Far East, Australia, and even indeed, Africa, a continent I hoped one day to visit myself.

So as we sped along, I reviewed what I proposed to teach and he seemed eager to begin. We intended to spend every available hour on the komatik exchanging ideas, with me offering him what little knowledge I did have on subjects he would need to further his education.

Toward late afternoon, we saw three houses in a cove and headed in their direction. Tuck knew what she was doing and brought us to the one with smoke lifting from the chimney. We got off and stretched, and I went to knock on the door, though it wasn't necessarily part of my own parish.

The lady of the house opened it and, after I introduced myself, welcomed me inside. Behind her I saw her three children and elderly parents, but there was definitely an air of anxiety. She told Clayton where to find the empty dog pen behind the house, and he went to feed the team and pen them up for the night.

It wasn't long before the reason for their anxiety came out: a week ago the father had taken his komatik to go hunting. He must have been caught in the storm that delayed our departure. It had cleared by noon today, but still she'd seen no sign of her husband. When Clay came back in, I alerted him to the situation. The first thing we did was kneel and I led prayers for his safe return.

What a shame I thought, as we rose, that this first house might soon be the scene of another tragedy. Her father-in-law kept insisting on hobbling to the door and stepping outside into the frosty afternoon to scan for signs of his son. I tried to keep the situation hopeful, so when he came back to sit morosely by the stove, I told optimistic Bible stories to take their minds off the impending tragedy. The wife busied herself putting on supper, but I could almost hear the minutes ticking by.

"Maybe Clay and I should go looking?"

She shook her head. "The Lavallées next house, they've gone, the b'ye and 'is older brother."

Nothing for it but to wait.

The fifth or sixth time the old father went to the door, he shouted, "I see 'im, I see 'im!" Everyone, children included, rushed out, though it was freezing, and peered into the dusk. Yes, a dog team with a komatik.

Dorothy, his wife, called, "That's 'is team, I recognize it."

Everyone bustled inside while Dorothy put the kettle on and stoked the fire. The children were jumping up and down with excitement. Clay donned his overcoat, sealskin boots, and mitts, ready to help when the team arrived.

The dogs dutifully pulled the komatik up outside the house, yapping and barking, and we rushed out. The man had been haphazardly lashed to the komatik. We undid the wrapping and Clay and I helped him into the house. He looked badly frozen, in fact, half dead. He could not stand on his own.

We got him onto his bed and left his wife to undress him and check out the severity of his frostbite. While Dorothy was in there, the old man found some seal meat for the ravenous dogs and he and Clay went to tend to them.

When Dorothy emerged from the bedroom, she grabbed an axe, gave it to Clay, and asked him if he would snowshoe down to the sea and fill a bucket with saltwater. Clay, of course, did as he was asked.

Then Dorothy sat with drawn face and told us her husband had apparently been out long enough to run out of food, and was on his way home "when the blizzard came on heavy-like." He had stopped in the cover of some woods and dug a snow cave under the branches of a large spruce. For two days he had lain there, not eating. On the third day when the storm lessened, the starving dogs broke into the komatik box and tore its caribou covering to pieces, ravenous for something to eat. He knew he'd be next. With what little strength he had left and liberal use of the whip, he marshalled the dogs, strapped himself onto the komatik, and lost consciousness, trusting the team to bring him home.

When Clay returned with the saltwater, Dorothy set it on the stove. "Best thing in the world for frostbite," she said. "His legs is no good. They're swelling up somethin' terble. I'm going to bathe 'em in hot saltwater. I 'eard it from my mother. It worked three year ago with Frances next door."

I myself wished that a doctor had been available but then, on this whole coast, there was not one. Every family, especially those isolated as this, had to be their own middahs.

Later as we were sitting down to a supper of hardtack and some of the cod I had brought in from our supplies, the two French Lavallée lads who had gone searching turned up. When the father opened the door, I saw their worn-out look. "We see not'ing. *Pas de signe*. De snow, she cover 'is track."

The lads were, of course, delighted to find that the dogs had brought him back safe. Dorothy invited them in to thaw themselves out and join us in moistened hardtack and fish. After the meal I led this little Catholic group in a prayer of thanksgiving for the safe return of its breadwinner.

With no beds here for us, Clay and I slept on the floor close to the stove, which soon went out. I found myself waking up, shivering, but I was so pleased that this first encounter had not ended in tragedy. Later, I heard that the husband had eventually been able to walk more or less normally.

The next morning Clay and I set off again toward St. Augustine. We made good time across the open ice between the mainland and the islands. At one point, rather than go out around a long cape that blocked the direct route, we decided to take a well-marked trail over it. Going down the far side, we applied the chain drag, which is a chain-rope loop thrown over the nose of the komatik. But still, we began sliding sideways, and finally the sled got away from us. We struck a buried tree trunk and I took a most delightful header into a deep drift of snow.

The dogs were brought up short and waited while Clay disentangled himself from some bushes and trudged up through the drifts to help me get to my feet again. Neither of us were the worse for wear and I found myself laughing. "Narrow escape!" I clapped him on the shoulder and we righted the komatik, thankful that we had lashed down the cargo well enough, and off we went again.

Because the days were still short, there was no possibility of getting to St. Augustine before dark. We both decided it would be safer to spend the night in a copse of stunted trees. I must say I admired Clay, watching him construct a kind of windbreak from chunks of snow with the snow shovel he had brought. Then we lit a fire, heated our tea, wrapped ourselves in blankets and a caribou covering, and fell asleep.

At dawn we were up again and before nightfall had sledded a good long way up the St. Augustine River toward the village of St. Augustine. Clay had been here before and pointed out the Indian reservation on the opposite bank. His cousins lived here so he knew who the lay reader was and after an inquiry got us to Mr. Martin's house. We were, of course, welcomed, and then, what a delight to discover that his two sons, Albert and John, had returned from hunting with a feast of caribou. Clay went off to stay with relatives here, while I sat down with the Martins to enjoy a sumptuous repast. I must say, having eaten very little for the past thirty-six hours, nothing ever tasted as good as that feed of caribou.

The next day being Saturday, I planned to make pastoral visits and then hold services on Sunday, for St. Augustine was lacking a priest to administer the sacraments. Before retiring, our host asked me if tomorrow I might visit a couple after Christmas whose baby had been stillborn. Apparently the wife was suffering from an attack of guilt. I'd be happy to do that, I replied, but then he added that it might be serious: she could not get out of bed, and they feared for her well-being. That night, lying on the bed they kindly offered me, I couldn't get to sleep for worry. How would I handle this new challenge? Finally, having sorted through every lesson from my university courses and finding none that helped, I drifted off into an uneasy sleep.

Chapter Nine

Clay took the day off to be with his relatives and I travelled round the small settlement on this side of the river on my snowshoes, or rackets. I knew the Roman Catholic priest ministered to the natives on the other side as well as taking care of any of his parishioners here. After a surprise lunch of partridge, or ptarmigan, at the Driscolls', another lay reader's home, I set off for the inner edge of the village where the depressed woman was to be found.

I found the simple home and the husband ushered me in, a finger to his lips. The couple seemed in a rather sorry state. After I had taken off my winter outfit, we went to sit by the stove where the husband poured me a cup of tea. His wife lay in their bedroom to one side.

"Aggie just lays there all day, Mr. John. She's no good for nawthin'. I don't know what to do with 'er. She moans about bein' a sinful woman. And there's no better woman alive than my wife." I could see tears starting to form in his eyes. "It weren't 'er fault. Our first baby, born dead. We've been wantin' children now for four year. But she works so hard, she's never been able to keep one. We both thought this was it." He shook his head, and put his head upon his hands.

I sipped my tea as I thought about the situation. Here again, I was at a complete loss. When I was growing up, such things were occasionally talked about among the children, but certainly, during my last years of school at New Carlisle Academy and those three years at Bishop's University, I had never come across anything to guide me in this morbid situation. But then as I looked at the man, I realized I'd better get started. Here I was, supposedly a man of God, just sitting and wondering what to do next. I forced any negative thoughts from my mind and rose. "Fred, I'll see Agnes now."

He nodded and gestured to the door, too sad even to move.

At the door to the woman's room, I turned back. I begged the Lord for something to spring to mind. Fred made as if to rise, and I gestured for him to remain seated. "I had better do this alone." Good Lord, help me, I prayed, but no help came.

I went into the tiny room — just big enough for the bed in which they both slept, a dresser against the wall, and a used chamber pot in full view. I sat down on the edge of the bed and Agnes opened her eyes. Such big round luminous wells, wet I supposed with tears. She blinked as though I were an apparition.

I introduced myself. "I'm stationed at Mutton Bay; this is my first winter trip down along the coast. I came to visit you," I said gently, "to bring the love of God and the good tidings of Our Lord."

She closed her eyes and turned her head away, mumbling "not worthy." No glad tidings would reach her now, I saw that. No good sitting and spouting the Bible. Useless. What on earth could I have been thinking?

And then it came in a flash. Try what I had done with the mad woman. If it worked once before, why not again?

I said, rather sharply, "Your case is not unknown, Agnes. In fact, it's well documented. And the cure is equally well known."

She turned back to me, frowning, and opened her eyes. She looked full at me, which is just what I hoped.

"But for the cure to work, you must get out of bed and stand."

I hoped this would work. I knew it would be no good asking her to kneel: it would sound too pious, too empty. "Come along." I reached out to help her up. "Your return to happiness is at hand."

She stayed looking and then as I moved my hands closer, she reached up and allowed herself to be pulled to her feet. Then, those bits I had read during one term about some obscure medieval practices came back. Facing her, I lifted my right hand above her head, and proclaimed in a loud voice, "In the name of our Lord Jesus Christ, I command you, Satan, leave this good woman forever!"

Then I struck her on the forehead with the flat of my palm, and she gave a moan and fell back on the bed, lifeless.

The door flew open and Fred stood beside me, staring in horror. I could see he was about to strangle me so I turned and stated, in a matter-of-fact voice, "Let us finish our tea, Fred. Agnes will recover soon. And you'll see the miracle." I thought that if I said it in a firm enough voice, he might believe me, although I myself had no great faith it would work. I then stepped smartly forward, almost pushing him from the room, and closed the door behind us.

As we went to the table, he looked at me with a kind of awe. "What did you do?"

I whispered quietly, "I told the Devil to leave her, as you probably heard."

"And you think it was the Devil?"

"You told me yourself that she was behaving in a manner quite unlike her. So who else?"

I had no idea how long I would have to sit, but I was determined to wait until she recovered; I didn't want to leave them in this state of uncertainty. And before I finished my second cup of tea and another hardtack biscuit, which I moistened by dunking in my mug, I heard a voice from the bedroom. "Fred. Fred, come quick."

He rose and hurried into the room, closing the door.

I stayed seated, fingers crossed, wondering: whatever would be the result? Should I beat a hasty retreat in fear of my life? Or would he be rejoicing with me that goodness had won out?

Well sir, goodness had indeed won, for she came to the doorway in her nightdress. "I feel, Mr. John, I feel so..."

"....much better?" I nodded, and rose. "I told you, the name of the Lord Jesus will work miracles, whenever it is called upon." Then we said a few prayers of thanksgiving and I went out into the freezing afternoon.

On Sunday, I had a remarkably good turnout for my two services here in St. Augustine. Mr. Martin and his committee had gathered the town. Both celebrations went well and I was pleased with myself, having had an unusual number of communicants — forty-seven, by my count.

Then, when I was saying goodbye to the parishioners, one rather shabby fisherman lingered behind. When the others had left, he drew me aside and in a low voice told me a startling story.

After he finished, I assured him that I would do what I could, and thanked him. I went back to the Martins, and after a cup of tea and private prayers, I lay in bed, tossing and turning. Every instinct told me to just get on with my journey. But what he said had shocked me. Apparently in a little known community of three or four homes, about six hours' sledding distant, he'd heard — and even witnessed himself — some strange goings-on. I admonished myself, I am here to do God's will: how dare I think of bypassing this pastoral challenge? Nothing for it, but I would have to make a visit.

The next day broke with heavy overcast, mirroring my own gloom, but no snow seemed in the offing, so Clay and I set off. He had not slept much the night before, he confessed, having hit it off with one of his cousins, a pretty girl whom one day, if the years were kind, he would marry. They had sat up most of the night talking about it and their future together. She was only sixteen — rather young, I remarked, and alerted him that some rather difficult times might lie ahead, but he did not seem unduly worried, being caught up in daydreaming about her.

We had a hard time finding the cluster of homes because, as it turned out, they were hidden behind an outcropping of grey granite, the top of which had been swept clean of snow by the incessant winds that blew hereabouts. However, that was the landmark indicated by the fisherman, so I guided the dog team around the curved inlet and at the end, we saw the houses.

I cannot say that I was afraid, exactly, but certainly apprehensive. How indeed should I handle this? I said a quiet petition to the Lord, hoping that He would give me strength and wisdom to do the right thing in an extremely difficult situation well outside of my own experience.

Their dilapidated houses gave me the feeling this was a group of rather unlucky fishermen. Who knew what they had to do to survive? I wished I had brought more food but I rejoiced that I had acquired a goodly amount of dried codfish in St. Augustine in anticipation that some parishioners might be in dire need. I headed for the house nearest the sea, for that was the one where the fisherman said its inhabitants needed attention. I called our dog team to a halt, left Clay to deal with them, and knocked at the door.

It opened a crack. The unshaven face looked at me askance.

Thinking fast, I did not introduce myself as a gentleman of the cloth, I simply gave my name and said, "We're not from here;

we're a bit lost. Might I trouble you for just a quick cup of hot tea? So's we can moisten our hardtack... and then we'll be gone."

He didn't budge. "My wife is... not well."

"Oh, sorry to hear that. Can we bring her somewhere? Our dog team..."

He shook his head. "She'll be fine. Well, come in. I got a kittle hot."

Grudgingly, he opened the door. I waved to Clay, who had looped the dogs' traces around a post near the door. Once inside, we tried to ignore the sight of his wife who sat in a rocker next to the stove, head drooping and drool coming out of her mouth. The listless hand clutched a tankard, mostly empty; the whole place smelled of homemade brew.

From behind a shut door I heard a child crying. "Shut up!" the man yelled as he was putting a spoonful of tea in the kettle. The crying continued and he called again, "Keep quiet or ya know what you'll be gettin'!"

The crying stopped at once.

I saw the whole situation in a flash. The fisherman had been right; these children were in dire straits. But what should I do about that?

I turned and looked at Clayton. He too seemed stunned by what he had absorbed of the situation.

I took off my coat and when the man turned from the stove he saw my clerical garb, and froze. I had worn it especially this morning for just such an occasion, though I normally dress like everyone else. So now I introduced myself and told him I was on a pastoral trip, visiting all our parish members.

"Well, we got nothing here, Deacon. We don't go to services neither. If you knock two houses up, them's more likely to put you up for the night. They'll 'ave your cup of tea too, likely."

"Oh, it's not lodging I'm looking for. I just..." I wondered what I could say. There were no police, nor magistrates, nor town council that I could report him too. I supposed that's why that fisherman had approached me after the service. None but the clergy hereabouts to deal with such happenings.

One of the toddler twins then began rattling the handle and banging and kicking at the door. The man moved swiftly across, threw it open so that it knocked that child on the floor, and turned to the other child. Through the open door, I could see that the girl had her waste in her hand and was smearing it on the rug to wipe it off.

"You little son-of-a —" He slapped the tyke on the side of the head, knocking her to the floor, and she let out squeals of dismay. Then he slammed the door, locked it from this side, and came over to me. "Now I'm asking you kindly to leave. As you can see, my wife is in no state to receive visitors. Ever since she 'ad them twins, she's not been 'erself. We never expected twins no-how. Too much for anyone to deal with, if you ask me."

Throughout, his wife had not moved. But as he spoke, her tankard clattered to the floor, allowing the few last dregs of beer to spill over the hearth.

I turned to go to the door, gesturing to Clay, who frowned at me. And then I was possessed by a sudden rage. Was I not a man of the cloth? Did I not have a duty to perform? Of course I did.

But what duty?

It was then that I spun on my heel, unable to control my expression of wrath. "Good sir, that treatment of your child is unforgivable. But I do understand the torment. And that of your wife. It has just become too much for both of you."

At that, he frowned, but softened.

"I think I may have a solution to all your troubles," I went on.

I stood there, trying to appear calm, doing my best, in fact, to adopt the friendly attitude Our Lord would have shown. But

I saw myself, feet apart, standing rigid, looking probably very self-righteous. Was this proper for a man of God? No sir! But I had no control over myself.

The man looked at me. "A solution? What kind of solution?"

"I believe I know of a fine home that would welcome your children and care for them as they deserve." I let this sink in, and he seemed to ponder it. He glanced at his wife, who was still immobile.

A crafty look came over his face. "When? When would they take them?"

"This very minute," I said, for some odd reason. "Yes, this minute! Now, while your wife is resting. Just quietly dress your children and give me their clothes and playthings. Clayton and I shall take them forthwith to the family I have in mind, and you need never be in trouble again."

What an astounding sentence I had spoken! I actually shocked myself. Of course, I had no place to take them. Of course, I had no idea what I would do with them. I had no experience of little children like that, save at Christmas and during holidays after little Earle was born. But this was an entirely different situation: two children, messy, dirty, most likely starving. Whatever was this young clergyman thinking?

The man seemed to undergo a transformation. He began to look shiftily around the room. Then he nodded. "Not a bad idea. I'll get them ready."

What on earth had possessed me? Perhaps the Lord had indeed spoken and I was just following His will.

In due course, the children were ready, but unfortunately, just as we were leaving, the gust of cold air from the open door awakened the wife and she rose. "Where are you going with my babies?"

"I'm taking them to safety, good lady, where they will be well cared for." With that, I grabbed up one child, Clay grabbed the other, and we hurried out to the komatik. Of course, by now, the two children were thoroughly frightened and screaming for their mother.

"You son-of-a-whore!" She rushed to the door. "You child stealer, you bastard!" She tried to run out after us, but thank heaven her husband restrained her, holding her firmly inside the door, trying to calm her down.

"They'll be well looked after!" I called back, hoping I'd be forgiven the manifest lie. We both leapt onto the komatik, holding the children as tightly as we could, and Clay shouted at the dogs. They took off like rabbits and away we went — with the taunts of the drunken woman trailing after us as she screamed her wild oaths into the late afternoon air.

Chapter Ten

After travelling a mile or so and seeing we had not been followed, we stopped in a sheltered cove out of the wind and tried to make our screaming kids relax. I had very little experience but fortunately Clay, the wonder, had brought up his younger brothers. I didn't know what we should give them, but we started a little fire, heated some water, and moistened some hardtack, breaking it into little pieces that Clay fed them with his fingers, giving them some warm water to drink as well. Then he set about fashioning a makeshift seat on the komatik for them between his knees.

My mind was, of course, working overtime. Whatever should we do with them? I was hoping I had done the right thing, but now what? Clayton, bless his soul, did not question my decision. In fact, he reinforced it. "We could'a never of left 'em there," he said as he fed them with little cooing sounds. It was plain they were starving; their crying gradually stopped with the attention Clay was giving them.

Without looking at me, he mumbled, "So what do you think we're gonna do now?"

"No idea," I admitted. "How far are we from the next settlement?"

"Next biggest could be Old Fort. A good day away, I'd say." He shrugged. "Never been this way before, maybe once when I was little with my cousins."

Oh dear, that meant spending the night with them, an eventuality that had not struck me before. "Well, we'd better find somewhere to stay so we can make them comfortable."

Clayton agreed, and we turned inland on a trail that had been fairly well travelled. I didn't want to get lost, for sure, but then again, I wanted us to have a comfortable night in the middle of a forest, or under some overhang, which is what in the end we found. We pulled up by what appeared to be a good indentation in a rock face, almost a cave surrounded by woods, perhaps often used, for this was exactly where the trail led.

We took our time before nightfall to arrange our bedding and to make a fire on which we heated more food for the twins and ourselves. The novelty of what was going on seemed to keep them from too many bursts of crying, Clay doing wonders at maintaining their good humour. I was not looking forward to the night, but the weather was with us, the night clear and frosty; with all that had been going on, we slept well.

The next morning, I could see that civilization must be reached as quickly as possible. The children had to be changed, bathed, their abrasions looked after, and then what? Would I bring them with me all the way to Blanc Sablon, or even l'Anse au Loup? And then back again, all the way to Mutton Bay? How on earth did I expect to do that? What a pickle! Before too long, the twins had eaten enough; Clay had even tried them on dried fish, which apparently they had been able to get down. "So we'd best be off," he suggested. We made sure they were well wrapped up and I got on the back of the komatik. Clay rode on the front with the twins between his legs, firmly strapped in. Off we went. The rocking of the komatik happily put them both to sleep.

Well, the answer would have been obvious had I given myself time to think. Of course, Gene and his family, that should be our first stop. Once he knew these circumstances, surely he and Anna Bell would take charge. I'd go on with the obligatory pastoral visits as far east as Blanc Sablon, and even beyond to L'Anse au Loup — not really in our parish, but since the Rev. Mr. Gifford was no longer serving at Forteau, which usually took care of L'Anse au Loup, we of St. Clement's administered there. So now, better make straight for Gene at St. Paul's River and eschew stops on the way.

A hard day's sledding found us beyond Old Fort and as night came down we both agreed that we should press on, for a nearly full moon shone in a clear sky; we could see our way with the reflective snow doubling the light. Not difficult, either, for we had come out in the morning onto the flat gulf ice and were following the shoreline. But then we realized we had better give the dogs another good feed, so Clay got out seal meat and fed them, and on we went. They often, if not always, ate twice a day.

So about two or three in the morning we arrived at the settlement of St. Paul's River. One house was nestled close to the mission building: the parsonage? When the dogs arrived they set up a chorus of barking, knowing this leg of their journey had ended. I banged on the door several times, waking Gene.

He welcomed me with open arms. "I've been waiting for you, John. I've been expecting you. Come in, come in."

"First, come and see what I've got here."

He was in his pajamas, so he could not. I turned to Clayton. "Bring them in. I'll come and help." Gene went in to light a couple of lamps while we undid the children's wrapping and picked them up as gently as we could. For some reason, they both remained asleep. When Gene opened the door again, his face fell. "What on earth have you got there?"

"Twins!" I said. "Lovely little souls. I'll tell you all about it, but first, let's get them in out of the cold."

He ushered us in and went to feed the stove more wood. We laid them down near the heat, but unfortunately they woke up and began to cry.

"Ssshh, please keep them quiet. Anna Bell is sleeping; she was up late with our own child. I don't want to wake her."

From upstairs came the call, "Gene? What's going on?"

I looked at Gene. His mouth opened and shut. He obviously had no idea what to say.

Of course the noble Anna Bell came down and took in the situation. Immediately she set about heating water to bathe the children and look after their cuts and bruises. I, meanwhile, recounted the whole story, with Clay nodding and throwing in such comments as, "There's no way Mr. John could'a left them there, Mr. Bishop. No way he could'a. He did the right thing, oh yis yis yis."

And then came the inevitable question: "Just what do you intend doing with them after Anna Bell has them cleaned up?"

I shrugged, rather helplessly.

"Well, let me say right away," Eugene declared, "that we are in no position to adopt more children. And that is that!" He was not only firm, but I detected a sizable annoyance growing. He went to pour us both a cup of tea, glancing at Anna Bell who was still dealing with the twins. Not used to being mothered by a caring woman, they began giggling and chuckling as she tickled them while she cleaned them up. Such a fine woman.

"First thing in the morning I'll have to wash these filthy rags," she announced. "We've got no clothes here for them. Maybe a parishioner will lend us some. We'll send them off with you nice and clean, I can promise you that."

Well, what else had I expected? No, I had thought the Bishops would take them with open arms, but I did see the impossibility of that now. Just think again, I told myself.

Had I acted too quickly? Should I have waited till my return trip? No, Clay had certainly made that clear. We'd done the right thing: there had been no time to lose. The question was, what was the right thing to do now?

Clay and I were given the spare room in the parsonage with two beds; we didn't wake up until noon. I had spent the first hours of my bedtime worrying, so in a sense my tardiness was understandable, but nonetheless I did feel guilty for a lot of reasons. I woke Clay and we dressed and went downstairs. I knew I would have to appear properly contrite.

Anna Bell was dealing with the twins, keeping them occupied and doing a good job of it. She had also made a sumptuous meal for us before sending us on our way. I had made it clear the night before that we'd carry on to the eastern end of the parish as quickly as we could, and at the same time look for a good home that might accept the twins.

Anna had cooked murres, nice plump little seabirds that Gene had been given in return for a wedding. She had turned them into a lovely thick stew with turnips, potatoes, and carrots, which they kept in the vegetable cellar of the parsonage. Gene perhaps felt a bit guilty for his peremptory rejection of my two charges. At any rate, we said grace and tucked into our meal.

"John," Anna Bell said, "Eugene and I have been speaking this morning. We have decided to keep the children while you travel east. It didn't seem fair to send the poor darlings off before we've had a chance to dose them up with good nourishing food, or heal their various bruises and cuts. I do think," she glanced at

Gene, "they had been knocked about quite a bit. I found welts all over their little bodies."

"I must say, John, you did the right thing," Gene admitted. "I'm only sorry that I cannot burden Anna Bell at this point, but I'm sure you'll find a family willing to take them."

"Oh yes," I replied brightly, at the same time pleased that Clay and I could finish this next jaunt unencumbered. I also felt optimistic that we would find somewhere for the twins; otherwise, why would God have placed them in my care to start with?

In due course we left in fine weather. In fact, the sun shone rather too brightly, for by evening my eyes were aching. Gene had told me he'd gone around to the major settlements at Christmastime with a borrowed team, so I was to visit the smaller places, making sure to stop in at every cluster of homes and bring God's word to those starved for any spiritual nourishment. The settlements became a blur: Salmon Bay, Five Leagues, Little Fishery, Middle Bay, Belles Amour (*sic*), and Bradore (from Bras d'or, Golden Arm) so many, up to Long Point, Blanc Sablon, Forteau, and finally L'Anse au Loup, my most eastern reach. But Salmon Bay stands out in my mind, where I found a home built only of wood and oddly enough, earthen sod. Several homes I had seen and visited during the whole tour were simply shacks, but this one in particular I felt the need to visit. The wind had blown the snow off the roof so I saw plainly the sod that covered it. The Sinnicks welcomed me; they lived in the one room, which was almost like a cave. As luck would have it, a storm blew through and kept us captive most of the day.

Nancy Sinnick was doing her best to look after us, but she had almost nothing that I could see in the way of nourishment, only bread and weak tea for breakfast, nothing really for lunch. So Clay and I brought in the rest of our dried fish, and some tea, molasses, and cornmeal we had kept for the dogs, but these good people needed it even more than the team. Imagine trying to feed three children and a grandmother, who lay on a mattress in a corner, never rising. "Mamma's not gonna last the winter," Nancy whispered, shaking her head. "And our oil's running out: I just got enough to light us ten more days, then it's the dark, God help us."

"I just wish I had that dog team," Maurice Sinnick said. "I'd be back every day fishing in that there lake." He had lost his dogs, I found out, because an injury to his leg meant he had not joined the seal fishery this year, and so not managed to get winter food for the team.

At the mention of a lake, Clay and I traded glances. "Lake?" I asked. "Why don't Clay and I take you back tomorrow, if you'll show us the way? We can spend the day fishing through a hole in the ice."

The poor man brightened, and his eyes even grew moist. The thought that members of the clergy actually did something more than offer a few pious prayers seemed to have touched him.

We ate dinner on the table neatly covered in a tablecloth made from flour sacks. Mind you, these sacks serve a multitude of purposes here, from dish towels to bed sheets, which consisted of four sewn together. The family ate with such delight, unable to keep their ravenous appetites hidden. I had heard of many in our parish too poor to buy thread, and now I was witnessing this reality, though I quickly put the thought out of my mind. No point in dwelling on the negative.

After the meal we sat around as I watched the wife pick apart an old canvas coat. I asked her why.

"Getting thread fer me mendin'. These clothes is some horrible. If I don't mend 'em, they'll drop offa us." They had run out of clothing for their eldest child who had no siblings for hand-me-downs. The lad badly needed a heavy coat, so Nancy was trying to cut down her old mother's, who would not be going out anymore herself, for sure.

The next morning after the storm had blown away, the three of us set off with our team for the lake some ten miles back in the interior. Maurice had brought a heavy axe, and I watched him walk across the lake ice with practised eye. At one end where a stream entered, he found the ice thinner so there we chopped our hole. While he went to cut some boughs for a windbreak and get us blocks of iced snow to sit upon, we started to fish. He impressed us with holding the line still: if it's for smelt in a salty inlet, you jig a bit to attract them, but for trout in a lake, the line stays slack, as trout are suspicious.

Out here in the vast silence, the snow-covered tundra rising in the distance to darkened hills with their smattering of spruce, and the wind soughing in the bare birch and alder at one side of the frozen lake, I did feel that sense of peace that I had been missing with my many pastoral duties. Is it not, I asked myself, the duty of a missionary to drink in His essence from time to time? To allow moments of calm for one to absorb His presence? I breathed deeply, gently leaving the line still in the hole. Nothing to do, at last; I tried to empty my mind of all those ever-crowding duties. Peace descended.

Clay broke my reveries with a shout, and pointed to my nose. "Rub it, Mr. John, frostbite." With the intense cold, he had often reminded me that we must check each other for such signs. Fortunately it was caught early, and after getting down out of the wind and rubbing it, the flesh returned to normal but burned as though I had placed a hot poker on it.

That fine day and the next produced not only spiritual food for the Sinnicks, but a good stock of trout to nourish them in the weeks ahead. Not only had I brought them a fresh incitement to worship the Lord, I reflected, but had done good work in feeding His flock.

After feasting on fresh trout and hot tea, I found myself sleeping soundly, albeit on the one patch of floor left. I couldn't believe how poor some of these livyers were in the Canadian Labrador. On my return through St. Augustine, I'd try at least to buy a stock of oil to light the Sinnicks through the rest of the winter. But now the room seemed snug and warm with its few furnishings, mattresses on the floor, two chairs and a table, handmade as all of them up here were. No draft entered the heavy sod coating that protected the modest dwelling. I wondered why more people did not resort to this type of building material — it was certainly warm and secure.

So now, returning from L'Anse au Loup, we set our sights once more on St. Paul's River settlement, some seventy-five miles to the west, visiting those houses we had not seen or stopped in on the way out, taking us three days. Time enough for Gene and Anna Bell to have found a family for the twins there, perhaps?

Oh yes, in my mind the problem of the twins had become acute. At one of the houses in Middle Bay, I had asked a carpenter to make a small device to lace onto the komatik behind our larger supply box, to act as a wind break. So I had little fear of the children's well-being on the return, but I wondered what could be done at Aunt Minnie's.

I think Gene and Anna Bell were relieved that I did not press them to keep the children any longer, and professed pleasure with the coach box that I had arranged on the komatik. We all had a lovely evening, discussing theology and planning what we might do the rest of the winter. I did have my trip westward to make and then we'd be locked in for April and May when the ice began to break but the waters were not yet open. Then, we promised to meet and possibly return together to Quebec in midsummer for the general synod. Gene would be finished with his tour of duty here, for he felt certain that now with a wife and child, the Bishop of Quebec would not require a third year in the Canadian Labrador.

So the next morning, full of trepidation, we loaded the twins, whose names, Tom and Tessa, had been given by Anna Bell at Gene's baptismal service.

"Well Tommy and Tessa," I said as we bundled them, crying again of course, into their special box on the komatik, "we're off on a wonderful adventure." But my heart was still perturbed, for I wondered what on earth I could do with them.

Chapter Eleven

The next morning, with the parsonage barometer rising and the thermometer dropping, we could expect a spell of good but very cold weather so we would have to watch for frostbite. Clayton and I set off toward St. Augustine, me driving and Clay behind, watching over our precious cargo. I steered the dogs carefully, staying mostly out on the flat gulf ice, rarely following any trail over capes or twisting forest trails. This made the going slower, but in some ways more enjoyable, for we had no fear of sliding or capsizing.

The wind had swept the ice clear for a good patch and we fairly zipped along. Again as during the past week, my mind turned to arriving at Aunt Minnie's with the twins. What would she say? Of course, she was too elderly to care for them herself. Then what about Lorna — how would she take this whole situation? I felt she could be relied upon to care for them for a few days while I tried to find some other home. But I knew only too well that most of the inhabitants had laid in just enough stores to feed themselves until spring breakup, no easy job in itself. Now was definitely not the time to burden anyone with two extra hungry mouths. Would my wardens help? Yes, undoubtedly they would spread the word among the parish, but again, based on what I had encountered to the east, I couldn't see much hope in that either. No way out.

I put the worry out of my mind and made myself enjoy speeding over the ice, passing barren shores, their low grey humps like stranded whales, swept in some places clear of ice, in others grizzled with coverings of low spruce on their granite backs. How lucky was I to have chosen this vocation — or have it chosen for me, as I always said, by the Lord above.

Knowing Clay was behind me keeping an eye on the twins, who were as silent as the passing scenery, I felt secure enough to let my mind wander. And then it hit me like a blinding flash: Of course! Why had I not seen it before? Spending too much time worrying, oh yes. That couple in St. Augustine who had lost their child — they would welcome these twins. Of course they would. I'd present it as God's way of saying, Don't worry, you will be looked after. I was so pleased at my inspiration, I turned and told Clay about it, and he too felt certain that they would be glad to accept.

After a rather difficult night in a spruce wood caring for the children, making a fire, and trying to heat food for their little tummies, we arrived in St. Augustine the next day and went straight to the couple's house. I had a bit of trouble getting the dogs to avoid the front and draw the komatik up behind, for I wanted to make sure that the happy state in which I had left them still held good and the wife had not lapsed back into her former despair. I walked around to the front door with some trepidation, and knocked.

The husband opened the door, and immediately brightened. "Come in, come in, Mr. John. I knew ya'd be back somehow." Holding the door wide, he called inside to Agnes. "Look who's 'ere? Our saviour: Mr. John. Get something together, we must feast him, fer sure."

I was about to enter into those welcoming arms when I shook myself. The twins — that's what I came for. I held up my hand and then tore around to Clay behind the house, undoing his charges.

"Grab Tessa." I picked up Tommy, trying not to be too rough in my haste, for I was anxious to bring them around. We hurried to bang again on the door and, as it opened, we presented our twins. They both stared in amazement.

"Look what the Good Lord has brought you," I cried. "You were not forgotten. When a single grain falls into rich soil, it yields abundantly," I said, misquoting the Bible slightly. "He has given you a set of beautiful but abandoned twins that anyone would be proud of. Two in place of one."

The twins were too befuddled even to cry. We set them on their feet and knelt to undress them, while husband and wife looked at each other, and then, to my delight, began to smile. "I told ya, Aggie, what'd I say? Good Mr. John, he has an answer fer everything."

Well sir, what a celebration we all had! The twins did look delightful, dressed in presentable outfits that Gene had scrounged for them at St. Paul's River. I almost wished they were my own. Fred and Agnes set about feeding them, talking excitedly how they would care for them, where they would sleep, and making all sorts of plans.

I had struck gold.

Well, of course, I couldn't wait to break the news to the Martins. They were pleased and promised that the parish would rally around with extra food for the couple and see the family well taken care of the rest of the winter. "He's a good man, Fred is," Mr. Martin said. "I warrant you, those twins will have the best home ever." And with that, we decided to relax for the rest of the afternoon. With my sense of accomplishment, I even gave myself leave to take a little nap in the corner before dinner while Clayton went off to see his cousins. We arranged to leave the next day after a proper church service, for which Clyde Martin assured me he could gather a good flock.

In the morning after a fine service, Clay turned up and I could see he had hardly slept the night before. In fact, when he took off his coat to have a bite, I saw decided traces of spruce gum. Hereabouts that meant only one thing: dallying in those log wigwams that graced almost every home on the Canadian Labrador. The local custom was to stack logs like tepees so they shed water easily; their interiors formed a kind of shelter, often for the dogs, or more especially for couples who were "having a sneak."

I said nothing. After a good midday meal, we set off westward toward home on the last leg of my eastern pastoral trip, roughly two days to Mutton Bay. I was driving and soon turned to Clayton. "I don't know what you were up to last night, but I hope you haven't endangered your immortal soul for a few minutes of gratification."

Clayton was clearly taken aback. After speeding merrily along, for the day was bright and the glass low, around minus twenty-five, I heard the words, "Look who's talking about his immortal soul!"

I was struck with such horror that I called the dogs to halt and leapt off the komatik. I faced the young rascal. "Just what did I hear!"

"I'm sorry, Mr. John. I must'a spoke out of turn."

"But what were you talking about?"

Clay looked down at his feet, not knowing which way to turn. "You got a good idea, I bet."

"I most certainly do not have any idea!"

"You and that maid you rescued from that ship." The thought struck me like a thrown rock. "All the fellas in the school talk about it. She's one pretty biddy. Everyone's clear on that, and you bein' one lucky fella. You got yourself a good looker, fer sure." He glanced up to see if this had made a better impression. "You can't try to pretend otherwise..."

"Pretend! And what would I pretend? Our relationship is perfectly proper. I cannot think where these rumours emanated."

"That night in Mutton Bay, when you was mummering. It weren't so proper that night, I heard."

I stood thinking. Good heavens, when I brought the poor girl home? Oh of course, they would imagine what took place thereafter. Well, what else would young lads think? I allowed myself to relax. "If that is all, Clay, I can promise you that nothing untoward took place that night. Or any other night. She was a little tipsy and I had to take charge, only to make sure that nothing did happen to her. But that was all. Our relationship is, I guarantee you, perfectly proper." Imagine! The little whippersnapper putting me on the spot, when it was he who deserved reprimanding.

Of course, gum on the backside is no proof neither. The only thing to do was let it all blow away into the arctic wind sweeping by as we stood there, the dogs seated obediently, waiting for their next rush.

I put my hand out on his shoulder. "No hard feelings. You did have a right to think the worst. I don't blame you. I'm sorry I brought the subject up, but you see, as your clergyman, I felt it incumbent upon me to mention it. But let us discuss it no more." For some reason I added, "Don't think badly of me."

"Oh fer sure not." Clay got back on the komatik. "Fer sure, Mr. John, I don't think badly."

I climbed on myself, and called to the dogs, only to hear his final words: "But she's the best looker around these parts, and you being without a wife, we 'spect to hear wedding bells afore the winter's out."

Oh Lord, what a thought! Lorna had a way of appearing in my dreams, but for that I could not be blamed. Should my ministry not be my entire focus? But then, I knew Clay would throw at me that Mr. Bishop had gotten married. Oh heavens, better to put these thoughts aside for another day and concentrate on getting us home safely.

By now we'd developed the knack of caring for ourselves, so when night fell, we bedded down in the shelter of some spruce, fed the dogs the last of their seal meat, and made ourselves a little fire on which we melted snow and cooked up a soup of potatoes and dried cod given by the Martins, thereby finishing off our food supplies. Then we rolled ourselves in our blankets and had a good sleep. But before I drifted off, Lorna's image returned in full force. Of course, I had no fear for her safety. But I wondered how these short winter days and the long dark nights were affecting her spirit. Would she soon be getting homesick? She came from a thriving fishing village on the South Shore of Nova Scotia, filled with activities. Living with Aunt Minnie, doing her household chores, and helping out other elderly villagers, all this might tell upon even the worthiest spirit.

When we awoke, we were greeted with the most ominous sky. Clay was gathering some sticks for a fire, but I looked into the heavens and called out, "Clay, we finished our food last night. And the dogs, too. Look." He glanced upwards and then, as if stuck in the rear with a great hatpin, he scurried around wrapping our blankets and piling everything into the komatik box. "We'd best make a run fer it, Mr. John!"

Oh yes, run for it we had to, for we both knew only too well from first-hand experience what happened to folk caught with no food and a storm of several days' duration.

We sped over the frozen waters of the great Gulf of St. Lawrence. The night before I had found my eyes paining, and had gone to bed with a headache; Clay admitted to the same. I remembered something my old father had mumbled about how, at my age, his father had whittled him a pair of Indian spectacles out of a couple of twigs which he tied behind his head with string. They limited the field of vision, giving only a slit to see through, and I resolved that, for my next trip, I would equip myself with these, because that blinding light reflected off the snow had certainly taken its toll. But I kept my mind pretty well focussed on our present problem: how to keep ahead of the snowstorm till we reached Mutton Bay.

Much as I tried to relax and enjoy this last leg of my eastern trip, I couldn't help running over what I had been told to do when caught by the weather. Clayton seemed unduly preoccupied, too. We kept urging on the dogs, with Clay cracking his sealskin whip. They did respond, I must say, and fairly sped us along but I fear, not fast enough.

The black clouds were gaining: they kept billowing up into the blue immensity of the heavens like giant weather monsters leaning forward as if to pounce at any moment. I kept looking behind until I got a crick in my neck. "We'll beat her," said Clayton, more to reassure himself than me.

"I hope so," I called back.

And at last, as we were about to be torn to shreds by the ever-increasing wind, the familiar cluster of distant houses draped haphazardly over the granite capes of Mutton Bay came into view. What an intense reaction flooded through me. Goodness, how I thanked the Lord for delivering us safely. How much I had missed everyone! I pointed to the village, and Clay yelled back, "Good to be home."

Nonetheless, that last half-hour seemed endless. The forward fury of the storm struck us, but being this close, I knew we'd make it. And of course, I just could not wait for the sight of

Lorna in the doorway when I knocked. Perhaps she wouldn't be there: more likely she was working at another house. I mean, why hang around Aunt Minnie's? Though she had always been careful to take care of the home as if it were her own.

At long last, after the blizzard had dropped our visibility down to a few yards, the dogs found Aunt Minnie's. "D'you know," I said to Clay as I got off the komatik and tried to brush off the clinging flakes, "my opinion of these wonderful dogs has changed. After that seal hunt, I just thought of them as a bunch of wild animals that had to be beaten into doing our bidding. But now I see them as courageous souls who would stop at nothing to get us to our destination."

"You're right," he shouted into the wind as he went off to pen them. "No finer team around, neither. And that Tuck! No finer lead dog in all Labrador." I stumbled my way up the drifted steps and banged on the door, perhaps too loudly. I was so excited to see Lorna, and of course Aunt Minnie.

Nothing happened.

I turned away, disappointed.

But then, the door flew open and there stood Lorna. I gasped at how lovely she appeared. She gave a squeal of delight and opened her arms. I went quickly in, closing the door. We hugged each other as though our lives depended upon it.

I had quite forgotten what it was to hold a woman in my arms. What a period of drought I had gone through! I heard her whisper, "I've missed you so much, Jack."

"Me, too," I admitted.

After a good long emotional hug, she stepped back and I could see there were tears in her eyes.

"What is this? I thought you were happy to see me, and here you are crying!"

At that, she began to laugh. And then I started to as well. The two of us bent over in paroxysms of joy, laughing and cuffing each other.

Clay opened the door, and began to grin. "Lorna, have ya got any store of seal meat for the dogs?"

"Yis yis, lots." She went behind the stove and reappeared with a goodly portion which she gave to Clay, who went off to feed them, and then make his way to his nearby home.

"I've got so much to tell," I said.

"And so have I." She went to the stove to boil the obligatory kettle.

I don't know where Aunt Minnie produced all the food for that wonderful dinner she and Lorna made. Afterward, we sat happily in the glow of the lamp, finishing our many tales. The big news of the village was that a former inhabitant, Phillip Vatcher, had come back from Quebec where he had been working. He had decided to organize a kind of special winter festival, recruiting some of the school children. Plans were under way for what looked like a thoroughly enjoyable Saturday: dog and snowshoe races, pole climbing, all sorts of activities for both men and women. Lorna's eyes shone. "He's so full energy is Mr. Vatcher, I don't know how he finds time, because he's got three children to look after." She had already told me that he had lost his wife in an accident in the big city. This implication sailed by me.

"They were hoping you'd be back in time, Mr. John," Aunt Minnie told me. "And it looks like you are. They'll be so pleased, because they want you as official judge. And you know what Phillip 'ere 'as done? He appointed Lorna as queen of the festival. None of us 'eard o' that afore, but it seems a fine idea."

I looked at Lorna. "Wonderful, Lorna, congratulations! The figurehead of the whole thing!" We'd had such events in Shigawake, but I'd never heard of them spoken about in any reports from the Canadian Labrador.

"Oh yes, and Phil has taken me for rides on his komatik, even teaching me how to handle the dogs. He gave me lessons with his rifle. Oh Jack, he's such fun."

I confess I felt jealous. But of course, I didn't show a thing. So now Lorna had an admirer. And it appeared to be mutual. Well, I told myself, good for her. A fine energetic family man, that's just what she needs. But then, what would that mean for us?

She must have seen and read the thoughts crossing my face. She reached out across the table and touched my hand. "Jack, there's nobody in the world like you, you know that."

Easily said, I thought to myself. And no, I was not at all sure of that. But I did not want to let anything interrupt the flow of good feelings.

Lorna took my hand. "Come." She rose and brought me upstairs. Then she opened my bedroom door.

There, in front of the bed on the floor lay a lovely, new, thick, hooked rug.

"You made that for me?"

"I did, Jack." She smiled and gave me a kiss on the cheek. "Now let's have no more of this jealousy — I know, I saw it in your eyes."

Just then, we heard excited knocking below and went down to find Clay barging in. He shook the snow from his coat. "Everyone's talking about the races, Mr. John," he said. "I just came by to ask if you're thinking of driving in the race?"

"Of course not. I'm the judge, Clay."

"Would it be all right then, Mr. John, if I borrowed our team to race?"

I laughed. "Of course, Clay, and good luck to you. I don't know how I'll remain unbiased, if you're driving our own team. I just hope to heaven you'll win, for the glory of the parsonage and the church!"

Chapter Twelve

Saturday morning arrived at last: the day of the big races. I found Lorna in a high state of excitement at the prospect. What did that augur for me? And I was also disturbed by a conversation I'd had the previous evening when the couple I had married in October, Howard Gallibois and Gladys, told me a troubling story. Gladys went to church in Red Bay, part of Tabacher, and one Sunday the Roman Catholic priest, Father Poudrier, had taken her aside after the service. She had told him that she was now with child and as agreed with her Anglican husband, if it were a girl it would be brought up in the Catholic faith. That was the practice hereabouts, and indeed in the Gaspé where I came from. Couples in mixed marriages often went to different churches.

Imagine her consternation when the priest gave her a big dressing-down and said that her children would be bastards because she had not married in "God's church." She was living in sin and the priest feared for her immortal soul. He even went so far as to say that unless she confessed her willful deed and received absolution, she could not take Communion.

Well, this was indeed a situation that needed dealing with. But how? Here again, amidst all the theology, New Testament, ethics, and biblical history that I had absorbed, nowhere was I told how to deal with a priest of a different faith within the bounds of one's own parish who was dog-in-the-manger about his pronouncements.

I tried to put this situation out of mind and let myself enjoy the proceedings as I walked down to the temporary stage thrown up by the enterprising Phillip Vatcher and his team of workers from the school and some local men. In the winter, it is true, there is not a lot to do, once the seals had been harvested and their pelts stretched, many high on the walls of houses. Women made the garments in winter, not men. Of course, men went back into the interior, hunting or cutting stove wood, but this week, in view of the coming races, most of them had elected to stay home, so Phillip had plenty of help.

I was pleased I had arrived back in time, and had been asked by my two wardens if we could sit together and discuss the rest of the winter. I had decided that Clayton, having absorbed a good bit of English, history, and geography on the trip, should stay and even teach a class of younger children while I was away travelling on my rather long western pastoral trip. This meant no driver for me and both wardens were mightily concerned.

"Not even Mr. Bishop went alone, Mr. John," Thomas Bobbitt said. "With all due respect, that's some risk you're taking, going all that way by yourself. She's one big trip."

"But our young people here need the teaching," I countered. "And I feel perfectly fit. I've actually been planning just such a possibility. On this return journey, I mostly handled the dogs myself. I'm pretty well acquainted now with how to make a fire on the snow and spend nights in makeshift shelters. So I'm not only willing but eager to undertake the journey by myself." They began to interrupt, but I held up my hand. "Yes, no doubt, it will be filled with danger, more so than my previous trip, but then you see, I can't be a party to someone else coming to a bad end because of me!" I grinned.

"Perish that thought!" said Thomas Buffett, the people's

warden. "But if you're determined, well, three years ago, Mr. Kerr, 'e did it as a young deacon and returned safely."

"And there are lots of stopping places," I added.

"Yes, but them winter storms come up powerful quick. You never knows."

After more discussion, during which I remained firm, we decided to plan on that eventuality, though their misgivings had planted serious qualms. Was I being foolish? Well, I had decided, and after services on the morrow, I would take Monday to prepare myself and Tuesday I would take the bit in my teeth, and set off.

At the site of the festival, and being the official judge, I was assigned a seat on the platform, or bridge, about ten by ten feet across. But I found the wind strong and preferred to stand by a fire some enterprising youths were tending. And darn it all, didn't that problem with the priest loom again into my consciousness, for I knew he'd be here. The only thing that made it disappear was the sight of Lorna in her best tuque striding happily along, cheeks red from the cold, jet black, freshly washed hair shining in the low sun, which was struggling into the bleak winter sky.

She went across to greet Phillip Vatcher, a fine-looking man, I thought, rather too fine for my own liking, with frank, blue eyes, fair hair, and well-defined, almost Slavic, cheekbones, wearing a confident air. They sat down side by side.

After judging three or four competitions without much difficulty, I watched the winners — in a procedure Phillip had laid down — mount the steps to the stage and receive a small prize from Lorna as queen, who kissed each on the cheek and gave a hug. I must say all the men seemed more pleased with the kiss than with their gift. I smiled at these displays, on the one hand happy that Lorna was now so fully accepted by everyone and so clearly admired, and on the other, bothered by some curious lurking jealousy.

The last event before dinner, after the slippery pole had dispensed with a majority of climbers (only one of whom reached the top) we arrived at the climax of the morning: the men's snowshoe race. Phil had planned the course to go about a mile out around the cape toward Entry Island, where another judge would make sure that the men weren't taking any short cuts, and then back to the finish line. By now even the sleepyheads had gathered, so there was a good crowd. I would say almost every inhabitant of Mutton Bay, old and young, had turned out, the older given pride of place next to the fire to keep them warm, the youngsters cavorting about, everyone having a good time. And didn't I spot Father Poudrier in his black garb?

Should I go right over and confront him? But how exactly? I prefer spur of the moment action in order to avoid agonies of indecision later. But right now, with all the fun going on, I just couldn't bring myself to go across and speak to him about this dreadful indictment of a marriage I had recently performed. No, wait a bit, I decided.

I stood at the starting line, gave the signal, and Phillip fired his gun in the air. At the crack, well over a dozen men set off at a good clip on their rackets. I had no idea anyone could go so fast. These were strong men, men who had built their muscles and endurance in the winter seal hunts and again in the summer's fishing. They had cut trees in freezing winter forests, trudged for miles behind komatiks laden with wood or caribou carcasses, hauled in huge seals, and travelled strenuous traplines. These were fellows whose endurance I found admirable and whose strength was undeniable. No finer breed of men, I reflected, ever trod God's good earth.

In no time, the tiny dots in the distance were seen on their way back. We all gathered around the finish line and even before they got within earshot, boys started yelling for fathers, wives for their husbands, little girls shrieked, old ladies clapped and as they came closer, we saw Archie Mansbridge in the lead. But he was rapidly being overtaken by a younger man, Ivan Green. Harry Robertson was a strong third, and it looked like a close race. I'm not looking forward to judging this, I thought, but I knelt at the finishing line sighted across the two sticks, and waited.

Mansbridge it was by one mere second, then Green, and Robertson, as the crowd erupted into shouts and cheers.

We all clustered around the stage for the presentation ceremony. Archie was given a kiss by Lorna, after which he wrapped his arms around her and proceeded to give her one back, a mighty one on her lips, which caused catcalls and consternation and lots of laughter. After he released her, he shook her hand, seeing as how she stood somewhat dazed, indeed shocked, but then she broke into a delightful peal of laughter along with everyone else.

Archie had put my stomach in turmoil, but I went forward as his judge and pastor and heartily shook his hand, congratulating him both on his race and, as I told him, on his kiss; this was greeted by everyone with more laughter and applause. We retired for our dinners.

And then I remembered Bessie Yarn, the head of the Women's Guild. I hadn't mentioned anything about her to Lorna, and now I wondered if Lorna might not be exacerbating the situation — again unwittingly. Now was not the time to warn her; I had to bite my tongue, and let events take their course.

After a good hour's break, the dog teams began to assemble for the main race of the day, potentially a dangerous one. Cleverly, Phillip had spread out the starting line to leave ample space between dog teams. I mounted the stage to watch and then helped Lorna up the steps; she had been away for dinner, invited out by Phillip and his organizers at their house.

"You're doing a wonderful job, Lorna," I said. "I'm mighty proud of you." I was about to go on, when she quickly whispered, "Thank you kindly, Jack," and turned to assume her regal role.

I spotted Clayton approaching with Tuck at the head of our fine team. I did so hope that, if he won, it would be by a good length so I'd not have to judge any close call. I waved and shouted out encouragement. Lorna saw him and left the stage to go and chat. After a moment, she patted him on the shoulder and gave him a big good-luck kiss.

That was greeted by catcalls and whistles by the other starting drivers. "We want the same send off," one called. "Not fair," another shouted, "we all got to have the same good-luck wish."

Oh no! What would the Bessie Yarns think?

Nothing for it but she had to walk along and kiss each of the fourteen contestants and wish them luck too. This send-off was of course exactly what made every contestant happy. I watched the wives — being myself overly sensitive. But no, they seemed all to take it in good humour, though a few may have felt, as I did, a curious twinge. As I turned, Bessie caught my eye. She gave me a reassuring look. Imagine how relieved I felt!

When Lorna came back to the stage, I heard a chorus of yaps and barks, broken by vicious snarling. Two dog teams had somehow become enmeshed. Their owners hastened with whips to break it up, but it was not easy. In fact, so fierce was the encounter that only after several minutes were they separated.

One dog lay bleeding and when it picked itself up, it could hardly stand. Its owner, Wilfred Organ, began arguing with the owner of the other team, Ivan Buffett. "Now look what you done! How am I gonna race with Murky here? She'll never run again."

Ivan replied to the effect that it was not his fault: dog fights happen, to which several agreed. Wilfred began to remonstrate with him and I could see this building into a real altercation, so I waded into the fray.

I lifted my hand for quiet. I asked the good Lord to throw me a few special phrases but none came. So I began, "Now as the official judge, I must plead for calm. It's such a beautiful occasion, a great festival day, and we don't want it spoiled with any squabbling."

This sounded as weak to me as it must've done to everyone else.

"We won't squabble, Mr. John," Wilfred said loudly, "but what am I going to do now, racing with one dog short?"

Then it came to me. "Only one thing. One fair and just solution. Ivan Buffett, you release one dog from your team and leave him behind, so you'll also go one dog short like Wilfred."

Everyone looked at each other. Was it not a solution worthy of Solomon? Well, not quite. But grudgingly, Ivan nodded. "I guess that's only fair. Okay, Wilf," he said, "I'll get rid of one of my best dogs, and then we'll all line up."

And so he did. The course ran down to Schooner Bay, probably an hour there, and an hour back. So we could amuse ourselves in the meantime. Someone had brought a mess of dried capelin and we toasted them on the fire which the lads kept stoked. Again, I saw the elderly Father Poudrier joining the celebration and I realized now I must finally take the bull by the horns and go talk to him.

Difficult situation, no doubt. I walked across to where he stood talking to a couple of his parishioners. He greeted me cordially, although we had not met before. After we had undergone a few pleasantries about the joyful day, the good turnout, and how all our flock were clearly enjoying themselves, I suggested we step aside.

"It came to my attention that the couple I married, a nice young man named Howard Gallibois and his wife, Gladys, were surprised by your reaction to their marriage, which I myself performed."

He shrugged. "She not be perform in God's church," he said. "So *pas correct*! She not correc'. I tell to them what is right, that is all." He turned away.

I could not let him off so easily. I could see that he was elderly, and I wondered what his bishop was doing sending priests of his age to this remote and dangerous life. Our bishop, as we all knew, chose young men who might be at ease in boats and on komatiks for ministering to a parish spread out over a vast distance. Father Poudrier likely moved only between his rectory and his little church perched at the end of the Red Bay inlet.

"But good father, our marriage rites are indeed very similar to yours. And, after all, we are all Christians, are we not?"

A hackneyed argument, I admit, too often repeated everywhere in doctrinal clashes between Catholics and Anglicans. But surely up here on the Canadian Labrador, I said, the strictures of the church might be loosened?

He shook his head. "Our church, she come from St. Peter. No other church have this authority. I do not speak what is not correc'. Me, I know what is right."

"But surely, Father Poudrier, you cannot mean what you said, that the wife will have bastards? That she is right now living in sin?"

"Precisely. My *archevêque* — that is what he tell us. You must to speak with your bishop, you, and sure he say you what is right. But before she marry wid me, she live in sin, oh yes oh yes."

I looked at him, frowning slightly. Could he really be so stiff and indeed prejudiced? I felt my ire rising, ready to lash out. If I didn't, I could see I'd be seething all day. But then I looked in his watery eyes. He was of the old school, and near retirement. What good would any anger that I, a young deacon, might pour out — what good would it do? I sublimated my passion, nodded, and held out my hand to shake his. He looked at it and turned away.

So much for that! No wonder our churches collide all over the world. Such a shame. But there was nothing that I, a newcomer to the fray, could do to change it. I resolved to reassure the couple that they were certainly married in the eyes of God, as indeed were thousands of couples all across our nation and indeed the world, whose union had been blessed by the Church of England. In the face of this old priest's intransigence, I would have to tell them to spend no further time worrying.

Someone shouted and in the distance we could make out a lone dog team travelling toward us. We all peered, and within minutes, others could be seen. The way back was obviously quicker, for a trail had been broken. I watched the leader closely, hoping that it was Clay. But no, neither at the head, nor number two, nor as far as I could make out, number three.

"Doesn't look like Clay is up there with the winners," I said to Lorna.

She shook her head. "Just keep hoping." She moved off as Phillip called her to meet someone new.

All the attention being on Lorna rather than on me as leader of the flock was an entirely new experience, one that I actually found somewhat disturbing. But later that night as I lay in bed, I saw that getting all the attention must surely be not good for one who had taken up my calling. I resolved to put away this ridiculous, and actually quite new, need for attention that had developed. Thrusting it behind me and at the same time recognizing my awareness of it might even improve my own attitude.

As the sleds came closer, we saw Clay was right behind number three. Tuck was doing her best. About half a mile away, Clay took a risk and moved onto another track. Slowly, he began to pull level with the third team. On they came, neck and neck, toward the finish line. This close race caused everyone to applaud and yell for those two teams. Unfortunately, the teams with one dog short were bringing up the rear. I resolved to offer them consolation prizes, which I could do as the judge of the competition.

At any rate, the winner was well ahead; the second, solidly behind him, was Johnny Jones; and then came two more together — Clay was one of them, being just a foot or two behind. Oh Lord, I thought, what if they go over the finish line at the same time? What would I do then?

But thankfully, amid the roar of the crowd and the screams of the children, Clay just managed to overtake Jones by a dog's length and Jones's team came in third. What a blessed ending to a wonderful day!

Chapter Thirteen

Monday morning's preparations for my departure on the westbound trip were marred by Lorna bursting in. She slammed the door and lashed out at me. "What on earth are you doing, Jack?"

I looked up and frowned.

"I've just been to the store. I saw Clayton. He told me."

"Told you what? That he's going to stay and do some teaching? He seemed pretty pleased at the thought."

"Yes, teaching. Not going with you. You seem to be planning on going alone." Her eyes were flashing.

"I am, dear Lorna. It will be a lovely adventure."

"Oh yes, a lovely adventure. With you frozen dead in some snowdrift. I won't have it!"

I rose from my packing. "Lorna, please don't worry about me. I shall be quite all right. Honestly I shall."

"But I can't let you go alone, Jack. I just cannot." She looked disconcerted, even distraught.

I went on laying out my clothes.

"There's only one solution."

"And what is that?" I was not used to being challenged in such a fashion.

"I shall just have to go with you, that's all."

"You?"

"Yes, me. Of course. I'm strong, I'm young. Phil has taught me how to handle a dog team and I am a quick learner. I can be your driver. Yes, that solves it."

"Lorna my dear, for you and I to go off alone together, sleep in the same shelter, it..."

"It what?"

"It would not... it would just not be proper, unless we were married." As soon as the words were out of my mouth, I realized I should never have said them.

She looked up at me, a twinkle in her eyes. "So? What's so wrong with that?"

She had me there. "You're not proposing that you and I somehow get married before I leave?"

"No, of course not. You'll have to postpone leaving for a week. There will have to be preparations."

I reached out and took her hand. "Lorna, it's not the time. Nor the place. I have a great long trip ahead, I have to minister to my flock: I have to take services, write sermons — you know what I told you about the last trip, there are so many unexpected problems rearing their heads on trips such as these. I cannot subject you to this kind of torture, as a beginning to our relationship."

"Our relationship began months ago," she said. "I'm ready."

"Well I'm not!" How harsh that sounded. I immediately regretted it. "I mean, I'm all involved in packing, preparations, girding myself for the voyage. It... it would just be the kind of diversion I cannot undertake right now."

She dropped her eyes. "Well, who else?"

"Nobody else. I'm going alone, and that's that." I returned to my packing.

She turned on her heel, went upstairs into her room, and closed the door.

Of course, I felt terrible. How had this come up? The last thing in the world I ever wanted was to hurt my lovely Lorna.

Should I go up and see her? No, let time go by. And time was at a premium right now. So much to do, to prepare the dog feed for three weeks, think of everything I would need and what I had forgotten on the other trip. I must bring some snow spectacles, more changes of socks, and another pair of sealskin boots somehow. I should have to buy them, for Aunt Minnie was too elderly to make another. Thankfully, my mind turned to these many details, helping me forget how harsh I had just been.

And as luck would have it, Clay came in soon after, wanting to show me the lesson plans he had worked out for his students. He was so excited at the prospect of teaching that I had to stop and sit with him. Lorna, I suppose hearing us talk, emerged from her bedroom upstairs, came down, and helped Aunt Minnie prepare a meal.

What a thrilling start to my great tour. The dogs were in fine form after their week of rest and were fairly speeding out across the flat, frozen sea. But what made it special, of course, was my lovely passenger, the belle of the festival, the much sought-after Lorna.

The state of affairs that existed between us after yesterday morning's conversation could not last. So because Harrington Harbour was only one day's journey away, I suggested she leave with me early this morning and go that far. Provided of course the glass stayed up and the weather remained clear. The prospect of her returning to Harrington Harbour pleased and, I would say, mollified her somewhat.

We rose at dawn and as the conditions were right, we set off together, rejoicing. After a time, I even let her drive the team. We were having such fun together, chatting merrily. The future was forgotten, as was the past; we just revelled in the moment. I refused to allow myself to think of how wonderful it might have been to spend the next three weeks with her travelling the whole parish. For the moment this thought arose, I realized how much my energies would be diverted. So I said to myself, just enjoy these few moments now.

After a splendid ride, we arrived late in the afternoon at Harrington Harbour. I directed the team straight to John Bobbitt's house. I pulled up outside, left Lorna to mind the dogs, and I went up to his door and banged. The tall, lean, elderly figure opened the door and welcomed me in. He had been expecting me, for I'd sent an earlier message.

"Who do ya think I brought you?" I asked him and beckoned Lorna, calling out, "The dogs will be fine; they'll stay quiet now they've had a long run. I'll feed them later."

She walked over, a tall, striking figure, striding confidently, and looked John Bobbitt in the eye as she shook his hand.

I watched him closely. "Who's this?" he asked. "Someone from away, for sure."

Lorna was enjoying it. "You don't recognize me, Mr. Bobbitt?"

His eyes narrowed, he rubbed his forehead, and then motioned us in. "For sure I don't, young lady. If you was from here, no fear, I'd know you at once."

I gestured her to wait while we doffed our heavy coats and boots and then I turned to our host. "You sure you don't?"

"No, Mr. John, can't say I do. But we're sure glad you're 'ere."

"Well sir," I said, "this is the maid to whom you kindly gave a room when I rescued her from off a schooner."

Well, he couldn't believe his eyes. "That poor woman who ya brung 'ere that night?"

"None other," I said. "You find her different?" I was grinning all the while, as was Lorna.

"Never seen such a change," he said. "Well, you're welcome, young lady!"

I introduced her as Lorna Maclean, and she spoke up: "I wanted to come and thank you for your many kindnesses. If you agree, I shall help you round the house, work hard for a day, or a week, or even till Mr. John comes back. Whenever you decide, I shall return to Mutton Bay, where I'm lucky enough to have lots of friends."

"So you're that young lady. Your fame precedes you, my dear young Lorna," Mr. Bobbitt said. "Seems you're not afraid of work and you have a willing personality. I don't know what you'll find to do around 'ere," he looked round his house, the quite untidy house of a widower, and she burst out laughing.

"Oh never fear, Mr. Bobbitt, I may find a few things that need doing. After I leave, this lovely house will be as clean as new. And now, gentlemen, why don't I get into your kitchen and rustle up a good feed. Myself, I'm mightily hungry. I had no idea, Jack, that a komatik ride brought on such craving." And with that, she turned to the kitchen and left John and myself to plan the next couple of days. I hoped to instruct some of the local children in impromptu classes, prepare for some fine services on the Sunday, and afterwards take off on my westward voyage, alone.

My first port of call was Pointa Murray (*Pointe à Maurier*). I had been able to scrounge, and also accept, donations from my parishioners at Harrington, so I was well provisioned as I went on. The Society for the Propagation of the Gospel in London sent me each quarter some thirty-seven pounds ten shillings for my expenses, which included the dogs and the mission boat. Most missionaries, for example in Shigawake where Rev. Mr. Kerr had gone from here, with no dogs or dog food to buy and the use of a local sleigh or buggy, were sent only three pounds. This was in addition to the tiny stipends we received from the diocese. I had purchased enough seal meat to keep the dogs happy for the entire journey to Natashquan and back. My aim was to go even as far west as the first young couple, the Foremans, whom Mr. Bishop had married, and then to return, visiting everyone that I could.

Sunday came and went and here it was a Monday afternoon, and I was finding this first day out on the trail invigorating, though I did miss Lorna's vivacious personality, her happiness, and encouragement. But on the other hand, I also welcomed the next few days of being alone. I had a good bit of thinking to do, without having to teach Clayton nor living up to others' expectations, so I enjoyed the rest, ordering my spirit to face the many problems bound to be facing me in my ministry.

Before the cluster of houses at Christian Bay hove into view, I felt the dogs quicken their pace and then, I too caught the scent. Seal oil, sealskins, seal remnants everywhere, came into view. In fact, though I pride myself on having a good memory, I had to admit I didn't remember any of this from my passing through on the mission boat with Gene. The five or six houses, decorated with many rounded frames for stretching seal pelts, did appear to me now quite different.

I pulled up at the largest house, probably the best place to begin. The dogs smelled entrails piled at the next house and it was almost impossible to control them until I gave them a taste of the whip. Then I fastened their sealskin laces around a rail and walked up onto the house bridge to knock. On it, stood barrels of rendered down fat, beside the frozen carcasses awaiting their transfer inside.

A short but wiry man opened the door and I was struck in the face by the overpowering smell of seal. The entire large downstairs room was filled with the processing. On the stove bubbled a big, black cauldron, making the room furiously hot. Normally, rendering is never done inside but at an outside foundry in spring. I imagined that this family had its own needs and was not averse to running counter to the main practices. At one side, a young lad was vigorously slicing layers of thawed blubber into two- or three-inch pieces, which he tossed into the cauldron. A couple of older girls, daughters I guessed, sat by a window stitching seal pelts into clothes and boots. A regular factory, I saw, all one family.

We introduced ourselves, and Wilbur Stubbert did remember me as the young deacon who had come through with Mr. Bishop. He introduced me to his wife, Mabel, and to his sons, who were cutting thawed seal meat into portions to freeze later for the dogs and for the family.

I could clearly see this house, indeed the whole cluster, was not ripe for religious services, nor could I really lead any prayers. Perhaps later, after dinner they might take a few minutes off. But now I observed only a hive of uninterruptible activity.

"So Mr. Stubbert, is everyone as busy as you fellows here?"

"I'd be a lot busier if it hadn't been for them rascals, the Bucklands!"

Oh dear, better take a deep breath. I took off my coat and enjoyed the heat for a few moments, allowing it to seep into my chilled body. The family continued working and I took in snatches of the problem as Wilbur saw it.

"This year, didn't the bugger go and put his seal net across in front of mine?" continued Wilbur as he handily and swiftly divested a mostly unfrozen carcass of its pelt and subsequently from this pelt, its blubber. "I had to keep movin' mine back, for no matter what I said, he left 'er there! Right in front o' mine! It was 'im gettin' all the seals coming through our channel. I finally had to string myself a net out there by Fakey's Rock (which I knew to be *Fequet's*) so I did get a good few b' the end o' the season." He flopped the carcass over and continued to work efficiently with his sharp, skinning knife. "But it meant me 'avin' to go way out in the boat, break m'self a way through the ice, chop a jeezly great 'ole, 'aul them nets up through it. If 'tweren't for me two sons 'ere, fine young fellows I gotta say, we'd a 'ad no seal at all, at all, this year."

In the free hour or two before supper to which I'd been invited, I went outside and walked well-trodden paths to a few other houses where I made myself known, ending up at the infamous Bucklands.

Howard Buckland was a man twice the size of Wilbur, twice the weight in any case. His house was also a hive of activity, though only three children were helping, along with his wife's young sister. His wife was cutting the thawed blubber into pieces for rendering, and the one son, who looked about eight years old, was wielding a skinning knife, separating the blubber from the sealskin. The seal was first sculped (pelt removed) and then skinned (fat removed from the pelt). Of course, he wore his arm-wrappers up to the elbow to protect himself. They were pleased to see me, for they let it be known that Christian Bay felt the lack of a leader, a clergyman, one who could resolve disputes and weld them all together in one single harmonious unit, which was the case with most communities. I felt encouraged.

So I brought up the question of the dispute with his neighbour.

"He don't want to 'ear of no compromise. It be all or nothin' wit' him. I offered to give 'em a bit of my rock to dry 'is cod in summer, if 'e'd let my flake stand as is. But no, 'e says my flake interrupts 'is boats coming back some terble. He wants I tear it down! Why not build yours out a bit on one side? That's do the trick, I keeps tellin' 'im. But no, 'e won't budge. So this year, I strung my seal net ahead o' his — I had an idea that *that* would make him budge, but still nothin'."

I gathered that here was a man open to negotiation, and now that I had arrived in their community, I felt I should not leave until the situation was resolved.

But again, no amount of Old Testament theology would help solve it. After ten years in this Canadian Labrador, I might well have become pretty good at resolving disputes. But for now I felt my youth and inexperience only too keenly. Oddly enough, my mind flashed to Lorna, how she would have had some good ideas. Women always know best, judging from the way my mother ran our household on the Gaspé Coast.

I left Howard's house, unresolved, and went on visiting. In the end, the community of Christian Bay agreed that on the morrow, after their dinners and time to clean up, they would gather for special prayers and a short service. That cheered me and I went back to the Stubberts for a supper of stewed sea duck, called an eider, that the son had shot the previous day. Actually, like the murres, it was a little too fishy for my taste, but anything hot and liquid felt good on an empty stomach.

I had been invited to stay at the Anderson house at one end of the village, which had no sealing industry going on. The Andersons had finished their sealing, being only a husband, wife, and two small children, and they offered me a mattress in the corner on which their old mother had slept. She had died a month previously and now lay well secured on a high platform outside to await the spring melt when they could bury her body. I agreed to say some rites over her for the time being.

I wondered where on earth they would bury her, for I saw no sign on these granite outcroppings of the depth of soil needed.

They told me their cemetery was back a good way in the hills behind. But, of course, the central issue now for me was to resolve the seal-net dispute. However, these journeys are always more exhausting than one realizes, and after I lay down, hoping to go over the problem, sleep claimed me almost at once.

First thing the next morning, I asked if I might be taken by my host, the amenable Dave Anderson, to see the site of the disputed territory. Everyone knew of the squabble, and I came to realize that a fair and just resolution would be welcomed. But what on earth could that be? I hoped with all my heart that when I saw the actual landing stages, something would come to me.

Again, of course, the problem related to open water, especially during the cod season, and right now as we walked to the lip of land in question and looked down, I found it exceedingly difficult to imagine where the shore ended and the ocean began. The heavy covering of snow over a uniform sheet of shore ice all flowed into one, merging the two stages with no clear delineation.

I asked Dave if he could try to explain the problem, which he did, motioning me down onto the Stubberts' stage. "He just needs to build that out to one side, one crib length is all ya'd need." A crib — actually squared log pilings filled with boulders — is what underpinned a stagehead, or wharf. "But the stubborn bugger, excuse me Mr. John, 'e won't budge an inch. No building out fer 'im!" He shrugged.

Well, we walked back slowly and I dropped in at a few houses again, in case I could be of help, either spiritually or physically. Then, I had my dinner with the Bucklands so that it wouldn't look as if I'd had both meals at the Stubberts.

The community gathered in the Andersons' house for my short service. After we had said appropriate prayers and even sung a couple of hymns, I motioned with outstretched arms and said I had a couple of announcements. I felt I had to solve the dispute one way or another, and I hoped I could hit on something, though I had no idea how it would be received.

"It has been brought to my attention in this lovely community — and I wish I could stay longer here, but the rest of my parish also needs attention — that we here are somewhat torn by a conflict. I think we all know who I'm speaking about. And I have a solution."

There was a low rumble as neighbour turned to neighbour. I saw they had expected no such thing, welcome though it might be.

"I have examined the location in question," I went on, "and here is what I propose. If Mr. Stubbert were to extend his stage to the right, he would have even better access to the water in cod season and not be impeded any longer by the other stagehead. So in the spring, because the Bucklands' stagehead is what seems to be causing the obstruction, I propose that the Buckland family — before the capelin and the cod come running and all of us net our fill of fish — that they themselves build out that extension crib for the Stubberts — with everyone's help."

I went on quickly, "Because the whole community should benefit from the ensuing peace, I want you all to pitch in and help build this one crib. That, as I see it, should do nothing but weld us all together: two weeks working together for the good of the whole, and..." I lifted my hand as someone was about to throw in, "of course, for Mr. Stubbert and his family. This is what I, as your clergyman, suggest."

I looked around the room. People were nodding, others whispering to their neighbours. I gave them a few moments and then I said loudly, "Is there anyone here who might object?"

A few heads shook, one or two people said no, and in the end, when I asked for a vote, it looked pretty unanimous.

"Now I have another announcement. It seems that young Jane Smith and Alf Blais have decided, with me arriving so unexpectedly, that it would be a good time to put on a wedding!" This was greeted with consternation by one family, I noticed, but on the whole the others were delighted and went over to congratulate the two of them.

On learning of the couple's decision this morning, I had approached the two sets of parents with the stricture that they seemed awfully young to be entering the bonds of matrimony that would bind them together for the rest of their natural lives. The boy's parents seemed in favour for they loved the young girl and had already treated her as one of the family. Jane's parents were less enthusiastic, for indeed their daughter was only seventeen. Oh dear, more difficulties! We discussed the matter at length, and in the circumstances, they ended up agreeing to the match. So I had offered to announce it myself.

"So now, everyone is invited over to the Smith home at four o'clock for the ceremony. After which, I have no doubt larders will be opened, and everyone can share in what should turn out to be a great celebration for the newlyweds."

And indeed, a lovely, simple wedding ceremony followed, after which the evening was spent, as is usual in these parts, with a fine fiddler, dancing, and lots of drink of various sorts, mostly homemade. I finally got to bed in the wee hours of the morning. But I felt pleased because this visit had ended with some solutions. I hoped as much for the next stage of my journey.

Chapter Fourteen

I found it difficult to get up after all the partying, but with the day bright though very cold, I ate breakfast and took off. No question of a barometer in Christian Bay, and this next leg of my trip went through fairly deserted territory so I left feeling nervous, hoping the weather would hold. The bravado with which I had started was evaporating; I couldn't stop myself remembering tales of travellers whose bodies had been found after the spring melt. I wrapped my scarf around my face, for the glass had fallen to minus thirty or more. The sun was blasting onto the dazzling snow, so I secured round my head the spectacles I had fashioned from a branch with only slits to see through, whittled by one of my parishioners.

We tore along all morning, and soon began to cross a stretch of deep bay, with the far cape a thin line in the distance. Much shorter to make straight for that, but did the ice hold solid all the way across? I decided to leave that to my faithful Tuck and, to cut off a few miles, I pointed the team straight across.

After a time of easy travelling I found myself dozing off. Something awakened me and behind I saw a great tower of cumulus bearing down from the southeast. The sky had darkened without warning because thunder's omen never sounds in midwinter, frozen land being too cold to encourage contact with electrically charged clouds. Coming fast, I saw.

If we were caught out in the open by a real thumping blizzard which might imprison us for three or four days, it would finish us off, me and my dog team. We had to find shelter. And find it fast.

But in which direction? The shore lay a good hour away to the north. Anxiously scanning it, I saw neither houses nor woods. Should I still head in there? Perhaps deep beyond the shore might lie a stand of spruce offering shelter. Would we make that in time? No, for spruce was not a surety. To the southwest out in the Gulf, I made out a couple of islands. A fishing shack or two might have been built there for summer fishing. Should I take a chance and head toward those, hoping for an abandoned camp? But was there time for that either?

Trying to remain calm, I pondered the situation. I watched the storm clouds bearing down, flat black underneath, and tumbling high and white above like some great animal poised to leap. Closer and closer came the front, pursuing me and my team, and with it, a chilling damp that ate through my clothes.

I knew fishermen often left their summer camps unlocked because nothing remained to be stolen or pilfered, not that anyone here would do such a thing. All right, try the islands, I decided. I shouted to Tuck, "Ak ak!"

She paid no attention. I called again louder and she glanced over her shoulder as if to say, have you gone mad? But she did veer out into the gulf in the direction of the islands. Those clouds were really sweeping down after us with minds of their own, as if bent on our destruction. Quite a buildup of wind, I knew, and just as I grasped that thought, the air became bitterly cold, almost beyond bearing. This was a race I was not enjoying, much as I had revelled in team competitions back at Mutton Bay.

I yelled for the dogs to go faster, but they continued at their normal pace. To me, with that storm bearing down, they seemed to be positively dawdling.

I called again, slapped my hand on the komatik, but to no avail. Nothing for it but a touch of the whip. I got it out and tried to crack it in the best teamster fashion. No such luck. I yelled again in frustration, and whipped hard at my pittuk dog, Rob, the closest, and the one ahead of him. They gave yelps and struggled to increase their pace, but without much effect. I screamed at the team, frustration boiling up. After a few more tries, I was able to make the whip crack. Tuck looked back again as if to say, what on earth are you up to, Jack? But she did increase her pace and the whole team began to speed along, fanned out before me, straining at their traces. I shouted encouragement, checking over my shoulder, and tried to shun any idea that we might not make it.

About half a mile from the island, the first flurries struck and the wind tore at us. We'd soon be stranded out in the middle of nowhere. Alarming indeed! But I made out a tiny black square against the sky. A house for sure. Out of reach, most probably. I shouted at the team.

Snow flew up from the paws of the scurrying dogs and a lump struck my eye, causing it to water. And then, would you believe, that froze on my cheek. What a pickle! I had dropped my scarf from my face to shout and now my nose and cheeks had likely gotten frostbitten. I knelt on one knee, leaning low to reduce the wind drag, and used my free leg to kick us along yet faster. I don't mind admitting I was scared. Then didn't the dogs stop? I yelled at them, but saw they were rolling over in order to get the snow out of their eyes, and off we went again. My mind tumbled with thoughts of what to do if we were indeed caught out here.

The snow swirled heavily around us. This whipped-up drifting made the going even harder. I began to panic. But what more could be done? Prayer seemed the only escape route. And pray I did. Out loud.

I felt a bump, which meant we had struck a reef of rock which perhaps indicated the edge of the island, and then the faithful Tuck raced on over the bumps that indicated, I was sure, uneven ground. Yes, we had reached the island. When I could hardly see anything before my face, the dogs pulled up the komatik in front of a fishing camp, nothing more nor less than a shack that had presumably housed a whole family in the lovely summer months.

I leapt up onto the narrow house bridge, or veranda, and thank heaven the door opened. I went quickly back and forth to bring in provisions, wondering what to do about the dogs. This could all pass overnight, or stay three or four days, not uncommon hereabouts. If I were to get out alive, the dogs must be cared for, fed, and kept safe.

Under a stagehead, I decided — surely there'd be a stagehead down at the water's edge. I made my way through the drifts and peered. Yes, piled with snow, the end blown clear, a good-sized stagehead. I came back to release the dogs from the komatik and bring them down. I tied the sealskin traces around the stagehead beam and one by one pushed each dog into the space under the stagehead, by the rocky shore. When the last dog was safe, I turned but could not see my camp. I wiped the snow from my face and peered again. Only thirty feet away, already it had disappeared.

Now what? Stay with the dogs under here? No, no question of that. But if I didn't hit the camp, I could wander for hours, and freeze to death. Against my better judgement, I struggled up through the drifts, falling a couple of times. When I squinted through the blizzard, I still saw nothing. Should I keep going? Suppose I missed the shed by even a few feet, I could pass it, go on and on, and end up lost, frozen, just another North Shore casualty.

Make a try, I thought. And then, somehow I struck the end

of the low house bridge. I clambered up, got inside, shook the snow off, and took in my surroundings. A barren room, with an out-of-date calendar and a faded religious picture, a dishtowel hanging on a hook by the stove. Yes, delight of delights, a stove. At least I would not freeze tonight.

But a stove needs wood. No wood inside.... Better check round the back, I thought, and forced myself outside again into the gale of snow. With an arm out, touching the walls to stay close, I made a circle of the house. No wood anywhere.

These islands produced no trees so all firewood had to be carted from the mainland — not a commodity to lavish around. So I had my nice stove, my dry matches, but no wood. The kindling I carried to begin fires in the woods would not last twenty minutes.

No way to heat myself a cup of tea. I got out cold bread and tacky molasses and sat on the floor to munch on it slowly. The house was already shaking, the wind whistling through the cracks between the boards. A fine home for the summer, no doubt, but hardly made for winter.

Seal meat for the dogs, yes. Better get it out to them before we're quite shut in, I thought, and so I unwrapped some I had brought in from the komatik. I forced the door open, but could see nothing beyond two or three feet. With the fierce wind and the snow swirling, I was facing a whiteout. No hope of finding my way to the dogs. I'd heard stories of men dying within ten feet of their homes in such conditions. I wanted none of that.

I pondered what to do, and then came up with the idea of tying a spare dog trace around myself. I got one from my komatik box, secured one end around the heavy stove, the other round my waist, and out I went.

After three paces, didn't I fall off the platform. But as the snow was deep, no harm done. I picked myself up and went in the general direction of the stagehead. After being quite surrounded by whiteness, my foot stepped on air, and I hurtled down, striking my head on a rock or chunk of ice, and blacked out.

How long did I lie there? I only know that when I came to, I found myself buried under snow. Dizzy, I struggled up, blood trickling into my eyes. But I heard a dog sneeze only a few feet away, and started to crawl on hands and knees over. Then I remembered, blood! Yes, don't go too near. They'll smell it. What would happen to me, then? I didn't trust them.

I tried to staunch the blood from my scalp. I never dreamed so much blood ran just under my hair. What a copious flow! But I packed snow on it and pressed hard. After a while in this blizzard, the wind whipping me with coarse grains that stung like salt actually froze the bleeding. Surely that would keep the smell down.

I picked up the meat, pushed it ahead of me, and crawled closer. I threw some in, and heard their wolfing sounds as they gulped it down. Using the sealskin trace, I pulled myself back to the camp, got inside, and shook off all the snow. Mitts off, I rubbed my hands together to warm them. Now my nose and cheeks began to hurt as though they'd been badly burned. Frostbite, yes, but here, out of the wind, they had begun to thaw and with that, the pain started. My head did not bother me much, though it kept throbbing. In this cold, the blood would dry and the wound be staunched.

Nothing for it but try to ignore the frostbite. Darkness had set in; no candles here, for sure. I always travelled with one so I found it and got it alight to give me time to wrap myself in blankets. Only slightly better than being outside, I said to myself, for the wind was driving the snow through cracks and under the door.

What a night it turned out to be — the worst of my life, without any doubt. I was afraid the whole rickety camp would blow over. Such a horrible force of wind, rocking the timbers, shaking the camp on its meagre foundations. At one point I heard a horrible crash: the stovepipe had blown down.

Fortunately I had no fear for my dogs, being under the stage. But for myself, the windows kept rattling, the timbers creaking and rustling, and the wind howling like a savage spectre. Yes, I admit I was rather shaken.

How I ever slept through that storm, I have no idea; I would awaken and drift off again. Perhaps the ghoulish shrieking and battering of the wind felt somehow comforting, knowing that the Almighty was much in evidence. Or was that just the result of my dreamlike state? Perhaps, if I prayed, I might finally have this visitation for which I longed.

The next morning before dawn, I awoke with great hunger. Lighting the stub of a candle, I was able to cut off bits of frozen salt cod from one of the chunks I had brought and tore at it with my teeth. I ate some snow because I was thirsty, and then I set about trying to plug the more ominous cracks: the komatik box I pulled against the door, and found a loose board which I leaned against the one window whose pane was missing. I jumped up and down, beat my arms around my body again and did deep knee bends to get the blood circulating. It felt as cold inside as out, but at least in here the wind did not gust so violently. My nose and cheeks still hurt from the frostbite and I rubbed snow on them, lots having blown in through the various openings.

No sign of the storm abating, so I contrived to sit near a window when the light grew sufficient and read the Bible, which might take me outside of myself.

Of course, with freezing fingers, I turned to Second Corinthians, St. Paul's most personal chapter, for I knew he too had done a lot of travelling. When he wrote it in Ephesus, he'd been there before and all around, even back to Jerusalem. I hoped to find something that might help me through the coming days. And before I had read far, in fact in chapter six, I found what I was looking for. I read it over and over, and then paraphrased it in my mind:

> *Indeed we want to prove ourselves genuine ministers of God in whatever we have to go through — patient endurance of troubles or even disasters; having to work like slaves, having to go without food or sleep. We want to meet all this with sincerity, with insight and patience; with sheer kindness by the Holy Spirit; with genuine love, speaking the plain truth and living by the power of God.*

And then I skipped to the next bit:

> *Never far from death, yet here we are alive, always "going through it" yet never "going under." We know sorrow, yet our joy is inextinguishable. We have nothing to bless ourselves with, and yet we bless many others with true riches. We are penniless, and yet in reality we have everything worth having.*

I wished I had my copy of *Pilgrim's Progress* with me, for this certainly fit with Mr. Christian's journey. In fact, I was reminded of Apollyon, the monster, whom I could very well imagine howling around this little camp. How did he overcome that beast? I think it was by persevering and meeting the situation head on and not turning back, and as I saw it, I could do nothing else. I hoped it would produce the same result. After all, I do remember the Christian saying, from the prophet Micah, "When I fall, I shall arise."

And that is how I got through the day: reading, leaping about beating my arms and hands, marching with my knees up, anything to keep warm, which I made into a kind of game, and then dozing off. I wondered how many days I could keep this up, being freezing cold and hungry, but the signs of abatement began to make themselves felt late in the afternoon. Might it indeed be coming to an end? Lo! By sunset the wind had died down and I ventured outside.

What a glorious snowscape! So very white, so pure, a late low sun struggling to throw a few golden rays across the contours, gilding the monochrome a deep bronze. I searched the horizon for sight of some kindred soul struggling like a polar explorer over the ice with his dog team. But of course I was alone, quite alone. And a long way from any habitation. I was tempted to remain standing against the wall, just drinking it all in.

But the dogs! Time to get their food. My head wound had long dried, the blood caked solid, so I considered myself more or less healed. It throbbed a little, but no sharp pain. I went to retrieve some of the seal meat and poured cod oil over it. The komatik itself lay under a great drift that camouflaged it. In the rapidly sinking sun, I cleared some snow off and got one of my rackets. I stepped off the bridge into a deep drift, and then trudged over to where I thought I might find the stagehead, where I heard my team rousing and stretching. Using my racket as a spade, I unearthed the wooden platform. I dug some more, got to the open cavern beneath, and threw in a good supply of seal meat. Although they hadn't been working, they fell upon it with their usual ravening.

Then I returned to my house bridge but before going in, turned once again to take in my location. Snow had arranged itself in exquisite drapings — delicate ridges scrawled across the island in some ancient Aramaic, or heaped up into tiny fetching peaks, smoothing out blemishes, blending land and sea into one vast softened parchment. Out across the gulf, the flat ice lay unbroken by any tracks, all wafted into whorls of indecipherable tracings, so pristine and pure. The setting sun, now lower, threw its beams and shadows at different angles, highlighting the ancient script written in the snow's own cuneiform, so delicate that it appeared virginal, almost holy.

I wondered if paradise were like this? We always think of it, or the afterlife, as being rather more like butterfly-filled gardens. But nothing could approach the utter purity and cleanliness of all this. I felt bewitched, intoxicated, even delirious with the extraordinary beauty that some great Writer of the Snows had scrawled into my northern landscape. Even the dogs had not stirred from under their stage to mar the pristine purity.

Yes, it was cold. I could hear the house crack as occasional gusts flicked their icy whips against its flimsy walls. But on the whole, calm prevailed, although I heard the faint tinkle of ice cracking over the thin air, icicles snapping, and those delicate sounds one associates with winter, which would be impossible to describe for someone who does not know the Far North.

Feeling immensely cheered that we had weathered this storm and that I had made the right decision to head for an island, I went back in and again chewed my way through some dried codfish, which apart from the salt was tasteless to the point of absurdity. But with my appetite returning somewhat, it felt good just to have tough gristle to chew on.

After the outdoor light had faded and the candle I had lit began to burn low, the sight of a moon out the window drew me to the door. I rose rather stiffly and slipped out.

The low half-moon sent sharp rays over the luminous drifts. The shadows themselves, now dark blue, gave me an alternative view from the earlier setting sun. I leaned back against the door, blowing out my breath and watching it drift up in a cloud and disappear. I revelled in this moonlit experience. Was I not blessed to be on this island set apart from all others, lonely and gaunt, casually draped in glittering snow on its great tableland of the gulf? Such a shame that only those who are handed God-given challenges, as I consider myself to have been, are the ones to whom moments of great joy are often bequeathed.

I looked up. Oh my! Such vast black interstellar spaces above, who could not marvel at them? Singly and then in growing clusters, the stars began to emerge. Those same stars were of course winking at my family in the Gaspé. Would I have a letter from them when I returned to Mutton Bay? In any case, duty prompted me to get down to writing them with a full report. When I had left in August, my mother had hinted I might be having a little brother or sister in the winter, and I was anxious to know the results of that.

Such a pity that our Lord had not appeared to mankind in northern climes such as this, for then he could have himself experienced such extraordinary fresh moonscapes. And those Northern Lights, which I have not mentioned for we have them in the Gaspé, though not so vivid as here, dancing across the heavens in displays of celestial brilliance. I never ceased to marvel at them, night after night, willowy wafting curtains designed surely by the Lord of all to show us His predilection for beauty and harmony. But then I reflected that He is in all of us, and through me, He must be also rejoicing in my solitary, but yet by no means lonely, happiness.

After a long time of standing, I'm not sure how long, I became conscious of being more than usually chilled. I went inside in and closed the door, and then proceeded to do some warm-up exercises, beat my hands around my body and leap about. I had to prepare myself for bed and knew I should not get under blankets this chilled. Whatever had possessed me out there, I wondered, as I began to pant with exertion? A big day lay ahead tomorrow, I knew, and I had to force myself into a good deep sleep.

Chapter Fifteen

The next morning being crisp and clear, I went to dig the dogs out of their snowbound enclosure. I brought them up, fed and harnessed them, attached their traces to the pittuk loop and, having already cleared and loaded the komatik, off we went.

It seemed almost a shame to ruin the beautiful snowscape with these crass runners cutting double clefts through the drifts. By the same token, although we headed out immediately onto the ice, the dogs found it heavy going. I got my rackets off the komatik and put them on so that I could plough on ahead of, or beside, the team. We made for the cape at the end of a bay and, rounding it, made slow progress, always keeping the shore to our right.

We spent the day keeping close to the shore. When we'd hit a patch of windblown ice, I'd get back on the komatik and away we'd go. Late in the afternoon, I did see what appeared to be some movement on the shore. The scattering of huts looked more like igloos, being buried under the previous day's drifting snow. Nonetheless, these were my parishioners, and in I went.

I was given a fine welcome, but I concede they were having their own problems just surviving this winter. The cod fishing had been good, but not the seals and so they had not managed to catch enough food for their dogs. I broke out what I could for supper, and afterwards led them in a short service of thanksgiving for what they did have. It was edifying to see how much they appreciated my presence and how they longed to be able to give me succour from what little stores they had, but I could take none of it. In fact, I only wished I'd had more to give them. They assured me it was not too far to the next large settlement, Kegaska, with its decent-sized community of Anglicans, and also to Natashquan, where I'd be able to buy more.

The next three days went well enough, and I did feel I achieved some goals of my ministry, even counselling two families. In fact, I met with the RC priest in Kegaska, a good deal nicer fellow and younger than the one down our way. So I felt ready to push on to the Foremans, the first family Gene and I had visited.

And so my trip went, one settlement visited after another, with my struggling through drifts, fighting the ever-blowing wind, twice losing the way when we had to go inland to cut off a large cape. I began to pay attention to the differing tracks in the new snow: the rabbits were easy to make out, and some I knew to be fox, tiny lines were mice and even a partridge or two's resting place. But after my brush with that icy winter storm, I was now rather more afraid of losing my way. I couldn't remember anything about the next settlement or indeed any of the names. Everything looked so different from a komatik in midwinter than from a mission boat in full summer. I searched my mind for clues to the next community.

It had not been easy to reach the Foremans' cabin before and now I found this even harder. I tried to remember the trail I had walked on with Eugene, and it did not feel as if this were right. Should I cast around? Go further inland perhaps, or back toward the coast? Those first days when I arrived here, we had chosen well-travelled trails and I had paid little attention to my orientation from the sea, nor indeed to important distinguishing marks such as stands of certain trees that would now help me locate myself. The last thing I wanted to do was get lost. Especially as another storm seemed in the offing. Would these storms never cease? Debilitating to get twinges of panic at every sight of great clouds rearing up in the distance. But then, one cannot always be a hero.

I did seem to remember having climbed a hill soon after the Foremans', and to my right I saw an odd and rather substantial hill. Thither I directed the dogs, but when we reached it, the climb seemed to be heavy with no broken trail. I persevered because from the top, I knew I'd have a good view.

The going became more difficult. The snow had blown up this side of the hill; in places the drifts were surprisingly deep. Tuck did not want to try it at all. She kept moving to her left to go around the peak and back down. I should have paid attention. But no, as is often the case with northern tragedy, I was stubborn and pig-headed. "Come on Tuck," I called, "radda radda," go right, and finally, she did keep at this really impossible ascent.

I walked behind the komatik, struggling, sweating, often on my knees, pushing as hard as I could while the dogs themselves, often over their heads in snow, tried to make it upward. By late afternoon, it seemed we were well and truly stuck. I castigated myself for being such an idiot. I dug with my rackets and tried to clear some kind of path, first for Tuck and then the komatik. Such a steep angle! However, after much sweating and shovelling, we got going again and, as the sun was setting, achieved the summit.

Yes, there in the distance, I did see three columns of smoke rising from deep in the woods. That must be them, I thought. Then again, would the Foremans remember me from the previous autumn, me being only a companion to the Rev. Eugene Bishop? Well, at least the smoke meant a house — any house would be welcome with night falling and the storm clouds streaming at us. I resolved I would definitely give myself a day's rest before turning and setting off on the long trip back.

But then I looked down. We stood on the verge of a steep slope, almost a cliff. Heavens, how would we manage that? Go back the way we came, I told myself. But that tower of cloud was fast approaching. I stood there, frightened, as the sun kept sliding sideways into the horizon, the dogs panting, and my mind churning with a thousand indecisions. Oh yes, even within sight of those distant stovepipes, this whole adventure could end in tragedy. Dreadful being such a coward, I told myself, so buck up, for pity's sake! Just make the best of it, put on double drags, or brakes, and slither straight down. Much faster, easier, simpler (if we made it, sure) and then no worries, we'd head off into those woods and find the source of the smoke, where I believed the Foremans to be.

Going back down the way we had climbed would be safer, of course, but then, would I ever find our way to them out around the point in the dark? I might have to bivouac for the night. The clouds were closing over, the storm almost upon us, nothing to light our way if we faltered. Chilled and frightened, I thought, well, give it a try — nothing like a thrilling run down the side of a steep hill. Probably the most exciting run I'd ever have. But, I begged, not the last!

I put on the drags, got the dogs to their feet, and down we started.

Was that a partial track leading off left? Yes, that might be less steep. We set off in that direction, a direction that Tuck also wanted. But before I realized and could correct for it, the dogs hit some loose snow and down we all went sideways — over a much steeper drop. Faster and faster we tore, and then the komatik straightened and actually overran the dogs. Down I went with it, clinging with all my might as we dragged the dogs on their backs behind.

Huge pinnacles of ice called ballicatters (from *"barricades"*) rose to face us at the foot of these cliffs on the sea's edge. I closed my eyes and prayed not to hit one, always leaning sideways to keep the komatik from overturning; the dogs were yelping, dragged on their backs as faster we went, sliding sideways until I jammed my leg down and righted it again so that now we tore head first out onto the flat bay ice and then, slowly pulled to halt. I tried to stand.

I was whitefaced, I'm sure, and certainly trembling. Lord, what a narrow escape! After catching my breath, I walked back to where the dogs lay entangled in their traces.

I hope I had not broken any dog's leg.

Fortunately, Tuck was unharmed and got up, wagging her tail when I released her. One by one, I lifted them, talked to them nicely, and got them sorted out. But then, I came to Grey. Oh dear, he couldn't stand, his hindquarters would not move. The runners must've struck him. It looked to me as though we had broken his spine.

Now what?

Bring him over and lay him on the komatik? Strap him on? Bring him to the settlement? But what would they do there? A spine, as we all know, is not curable. But leave him here to slowly starve and freeze?

Oh what a wretched rogue and peasant slave I am, I cursed as I mangled Shakespeare. How could I ever forgive myself? I had actually damaged one of my seven wonderful companions — whose brave hearts and sturdy legs had carried me so many miles? And only through thoughtless stupidity – how horrible. I stood above Grey, chastising myself. But dusk was falling and the storm looming.

Nothing for it, but to get the revolver my church warden had given me in case I ran into intractable situations. Wearily I plodded over to the komatik box, rummaged around, and found the gun.

What would the other dogs think when they saw me? But then I knew my mission came first. My parishioners needed my care. I could not, for their sakes, endanger my own life or that of the team.

I loaded the revolver.

The dogs sat panting, their traces still not fully untangled. Fix all that later, after my unthinkable task was done.

I knelt by Grey who looked up at me: I could see he was in pain. I bent down, and touched my forehead to his, almost hoping he would tear my throat out before my dreadful deed. But no, he lay back on the snow, and waited.

I rose from my knees, pointed the revolver down at his head, and pulled the trigger.

Grey's blood spread a great stain on the white snow.

I walked back and sorted out the harnesses. For some reason, the clouds had not poured out their vengeance yet. As if sleepwalking in a nightmare, I hitched the team, got back on the komatik, and gave the shout to move off. No point in wasting precious time in burying the poor dog; the coming snowfall would do it for me. On we sped across the windswept ice and then toward the black forest. Before we entered I checked for the direction of the smoke. Heading that way, I came upon a kind of roadway hewn through the stunted trees. In single file, the dogs quickened their pace, smelling the smoke and human habitation, which meant a good meal.

Finally we arrived at the group of dwellings, when night, black as my own soul, fell upon us like a smothering curtain. I got off the komatik, banged at the door, my heart leaden. The Foremans opened it.

"Mr. John!" Ralph cried at once, "Welcome. Welcome!" He

ushered me in. I knew the team would not go rushing off, for they were always fed at a house. I left them outside and stepped into the modest log cabin.

Esther came rushing across, shaking my hand, but then she could see that all was not well. "What is wrong, Mr. John?" she asked, concerned. "Has something happened?"

I nodded. "That cliff back there. I should never have gone over."

"But whatever happened?" Ralph asked. "Did ya have an accident?"

I nodded again, too heart-broken to speak. "Yes, an accident..." I stood mute, and then realized I should not subject them to any more of this self-flagellation. "My fine dog, Grey, broke his back, and I had to shoot him." I stood, mute, doing my best to control the tears.

In the rocking chair next to the stove normally reserved for Esther and her newborn, I couldn't stop shaking. The couple had been more than kind and very understanding. The stove had been stuffed with their best birch from the interior and threw off a good solid heat that warmed my bones. I just had not realized how much the accident, the frightening race down the mountain, the brush with my own destruction, and then, the tragedy of my lovely dog Grey, how much it had all affected me. Indeed, I wondered then if I would ever get over it.

Ralph had seen my state, and after having got me by the fire and stoked it well, he had taken my team, unhitched them, and put them in the dog pen of his next neighbour who had gone off on a five-day jaunt to look for game. It became clear that if the man shot no game, the little settlement might even starve, for the month of March was coming to an end and with it their meagre provisions. How could I ever conduct a service for them all in my state, and with their starvation approaching? The winter storm had struck hard here too, rattling their windows and shaking the timbers.

"Mr. John? Mr. John!" I opened my eyes. Esther stood before me, a mug in her hand. "Mr. John, I know it's not a woman's place to serve you this, but Ralph whispered to me when 'e went out. 'Tis left over from the celebration when I 'ad my baby. Rum, just a tot. Do you no harm. From what I see, might even do ya powerful good."

I shook my head. "No thank you, Esther. I could never take a service after —"

She interrupted, "No question of a service tonight, Mr. John. They's... they's just not ready. And the storm 'as come. Tomorrow. Tomorrow would be better. You 'ave a good sleep tonight, and tomorrow we'll gather. In fact, in the afternoon, you can give us all a fine service. After that, maybe we'll put together what little food we 'ave left and celebrate. Yis," she said, obviously having made up her mind, "Yis yis yis, that's just what we'll do. A service, and a celebration. We needs it, for sure."

I was so overwhelmed that I reached out and touched her arm. Then I took the rum. "Well, if you say so." I couldn't stop my teeth chattering as I spoke, and it made me giggle. She laughed with me. Then I took a good slug.

I coughed as it went down. But no doubt, just what I needed. After a few minutes, rocking by the fire, letting the heat seep into me, sipping my rum, I felt more myself, so that when Ralph came back, he smiled.

"Well, I see you're on the way to recovery, Mr. John. Mighty good thing for all of us." He took off his outer things and hung them on hooks. "Your dogs is fine. I found the seal meat where you told me and they're 'aving a good feed. Poor fellas, I think that there accident shook 'em all. I never seen dogs so quiet. They was almost polite when they tore into that there meat."

I smiled again. "Well, I guess something good came out of it after all." And I found myself chuckling.

How could I laugh — when I had just, through my own stupidity, my own thoughtlessness, destroyed one of my seven finest companions? But laugh I did, and all three of us joined in. In fact, Ralph himself went to the corner, squeezed the last drop of rum out of the container, and came over to sit beside me. We chatted and drank like buddies, and I found myself (the rum loosening my tongue) pouring out my own shame and guilt for what I had done. Ralph readily sympathized and told of other accidents, none by any means the fault of the driver. Esther contrived to make us some weak soup for our suppers. I knew I would later bring in my provisions. But for the moment, this fireside moment, this welcoming home, it was the best thing that could have happened to me, after my ghastly mistake.

The storm was passing, and the next day after a simple dinner of tea and moistened hardtack, and even porridge from my supply of oatmeal, the households gathered for a lovely service. After that, their modest celebration began. I joined in, hoping their warmth and good comradeship would wash away the pain, and that by the next day I would be ready for my long return.

But with only six dogs... would we make it safely? I'd have to walk a good part of the way. I put such thoughts out of my mind. Tomorrow would have to take care of itself.

Chapter Sixteen

Tonight, Harrington Harbour.

I sprang out of bed at the thought. My long return journey was coming to an end. These last days since visiting the Foremans had, if anything, put me in fine fettle: I must have trekked a good halfway on my rackets. Heavy snows came and went as expected, and after each storm, I had to break a trail at the head of my reduced team. Two or three nights I did sleep out of doors, finding shelter among spruce trees or once, even nestling down in a snowdrift at the base of some high rock. The snow, I found out, makes a wonderful insulator. Last night, I slept the soundest of them all.

At first, I had fought the dreadful image of Grey lying on the snow, but then, I fell upon an important trick: let in a special image — that of glorious red cheeks, black eyelashes, dark eyes, glossy black hair: the lovely Lorna. Her lilting laughter made even poor Grey disappear.

Released from my torture, I felt in a better position to minister to my parishioners. Because I wore the collar and the marks of the priesthood, I had been treated with a devotion and respect I had not earned. That knowledge alone sustained me on the long, often lonely, but never boring, route home.

My memories of the settlements tended to blur into each other: the Mingan Islands, Natashquan, Kegaska with its Hudson's Bay post and cheerful manager (called a "factor"), Saint Peter's

Harbour, and many other smaller places I visited. Some were admittedly more charming than others: Christian Bay (where happily I found that my solution had put everyone, including the Bucklands and Stubberts, in a good humour), Old Edwards, Blais, and Mainland — so-called because on the islands where they went fishing, fishermen would refer to their winter homes as Mainland.

As I set off across the bay for the island with Harrington Harbour, I grew anxious. Was it because I hoped Lorna would still be at the house of John Bobbitt? Or had she returned to Mutton Bay? And what of Phil Vatcher? Had he now won her heart? I certainly had no claim upon her myself. With a shudder I remembered how brusque I had been when she had welcomed the notion that we should travel together as man and wife.

All right then, did I really want to get married? Such an enormous subject — each time it arose, I put it aside. I recalled my mother's second thoughts as recounted by cousin John that first Christmas of my university stint, when she'd left the day after their marriage. And I told myself, my first duty did lie here in this enormous parish. The whole drama of matrimony, with its many accoutrements, might be too diverting: learning to live with another, all the family implications, children that surely would come, no, I felt I could not handle it all just at the moment. But of course, that could change.

At last, I rounded a cape and there on the low promontory, I saw the gathering of snow-covered houses. Among them rose the skeleton of the new church building. Once the weather got warmer, I knew from the locals' enthusiasm that the building would take shape quickly. The uprights wore jaunty caps of snow perched on interlocking rafters, only now a proud symbol but one day to be inhabited as a house of God. I swelled with pride, even though it had been the Bishop himself who had chosen the spot and the previous pastor, I.N. Kerr, who had done the organizing. Of course, our wonderful lay reader, John Bobbitt, had helped generate the energies poured into all this during the summer.

Faithful Tuck brought me right to the door of John Bobbitt's large house. I dismounted and walked up onto his house bridge. Would Lorna's face be at the door to greet me?

I knocked.

I glanced back at my dogs, tongues hanging out after the pull up the hill, waiting patiently. Behind me I heard the door open and whirled.

John Bobbitt held out his hand. "Mr. John, welcome! It's good to 'ave you back. They'll all be pleased to know you're safe after that big trip o' yours."

I went inside and he put on a kettle for tea. I was dying to ask about Lorna, but John kept up a babble of information, until finally, I discovered that Lorna had only stayed three or four days. "But when she left 'arrington, this 'ere house was as spic and span as when my wife lived in it, if not even cleaner."

I smiled. "She's quite a worker, our Lorna."

"That she is. We got the best of the bargain, Mr. John, when you went to rescue 'er from that there schooner." But then John let it drop that Phil Vatcher had come over on business, and the minute he had arrived, had called in. Because the house was spotless, John had suggested Lorna return with him and the next day, off she had gone in Phillip's komatik.

That news gave me quite a jolt.

But again, I just had to put it aside for I knew very well I had no great call upon her attentions. I did, however, want to get to Mutton Bay and see her as quickly as possible. So many disturbing questions popped into my mind. But now, Wednesday, I would have to wait for my Sunday services: Holy Communion in the morning and Vespers at night.

After I had unloaded the komatik and gotten through the various arrangements necessary at the end of my long trip, I came upon the idea of holding a sunset service in the skeleton of the church. It would help also get my mind off Lorna.

And so we did, the next night: a most beautiful evensong out on simple flooring that had been swept clear of snow. We prayed in the gentle breeze, a glorious sun throwing its crimson rays from under dark layers of cloud over these snow-covered capes. A couple of quite strong voices led us in hymns of praise and thanksgiving. I concluded with the "Song of Simeon":

Lord, now lettest thou thy servant depart in peace, according to thy word;

For mine eyes have seen thy salvation, which thou hast prepared before the face of all people:

To be a light to lighten the Gentiles, and to be the glory of thy people Israel.

And then I myself sang the lovely antiphon:

Guide us waking, O Lord,
and guard us sleeping;
that awake we may watch with Christ,
and asleep we may rest in peace.

A perfect way to end the service I thought, and a couple of parishioners even commented on it, too.

I found it odd that the builder who had done so much groundwork on the structure did not attend this service, and

I inquired after him from our church warden. John Bobbitt hesitated in his reply and not until I spoke to his cousin Dan Bobbitt, the husband of our tireless Sunday School teacher, did I find out the truth. The builder, Levi Wright, had been insisting that the church was higher, or taller, than need be, making it hard to heat in winter. He had proposed lowering the ceiling, which would make it cheaper and more comfortable in winter. Not from here, Dan had come over to lend his expertise. On the other hand, John Bobbitt had opted, quite rightly in my opinion, for the usual proportions that had turned out such a nice church in Mutton Bay the year previously: this conflict I saw now needed solving.

If it were not one thing, it would most certainly be another.

The next afternoon after a splendid dinner of murre stew made by his daughter, John and I received the builder, Levi Wright, whom I hadn't met. With his prominent nose, bright eyes, and tuft of hair, he looked to me like a squirrel: a small man, strong as iron apparently, who knew his carpentry better than anyone around. John by contrast was tall and also lean, but in spite of his size had a gentle voice — I often had to lean forward to hear him, a noble-looking man, both in spirit and in body.

They both knew why I'd asked them to come, and began by defending their positions on the height of the church rather too vigorously. I got up and went out to the stove to get a teapot and cups. I needed time to think.

When I came back, I found them having happily diverted their argument into a discussion of ghosts. Not the subject, I assured them, for churchgoers. But I was curious, of course. Often the subject of the phantom ship had been broached on the Gaspé Coast.

"Well if you wanna talk about ghosts," Levi said, "here's the man knows more about them than anyone. He's a great believer in tokens and phantoms."

My interest quickened. "You John? A man of the church?"

"Well sir, it isn't exactly that. It's this 'ere boat I lost."

"Called the *Flying Dutchman*," said Levi, "after that there famous boat." We all knew the legend of the ghost ship that could never make port, being doomed to sail the oceans forever. "Now after he'd lost it, 'twas seen all over the gulf at different times, oh yis yis yis."

"You lost a boat?" I asked John. "How so?"

"Well sir, I bought this here boat in Sydney and I's trying to take it back to Newfoundland. Bless my soul if I couldn't find not a single man to accompany me. So I said to m'self, all right, I'll sail 'er alone. And sail 'er across I did. But it was a long trip. And at one point, the sea got up rough, so I lashed the wheel tight, went below, and Lord 'a mercy, didn't she run onto one o' them shoals?"

"Oh heavens, John, what did you do?"

"Well, finally, I had to jump off, fer she was lost, fer sure. I knew how to swim, not far to the island there, you know, Levi?"

"Yes sir," Levi went on, "but that ship, she's seen all over, fall of the year or spring after the ice opens — whenever the weather's bad, she's seen in a storm or in a fog, sailing along with a ghostly figure at the 'elm. Everyone knows the story of John Bobbitt's *Flying Dutchman*. Everyone on the Canadian Labrador, oh yis yis yis." He slapped John on the shoulder.

"Maybe so, maybe so," John said, "but I sure wish I had 'er back. And that there light was seen many times, I heard, up by Shecatica Island."

"Was it," I asked, "like a burning ship? We have a phantom ship in Chaleur Bay often seen from land by quite a few people. Never seen it myself, though."

"No, this weren't no burning ship. Just a round globe, like a puncheon."

Well now, better face the main issue.... "Gentleman, here's what I think. I hope you won't mind, Levi, but I do want the church to be of a decent size. I don't think —" I held up my hand to forestall his argument, "I don't think the community here would like to have a little runt of a church which could be the laughingstock of the Canadian Labrador.

"You see, Levi," I went on quickly, "what John hasn't explained: there are pretty sound geometrical reasons for the proportions of the Mutton Bay church, and indeed most of the Anglican churches across our country. So would it not be a mistake for this noble community to find itself with a church that doesn't match any other?"

They were both silent, polite. I waited. The onslaught would surely come. And how would I deal with that?

Well, Levi was the first to agree. He began nodding to himself. "I was just trying to save yez some money in the winter. But now that you say that, Mr. John, I'll be behind ya one 'undred percent. And that's the proportions I'll build 'er to, whatever John 'ere wants, John o' the *Flying Dutchman*!" He laughed and slapped John on the shoulder. And thus it was resolved to everyone's satisfaction.

Sunday dawned, a lovely day, unusually hot. The glass rose above freezing, and the eaves and roofs of the houses began to drip with spring runoff.

"Do you think spring's on its way already?" I asked my host.

"No sir, just a real warm spell, often lasts two to three days, and if it goes on tomorrow and Tuesday, I'd counsel you not to try and make it through that slush toward Mutton Bay. You'll have to wait till she freezes over again."

My heart sank. More waiting before I could get to see my

Lorna. My Lorna? What was I thinking? Indeed, wasn't she just a good friend? Why on earth should I want to rush back home and see her? I put such desires firmly out of my mind.

"We'll have to get shoes for your dogs, o' course," said John. "If she freezes over, that ice there, it'll cut their feet good. I'll see if someone I know has pairs for 'is team that 'e could lend you, and you could send 'em back by the next komatik."

Shoes for dogs? I'd never heard of such a thing. Of course, in the deep snow in the winter, there was no need. But now, with sharp, cutting surfaces of ice that followed a freeze-up, I had better do as I was told. For I wanted nothing to go wrong on this last stage of my journey.

Chapter Seventeen

"There's a letter for ya, our post fella Joseph Hébert brought it last week."

Could it be from Lorna? I'd just taken off all my outer things. Aunt Minnie had been delighted by my arrival: she and Lorna had been worried with me being away so long. Anxiously, I went across to the sideboard. "So Lorna's out working all the time these days?"

"Oh yis yis yis. That Phillip Vatcher, he keeps 'er busy with his two kids. And she helps Captain Blais with 'is store, she never stops." I looked up. Was I hearing that correctly? She was working now at Phillip Vatcher's? Aunt Minnie must've caught my look. "Oh yis, but she makes sure I'm well looked after 'ere, don't worry about that. The 'ouse is spic and span as ever was. I don't know 'ow she does it all." Off she went into her room.

I took the letter over to the table by the stove, shivering with apprehension, or was it because I was still chilled from the journey, though it had been a lovely crossing from Harrington Harbour. The crackling sounds of the runners on the newly frozen crust of ice had been delightful. The six dogs, knowing we were getting close to home, needed no encouragement — they had fairly sped along. Out on the open plain of the gulf, the most inspiring landscape imaginable, I knew that to many it might look just forbidding, desolate, cold, and sterile, but I drew from it a strength, an awareness of my own self and my companionship with those trusty dogs.

At the same time, I had been possessed of a fierce loneliness, a longing for a companion, well not any companion, only my laughing Lorna. How lovely it would be to see her again! I had banished thoughts of other suitors, just dwelling on our trip together to Harrington Harbour, and how much fun we'd had. As we had then sped along, I allowed myself to revel in the vast space that surrounded us, that great arc of pale immensity above, and to my right, some distant tumble of clouds romping about the horizon. The crisp wind had kept me alert, not freezing as previous gales that had so often bitten at my nose and cheeks. And now, the end of March, spring breakup was close at hand.

I took the letter and opened it: my father's writing.

Was I delighted, or let down? I turned the envelope over. Amazing how the system works now: my father told me that in early days, they had no such thing as stamps. And then, when he'd written from Montreal, it had been costly, no universal postal system in action. And now, a letter from Gaspé to here only cost one cent.

Dear John,
You'll be pleased to know you got a baby brother, Eric we call him. He's got all his fingers and toes, and seems a smart little fella. I fear he'll be the last, so we're all mighty happy. Born at Christmastime, so he might even follow in your footsteps. Clare and Mack are doing a fine job of farming.

He went on to describe in a short paragraph how well the sisters were, how everyone was faring, that Lillian was off studying with a view to becoming a teacher.

I was delighted at the news of little Eric. But a thought struck me: Lillian might even enjoy, as her first job, accompanying me next year to these shores, were I to continue, as is normal with a new deacon. In the summer, I expected to be ordained into full priesthood, and so in charge of the parish. It would partially fall to me to find teachers. Oh yes, Lillian would be ideal, and what fun we'd have together.

I was just folding the letter when the door burst open, and there stood Lorna. I got up quickly. She shut the door. We looked at each other. What a shock — no dream on my wilderness trip came close to her actual reality. I rushed over and clasped her tightly. She responded, after a second or two, and we clung together as in the old days.

As we broke apart, I noticed she wasn't looking me in the face. She didn't take off her coat. "Someone saw you coming home. When they told me, I threw on my coat and rushed out. I thought the two girls would be all right for a few minutes while I came to say hello."

"Dearest Lorna, you look... you just look... wonderful."

"Not so wonderful that you couldn't have come to see me first?"

"What do you mean, at the Vatchers'? I've just walked in, taken off my coat and read this letter from the family. I have a new little brother."

"Oh. That's splendid. What's his name?"

"Eric."

"I had a letter, too. From my family. They are hoping I'll come back in the summer." She glanced at me.

I looked back. "That's a good idea. They must be missing you. Although I have no doubt that Frank, my friend from the schooner, would have brought news of your safe escape when he returned to Nova Scotia."

She nodded. "They did hear about it. And he told them

about you." She relaxed somewhat, staring at me the while for my response. "Did Aunt Minnie give you of a cup of tea?"

"I've just biled the kittle," Aunt Minnie called, coming out of her room. I don't know if she'd gone in there to be discreet.

"Well, I'd best be getting back. I cannot wait to hear all your news, Jack," she said and looked me full in the face.

Those large eyes. What they did to me! They made the bottom drop out of my stomach. She threw on her coat. "I'll be back for supper," she said, "and I shan't go out again."

"You work after supper as well?"

She nodded. "I usually get the children into bed, for Phillip." She turned and out the door she went.

I walked back to the table and sat quietly while Aunt Minnie poured me a good cup of tea, and put it front of me a fine slice of homemade molasses and raisin bread. I had a deal to absorb from this brief encounter.

My return gave me unbounded energy. After I finished my tea, I went off to see my church wardens. Thomas Bobbitt had gone off hunting back behind, but Thomas Buffett was at home and in fine form. He told me that the services had been going well in my absence, though not as well attended as when I was here. Everyone had been eagerly awaiting my return and there'd be a good turnout on Sunday. I inquired also after Clayton, teaching in my stead over in Tabacher. I resolved to take a run there in the morning, and perhaps even have a service this Sunday. I needed to set up my own teaching schedule for April and May and perhaps even into June when the waters would finally open up. Then Gene and I could sail once again the length of the parish in the mission boat. I also dropped in at the house of Mrs. Stiles, whose child had developed whooping cough and might be taken from her sooner rather than later. I prayed with her and got back in time for our supper, to find Lorna busily making a splendid meal for my return.

She and Aunt Minnie were gossiping gaily, Lorna laughing, teasing her landlady as they worked. I wondered if her happiness was due to her afternoon with Phillip, or to my return. Well, I would find out soon enough.

"What are you girls cooking up?" I asked.

"Never you mind!" Lorna exclaimed delightfully. "You'll see soon enough. Could be one of your favourite suppers..."

I loved to see Lorna in this good mood. I went to clean up and came back to sit. Lorna brought over our food and the three of us bowed our heads as I said grace. So much to tell of my trip, but I preferred first to hear news of the village. Aunt Minnie proceeded to give it in great detail, nothing of great import, but I loved it — almost like hearing about my own family in Shigawake. For the moment, I felt well and truly home.

I told them something of the brighter events during the trip, but I resolved I would keep the more frightening aspects for Lorna's ears afterwards. Once we had eaten and I had helped clear up, Aunt Minnie professed she was tired and retired to her room. I wondered if she was leaving us to talk, grateful for her probable discretion.

"I'm worried about the Vatcher children," I mentioned to Lorna. "Perhaps you should now go and see to them." I suppose, like some ridiculously jealous suitor, I was testing her.

"Jack, the children can be looked after by their father this once. I've told you before and I'll tell you again, you come first." She glanced at me, and then down at her cup of tea, and proceeded to take a sip, obviously waiting for me to respond to the hint.

"Well, my dear Lorna, I did miss you, but so much happened while I was away. On a couple of occasions, I even thought we might never see each other again, for such were the disasters that befell me. One night a storm pursued us across an open bay, and I genuinely feared for my life."

She looked up in alarm. "Oh dear Jack, should I be hearing all this?"

"Of course, I'm here, aren't I? Back, safe and sound."

"And you did miss me?"

"Of course I missed you. I thought about you often, in fact. But let me tell you about this one night when I thought it was all over."

"Go ahead, tell me." She watched me with large eyes, waiting.

I told her about it in vivid detail, building it up to be even more life-threatening. I suppose I was trying to make up for what had been, perhaps, my rather feeble responses to her questioning.

"That's so awful, Jack," she said after I finished. "I don't think I could live through another winter of you going off like that."

"Well, perhaps you won't have to. We'll just have to see what the bishop has in store for me."

Again, she looked down. I think I was failing whatever tests she seemed to be setting. I started on again about another escapade, when she interrupted. "I had no idea what you went through, Jack. Though some nights, I believe I was almost in contact with you, somehow. You know, even that very night of your storm, I'm sure it was then that I woke in a panic..."

I softened. What a wonderful woman she was.

"And now Jack, how did you miss me?"

"How?" I grasped for meanings. "How do you mean?"

"Well..." She paused and looked at me. I guess she saw I was genuinely asking for help. "Did you ache for me? Did every bone in your body cry out, day after day, minute after minute, so that the pain was more than you could take? So you had to find things to do, just anything, just to get rid of the great emptiness?"

"The emptiness?" What should I say? I had to be honest, no doubt about that. I had no desire to base this, my most important relationship, on lies. "No, no, I can't say I did. No, it wasn't like that at all. But I did miss you, even terribly." And then, quickly, to divert the conversation, I went on to talk about the time I had to shoot Grey. I really wanted to get it off my chest, and she was the only one I could confide in — I mean, really tell what was in my heart. So I began on that story.

As I talked, I noticed her nodding to herself, and then she reached out her hands and clasped mine, bowing her head, her hands clinging so tightly that I faltered in my description of that horrendous downhill slide, leading to the injury of Grey. Slowly I came to a halt. "Is something wrong, dear Lorna?"

She sighed. "No dear Jack, it is as it should be, I suppose. I have to learn to live with that." She looked up. "And now, if you don't mind, I shall have to retire. I've had a tiring day, as I know you have too, and these frightening tales wear me out even further. Please forgive me. We shall see each other tomorrow, of course."

She rose and walked slowly to the foot of the stairs, seemingly in a daze, or rather, in some deep contemplation. She paused, without looking back, and then slowly, step by step, mounted to her bedroom, alone.

Over the next three or four weeks when the weather kept me pinned to Mutton Bay and Tabacher, I fell into a kind of routine: fulfilling the many tasks I set myself: teaching school, giving services, ministering to the sick, and adjudicating family problems. But it was hard to keep on top of everything: I think my journeying had taken more out of me than I had suspected, as much fun as the adventure had been.

April was cut in half by Holy Week, which culminated on Easter Sunday on the eighteenth. The week before, I had read the Palm Sunday Gospel, about thirty minutes on the Passion of the Christ, so dramatic! We even stripped the altar for Good Friday, a day when nothing is done in the whole village, no work of course, no cooking, absolutely nothing. The next day we had a baptism at the Easter Saturday candlelight vigil. Excellent turnout on Sunday too, with everyone dressing up, including the stately Lorna Maclean, who towered above the other ladies. I was so proud of her, looking so imposing and, in fact, gorgeous. A regular attendee at church these days, she didn't throw me off my duties; I looked forward to her sitting there, listening seriously to my sermons. Easter Monday then brought forth celebrations, mild of course, not a lot of drinking, but tea parties and visiting, even a few dances.

Lorna and I had more or less settled into a routine that seemed on the surface not to have changed. Yes, I had been troubled on that night of my arrival; yes, I had lain in bed worrying whether or not I had hurt her somehow, wondering how I'd failed what must have been some form of testing. But then, over breakfast the next morning, she had said no more and went about preparing for the day as usual. It wasn't until a couple of weeks had gone by that I noticed her activities had changed. She hadn't let me in on that, but Aunt Minnie did, one afternoon.

"She's off working at a number of different houses now," said Aunt Minnie, "and she helps down at the fishing co-op, cleaning the place for the summer's cod fishing, and she's back helping Captain Blais, and over at the Rogers, too. I know they give her things in return, and she trades them up!"

"She trades them up? How do you mean?"

"Well, she trades this for that, this fish for one bigger or better. She's a smart maid; I think she's laying up a store for herself."

"What makes you think that, Aunt Minnie?"

Aunt Minnie just shook her head and went about her business. I resolved to talk to Lorna about it, but then thought it might be too much of an intrusion. So we kept to our routine, though our evening chats were cut short because she disappeared every evening after dinner.

"You're putting the Vatcher children to bed again?"

She nodded. "I don't go there during the day anymore. I have to work harder, somewhere that gets me better bartering."

"Work harder? Why ever do you have to do that, Lorna? You have a safe haven here."

She shrugged. "Don't you worry about it, Jack, just keep on with what you're doing; you're making a fine job of ministering to everyone — torn in ten parts, I do see that too. You just keep on. And so shall I."

I found this rather ominous, but then not long after Easter I got an early morning visit from a young man I had often seen in church, a Perce Mansbridge.

"Good day, good day, Perce," I said. "Something troubling you?"

He nodded. "I been up the coast visiting relatives." He looked distinctly worried as he took off his hat. "I seen a flag up at that there settlement on Gros Isle," he went on, without the usual polite preamble. "Seems like they might need your services." People when marooned, not able to go for help, often hoisted a flag. "But them ice conditions, terble dangerous. Didn't know whether I should tell ya or not."

"Thank you, Perce, of course you should."

"But she's a good long way off with these 'ere ice conditions. Don't know if you want to take it on, or even if you should. Trouble is, they's me relatives. The fella's a cousin and..."

"You were quite right to tell me," I confirmed. "That's my calling."

"You thinking of going, then?"

"I'll have to. No other way. Today it's only the little ones I'm teaching, and my assistant teacher can handle it."

"I better come with yez then. Fer that ice is dangerous, no telling when it'll give out. Some places the melt's as big as a lake over that ice."

Could I really ask someone to risk their life with me? "No thanks, Perce, I'll be all right."

"I knows why yer saying that, and it don't make no spot o' difference with me. I'll come too."

He suggested we borrow his uncle's team of nine dogs, the best anywhere around, because he said we might be needing that. Packing hurriedly, we set off together, after I told Aunt Minnie where I was going. I asked her to say my farewells to Lorna, for I knew she'd expect me home for supper. I didn't want to see her right now for she'd worry at my leaving. We'd be meeting the most dangerous ice conditions ever: broken floes, drifting ice pans, and the dark ocean beneath. But duty did call.

Chapter Eighteen

The three of us sailed along over the melting surface of the gulf. Perce had explained that his cousin's wife, Becky, was about to give birth any time now, so I insisted we bring the middah along because, like as not, the island settlement was too small to have an experienced one to hand. He agreed, and we enlisted the services of Alice Gallichons from Old Post.

"She's some pretty, that Becky," Perce went on to explain. "I was really getting close to having 'er marry me instead, but then Howard won 'er fair in square, 'e did. Put me in a bit of a spin for a few months... but now, she's still part o' the family..." All this was explained while we sped through what seemed almost a lake, and I feared that we'd go right through the thin ice beneath.

When I voiced my fears, Perce replied cheerily, "That's just the melt; she's solid under, no fear o' that. We'll make our way..." At least he appeared sanguine; not so, I. Then he went on, "Why Becky went off to live with 'er own folks on that island I'll never know. Mrs. Stiles, she's not handy with birthing, no doubt about that. Never was. Not like other women 'ereabouts."

I couldn't stop myself watching the water on either side. I noticed my hands were gripping the komatik box much too fiercely. I tried to get myself to relax.

Alice Gallichons had been sitting well wrapped up, hardly speaking. But now she responded, "Not simple, births. I know a good few who wouldn't touch 'em. For us what likes it, nothing easier. But if she's given birth already, who knows what to expect. They might *both* be gone."

I burst in, "No no, let's think the best, that's why we're going after all."

These nine dogs certainly made up the finest team in Mutton Bay: the way they worked together as we forged across this shallow ice lake, in some places deep enough to give their bodies a good soaking. Hard pulling.

I tried to cheer up. "They seem to be enjoying themselves, Perce," I said.

"For sure," Perce replied, "Just hope the weather holds for the return, though."

Now why on earth bring that up? Every day, we all knew that the full melt was coming closer. Crossing from that island would become even more dangerous, if not impossible. But our little rescue trio, clinging together, rolled along. Around dinnertime, we climbed over a cape and saw before us a jumble of loose floes enclosing, in the distance, Gros Isle. We stopped to take it in.

I shook my head and just gave up.

Perce took it upon himself to decide. "I reckon we'd better go round the shore to get closer, no matter if we have a hard time with them ballicatters" — rough edges and pinnacles of ice thrown up by the spray with more snow piling on top. "See that there shelf out there?" He pointed to the white sheet stretching out to a line of dark water in the gulf. "Wind keeps pressing that shelf in, crams these floes together, so we might manage."

We set off, gritting our teeth, and me invoking the Lord's help as strongly as I could. With the broken floes nestling close, I still saw ominous cracks between them and frightening openings of black water. As we crossed onto some floes, they sank and I felt the komatik go down. Not enjoyable one bit. The team would start across a pan, and then veer sharply off: lots of experience travelling this spring ice, I gathered. And I had none. Lucky Perce had come along.

We finally made it over to the island. Perce guided our lead dog, Nipper, toward the cluster of rough but sturdy dwellings. We clambered off at his cousins' and I stood up to stretch, my worry building. What would we find when we entered?

"You fellas go in," Perce said, "and I'll take these here dogs round to a pen."

Aunt Alice stamped her feet to get the circulation back. "Please, you go on in," I suggested and, divining somehow the reason for my reluctance, she went and knocked. A young man, same age as Perce, opened the door and his drawn face lit up. "Come in, Aunt Alice, come in." She hurried through, shutting the door.

Perce soon came round the corner of the house looking as though he had just seen a ghost. Wordlessly, he beckoned. I followed him and he pointed up.

High against the outside wall hung a bundle wrapped in white canvas. What on earth could that be? He returned my look and I saw in his look the awful truth. "You think... that's the baby?"

He nodded and closed his eyes. He swayed and I came to steady him. "It may not be," I said, rather fatuously. "Come."

When we went in, I knew Perce had been right.

The middah had doffed her outer clothes and was hurrying from stove to bedroom. Through an open door, I saw the bed on which Howard's young wife, lay. Becky's mother, Mrs. Stiles, a heavy-set grey-haired woman, was wringing her hands and obeying the terse commands of the middah as best she could. As I took off my coat, I saw an unspoken sorrow pass between Perce and his cousin Howard, slight of build with a broad, intelligent face and brown hair. "I saw outside..." Perce began.

Howard nodded. "Last night. We did what we could. A little maid she was. Gone. Didn't tell Becky." He glanced at me. "She keeps asking for her."

"So Becky's all right?" Perce asked. I could tell from the shake in his voice he was close to panic.

"Not too all right, I guess." Howard shut his eyes, bowed his head, and tears began to run down his cheeks. Perce gave his cousin a firm hug, doing his best to hide his own grief.

What a difficult state of affairs for an outsider!

"Is there something we can do?" Perce asked Aunt Alice.

"Just keep out of our way." She hurried into the bedroom with towels and a bowl of water. The mother stood shaking her head and then followed the middah. I began to hope silently for Becky's survival, now our paramount problem.

When his mother-in-law came out of the bedroom, Howard calmed himself to ask her, "You think, Momma, you could get these fellas a cup of tea?"

She brightened. At last, something she felt comfortable about! "Yis yis, so sorry, such a twenty-four hours, I never knew whether I was comin' or goin'. Of course, I'll get yez a cup o' tea. And how about some bread and molasses?"

"Thank you very much, Mrs. Stiles." I added that I was the new clergyman in Mutton Bay.

She nodded. "Oh yis, I heard about you, Mr. John. The folks all like yez. I 'ope it's only one funeral you'll be 'olding 'ereabouts."

"Mrs. Stiles, the power of prayer, combined with a good middah, can often work miracles," I said as firmly as I could. I noticed both she and Howard seemed to cheer up somewhat.

After tea as we were talking in low tones, the middah came out with the news that her patient was resting. A good chance, or so she said, that she would pull through, but I saw from the look on her face that she did not believe it. "What she needs is some rest, and good red meat." She frowned. "But meat we don't 'ave." Becky's father had gone off looking for caribou two days before, but had not yet returned.

"Oh yes we do," piped up Perce. "I brought a good three or four pound. My uncle went inside and shot a big buck last week, and we froze it." He jumped up. "I'll just fetch the parcel, and bring in our bags."

I knew I had better get going. "Is she asleep?"

The middah shook her head. "Dozing, most like."

"Would it disturb her if I went in?"

"She keeps asking for her baby. Dunno what to tell her."

I paused. How should I handle this? She'd have to know sooner or later... "Perhaps I should enlighten her on your behalf? I can describe how her little maid is safe in the arms of the Lord."

They looked at one another and then nodded. I rose with some misgivings, for I still did not feel confident in such situations.

I entered, shut the door, and pulled the chair close. I leaned forward. "Becky, I am your clergyman from Mutton Bay. I want to tell you..." She reached out and grasped my hand. "I want to tell you that your little maid is now sharing a far greater joy than any of us could imagine."

She gave a cry and rolled onto her back, staring at the ceiling. "I knew it, I knew it. They didn't have to tell me. I just knew."

I let the silence fall for a moment, and sat back. What now?

"Gone... gone... she's left me forever..." Tears gathered in her eyes.

"Becky, Becky, right now, Our Lord is rocking her, and choirs of angels are singing her to sleep. She is, and will be forever, surrounded by Heavenly Grace."

She said nothing, staring at the ceiling. I realized that somehow, these words were not as great a comfort as I had hoped. Try another tack. But what?

I leaned forward again. "Becky, you're young, from all I hear you're throbbing with life; the middah says you'll soon get better. You will have many more children, without a doubt. I can see it plainly." I stopped as she turned to look me full in my face. "I know this seems impossible now, but many mothers have lost their first child, and gone on to have wonderful families. And you know this to be true, don't you?" I paused. "Don't you?"

Becky nodded. So the words had reached her.

I went on gently, "And now, for the sake of those many beautiful children you and Howard will have, you must try to sleep. We'll come in later to pray for your own safe journey back into the land of the living once again, and continue to be a glorious — and from what I hear from Perce — very lovely lass."

I actually saw a slight smile flicker across her lips before she closed her eyes. I stayed sitting until I saw her breathing relax; she had gone to sleep.

During the night the fog crept in with the stealth of an arctic fox and by morning, we were completely surrounded. Even had we planned to leave, and of course we could not with Becky's health hanging in the balance, we were marooned.

She had lost a lot of blood; Alice was unable to say whether the point of no return had been reached. During the night she had made a thick broth from a portion of the caribou and had been feeding it to her. The flow of blood had stopped. It was now a question of whether the good Lord would keep her alive, or take her up to join her lost child.

In the early morning, my first instinct, to read the Bible at her bedside, was actually not such a good idea: it might just depress her. So instead, I prayed silently: a form of deep thought as I sat by the fire, and sometimes at the foot of her bed. I had no idea if any of this would do any good, but was mightily heartened when, in the afternoon, the middah told me that Becky had whispered that she liked my presence in the room and was deriving some strength from it. So far, so good.

Although the fog was still forming a heavy wall around the house, Perce and Howard went outside midmorning with shovels. Although they said nothing, I knew they were preparing a grave. Late that afternoon, in a simple ceremony, I consigned the baby's body to the frozen earth. We reported back to Becky, and although the sorrow was intense, I could see that this ending might help her recognize that her own life lay ahead.

Chapter Nineteen

With the rise in temperature, the sooner we left, the better. After a good breakfast, I went outside to check the weather. The fog had crept away, only to be replaced by lightly falling snow. Then I noticed some odd-looking devices on the komatik.

"What have you been up to?" I asked Perce.

"I had the idea to attach some floats." He must have seen my frightened look because he added quickly, "Oh, just in case of emergency. I seen it done before." He shrugged. "You never know, that's all."

I went in for the last time to see Becky and found her improving. Amazing how the young recover! During the night, Aunt Alice had been able to feed her more cooked caribou. I kissed her on her forehead, saying that I wanted to baptize her newborn next year, at which she smiled. Yes, a pretty girl, I could see her loveliness returning. We said our goodbyes, piled on the komatik, and headed off.

The trail soon brought us to the point of shortest crossing over to the mainland. With the snowfall it was hard to see across, but the sight that greeted our eyes was, to me at least, frightening in the extreme. In the night, the wind had shifted and the great flotillas of drift ice were no longer wedged against the shore. How on earth would we ever get across? I looked over at Perce. He was anxiously scanning the strait, then walked to a higher point of land, where he stood surveying the pans. Then he came back. "Darn thing is the snow. Ya can't judge the thickness of the ice. We're just gonna have to make a try."

My heart was in my mouth. But shouldn't we wait? At least until some boat could break through to rescue us? Or another freeze-up came? Indeed, I voiced this suggestion, and added, "Or just wait till the wind shifts back? It might pack the ice floes again."

"We could wait forever," Perce said. "The sooner we get going, the sooner we'll get to that mainland."

Well sir, we got ourselves on the komatik, Aunt Alice on the after part for she was the heaviest, Perce and I hanging on just ahead. "It will keep the nose up," Perce explained.

The dogs seemed anxious to be off for some reason. When he shouted, whip at the ready, they charged across the ice, mostly unbroken near the shore. But after a hundred yards, we started crossing from floe to floe, choosing whatever gap was the narrowest. We veered this way and that, and I almost began to relax — when the next ice floe as we struck it, tipped right up. Oh Lord! I thought, just when we least expect it, down we go!

Perce cracked the whip and the first three dogs dug in their claws while the dogs behind swam in the drink, but the lead dogs pulled them out until they too got a grasp. The komatik had splashed into the water, but we held on for dear life as it started to sink, and our tremendous team with all their strength pulled us up onto the lip and out onto the pan.

Heavens, I thought, I don't want many more of those.

"Fun, eh?" Perce called excitedly as the team then veered to the right to get on to another equally flimsy fragment. But no amount of loud encouragement would make me feel less than absolutely terrified — not so much the fear of drowning as an irrational panic that gripped my very soul.

"Look!" I pointed. Sure enough, through the snow we could

see the contours of the mainland shore not a hundred yards away. But between us lay a good spread of black, icy water. We were on a broad floe that seemed safe, so Perce called the team to a halt. We got off the komatik to stretch and prepare for whatever may come.

"I don't think we better try swimming that," Perce said. "I see some good floes there to our right. We'll try them first."

We clambered back on the komatik, and Perce rallied the team. With great agility and force, they leapt the gap of three feet onto the next pan and our sled straddled the widening gap.

The same with the next pan, and the next, all gaps being three or four feet across. But we were getting no nearer the shore. The snow was now coming down hard. Any view of the mainland and its ballicatters was lost.

"What happens now? Do we go back?" I asked.

Perce turned and pointed. Behind us, the floes had separated even more. In fact, they were drifting out. Just deep, widening water behind us, and an open stretch ahead.

We stopped and considered. What would be our best direction? We could hardly see through the falling and driven flakes. The mainland lay across freezing water, black as agate and probably deep. Lord, I was petrified. Our floe seemed to be drifting away, too. We had to decide fast. But decide what?

"We'll give her a try that way." Perce pointed to his left. I shuddered, crossed myself, and got onto the sled with Alice. But the gap to this next floe was widening. The team charged ahead, leaping into the water and swimming across a fully eight-foot-wide gap, struggling up like drowned rats and behind them, in splashed our komatik. Down we sank.

But then, our weight being on the back, the front runners were up. I clung to the rigging and also held Aunt Alice on tight. Our team struggled hard, with us now sinking and getting drenched but somehow, the dogs pulled us over the lip and onto the pan.

Another floe lay across more icy water, but we were gasping and spluttering. Enough! I thought. But the dogs raced on. They leapt onto the pan, which rocked and then as the sled hit, tipped precariously. Yes yes, finally we'll tumble sideways to our fate. Perce leapt off and, on all fours, tugged at the komatik to keep it from slipping into the drink. Miraculously, to our left, I spotted the contours of the mainland — only fifty feet off, beyond this pan. But no! Between us lay another threatening channel. Our lead dog Nipper turned and, with a new burst of energy, set off hard and fast.

Beyond this floe, a good twenty feet of menacing blackness lay ready to enclose us and send us to our Maker. Surely here we'd end this whole bizarre episode. Perce called loudly for a halt, but for some reason, Nipper did not stop, nor did she heed Perce. The dogs threw themselves into this crossing, and surely our komatik headed straight into our agate sepulchre.

Without slackening their pace the team splashed in and swam hard. It all happened so fast I had no time to do anything but hang on. The sled dove off the shelf, and down we sank. Down, down, and as the water was about to cover our heads — all over, I thought — the lead dog reached the shallow bottom. She and the others dug in their claws and kept hauling hard. Up onto the ice they strained, pulling us surely forward, and lo the komatik struck bottom, and before our heads disappeared under the surface, we began to move forward and up, and finally, onto the shore. The shock had taken all our breath away and we gasped for air.

But we had hit land. Our team had pulled us to safety. With a wild, happy whoop, Perce called for a halt. But Nipper again ignored his commands and the team tore onward until — what did we see? — a rickety shack. Presumably it had been placed here for just such emergencies. The team pulled up at the door. We tumbled off and dove inside, sopping wet, freezing, chilled, astonished at our good fortune. The door had been left unlocked, and this time I did see firewood beside the stove.

I shall be forgiven if I say that normal proprieties observed all over the civilized world no longer held good for us. Hurriedly, we stripped down to our underthings, Aunt Alice included. Perce had quickly built a fire and, hanging our sopping clothes around, we huddled close, teeth chattering, and slowly began to lose the deadly chill in our bones.

We arrived home late that night, damp and uncomfortable, of course, but so happy to be alive. We took Aunt Alice home first, and then Perce headed for Aunt Minnie's to drop me.

Lorna had not gone to the Vatchers after dinner but had stayed home waiting, on the off-chance I might arrive that night. She felt certain, so she told me, that I would not shirk my responsibilities for tomorrow's Sunday services. We hugged briefly, and she exclaimed, "Lord, Jack, you're sopping wet!"

"Not as wet as I was before."

"Get upstairs this minute, and change," she ordered. "Bring me your wet clothes. I'll stoke the fire. And then you need some hot soup."

Aunt Minnie's door opened and out she came in her dressing gown. "Has the poor lad come back?" And then she saw me. "Whatever 'ave you been up to?"

"Well, Aunt Minnie, I have a lot to tell you. Suffice it to say that Becky Green is recovering, but I've been ordered upstairs to undress, and undress I shall. I'll be back down with the whole story in a few minutes." Indeed, I felt so happy to be back and lucky to be welcomed in this fashion.

As I was changing in my bedroom, a curious thought struck. Would I not like to have Lorna always there, welcoming me after every expedition? Oh yes indeed. I resolved to do some serious thinking about this over the next few days. And with that, I put on warm, dry clothes, went below, and recounted our whole saga.

Sunday night in early May, I was lying in bed having a bit of a read. My Vespers service had been short, for thunder heralded the beginning of what might be the major storm of the spring. Everyone counted on a great rainstorm to wash away the winter's debris and carry it out to sea. It never failed to turn up at just the right time. It would drench the communities so heavily that they could start afresh with a clean slate for the summer. During the long winters, most families just emptied their slop pails out behind the house in the snow and everyone counted on this deluge to take it all away, detritus from dogs, everything.

After the service Lorna and I had hurried home, expecting the downpour any second. But instead of that, sheet lightning lit up the sky and thunder boiled around. Nothing I enjoy more than a good thunderstorm, and I hadn't seen one since last year. So I got into bed and lay looking out my window which faced up the sloping hill toward a couple of houses and the low mountains behind Mutton Bay.

The thunder continued to rage and all at once, a great jolt struck — I swear I saw lightning knife down into the next house, which shook under the impact. I stared for a second, then leaped out of bed and tore down the stairs. Behind me, I heard Lorna call out, "What's happening?"

I shouted, "Lightning struck the Evans house. Come help." I threw on a coat, hauled on my boots and ran out. As I raced up toward their house, the door burst open and Mrs. Evans emerged, lugging the body of her husband, which she laid on the house bridge. The children came out after her. "It struck us. The lightning. He's gone, I think." She began to cry.

I tore up the steps to look at Mr. Evans, and then glanced in the open door. Flames had caught the curtains at one side, and I could see broken dishes scattered around the room. Lightning for sure. "Where's the water?"

"Around the back in a barrel."

"Buckets?"

"One under the sink. One out back by the rain barrel. Fred," she kept calling, "Fred! Speak to us."

I started into the house, then thought better of it and charged around to the back to get water from the barrel. Lorna arrived and I called out, "Ring the church bell! Quick, get everyone out, we need a bucket brigade." I grabbed a bucket and ran back in, threw it on the curtains, which helped, but the fire had caught the hooked rug, and smoke was billowing up. "Is everyone out?" I yelled at Mrs. Evans.

"No, no, Fred's mother, she's upstairs."

Heavens, someone still in there? Two men had rushed up and I handed the bucket to one, pointing to the barrel around the back. Then I tore inside.

The smoke was filling the main room and surging up the stairs to occupy the hall above. I started coughing, so I dropped onto all fours and crept up below the layer of smoke hanging under the ceiling. Was this madness to climb into a blazing house? Yes, but so what? On hands and knees I made my way up the steps and got to the second floor, hoping the landing would not catch fire, finishing me off. I scrambled to the first door: the bedroom was empty. The second. Empty. Pray God this place wasn't going up in a great explosion, as I had seen in the Gaspé. I came to another door, and an old lady rasped, "What's happening?"

"Quick, Mrs. Evans, the house is on fire, you've got to come down. Right now!"

"No no I can't, I'm not dressed. Get me my dressing gown."

"No time!" I went into the room and when she reached out I grabbed her arms and tugged hard. "Get out of bed, quick, you have to come down."

"No no," she shrieked. Funny people in an emergency: more concerned about propriety than saving life. I pulled her hard and she tumbled out of the bed onto the floor. She screamed, "Stop it, stop it!"

I grasped the mat on which she had fallen and, in spite of her loud protestations, tried to keep under the thickening smoke as I dragged it toward the stairs. "Come now, Mrs. Evans, we have to get you outside." I could feel the scorching heat.

"No, no," she howled, "I'm not dressed."

I heard the flames crackling and items falling. Nothing for it but to pull the rug, with her on it, down the stairs. I tried to block the sounds of her yells and the thumps her body made as it struck each step. A few bruises versus her life, indeed.

I got her to the bottom and hauled her quickly out onto on the house bridge. Then in the fresh air, I was able to rise and so I lifted her up and half-carried, half-dragged her, howling in pain, to safety on the grass.

"Emma, Emma, gimme a coat!" she cried.

Already the church bell had been ringing and men were gathering. Most of them brought their buckets because, as I learned later, lightning often strikes houses here where there are no tall trees. Fortunately, we were not a hundred feet from the water, so full buckets had begun to pass up the line, with empties going down.

Lorna came running across to fall in beside me. "They all safe?"

I shook my head as I slung the full bucket up to the next man. "Fred Evans is dead. Struck by the thunderbolt. The others are fine. I got the old lady out." I was panting, of course, but I said, "You got the church bell going, good girl! With the village coming, think we might save their house?" I looked up into the black night. Why, oh why had the rain not started?

"We need a second line," she said, "the Morency house over there, it needs wetting down."

"Good idea!"

She was off like a flash, grabbed three or four other men, commandeered buckets, and made a smaller and thus more widely spaced bucket brigade to protect the Morencys. My only thought, as I kept handing up the buckets, was how well we worked together, Lorna and I. It did augur well for our future together!

And then down came the rain. Torrents. The village was safe.

Chapter Twenty

Not too long afterwards, the ice cleared enough so that we could expect the schooners to arrive any time soon. Owen Cheveller dropped in and suggested we set about preparing our mission boat. June was now beginning and most of the children had been taken out of school to help the family get cod traps ready, knit new nets, repair the old ones, and set up the fishing boats. So Friday I called a halt to school lessons and the next week began working on the *Evangeline* with Owen. It needed a new coat of paint and some repairs to the hull; I had always felt that the interior could do with a bit of love and care, as well.

Such a relief to have my mind no longer clogged by figuring out how to keep two schoolrooms full of obstreperous kids busy, active, productive, learning not only their ABCs but something of the history of our country, what lessons we could take from the Bible, and other information that I might present vividly enough to keep them interested. Owen and I worked side by side, and my thoughts turned toward my most pressing, and needless to say enjoyable, preoccupation, my relationship with Lorna. The last couple of months, we had both been inordinately busy, anchored as we were to our home base by the breakup of the ice. Now that I was able to concentrate, I realized we had grown a little more distant — certainly something I had better see about.

But more than that, I really wanted to take a good look at our future together. Over the last six months, I could see that she really did care for me, even deeply. I admit, quite frankly, that I hadn't paid as much attention to this as I should have. Oh no, much too interested in my new ministry and caring for my flock: they came first. Whereas I believe that, for a time, I may have taken first place in her life. Must that not have been difficult for her — without that devotion being returned hundredfold, as it should be, were she my wife?

What a thought! My wife. The idea grew upon me, as I painted the boat rather mindlessly, exchanging fragments of gossip with Owen. Oh yes, looking ahead, clergymen needed families. And I have certainly never met any girl who overwhelmed me as had Lorna, even, as I reflected, from the moment on that schooner when she came out and I set eyes on her, beaten and bedraggled, a lass in the direct need of love and attention. And yes, at that time, that is what I gave her. But since then, had I not taken her for granted?

How should I rectify this situation? Make a full confession that I had not been as attentive as I wanted? Tell her how deeply I also care? Yes, both these might help. But to what end? Inevitably, however I thought about it, I came up against this main question haunting me: should we get married now? And my first instinct was to shout, yes!

But then what? When, or where? Probably down with her family in Nova Scotia. Or perhaps in the Gaspé? Or why not here, among these good folk whom we now know so well. What a range of options! Yes, and then I castigated myself. You idiot! Don't you think that she will have her own definite desires and points of view? Leave that to her. The first problem, I told myself, is when and how to propose. If indeed that was the course of action I must take.

The week went by with me tormenting myself in such fashion. The boat got painted, and I set about the interior cabin. I wanted to enlist Lorna's aid because I knew her feminine touch would add a great deal. But I vacillated back and forth. From the few conversations I've had with newlyweds, I realized this uncertainty was not unusual. It usually turned out to be a prelude to the actual wedding. Though in some cases, decisions had been made *not* to go ahead. So shouldn't I look first at the reasons why we should not get married? And of course, my own mother's second thoughts the day after her wedding carried some weight.

Well, I had gone over them during the preceding week, especially facing the fact she had been violated on that schooner, but I knew that would have absolutely no weight if the Lord were himself to decide. And now Friday morning, with so much done and only another week before the boat would be ready for its trip down the coast to St. Paul's River, I'd have to come to a decision and act on it right away. And to confirm that prediction, didn't the first large schooner of the season pull into our harbour at Mutton Bay and drop anchor?

It was a bit larger than the schooner from which I had rescued her but it did bring back in full force that scene with me rowing out in a fisherman's boat to do battle with the captain, and the ensuing rescue.

All morning, I'd seen fishing craft rowing to and fro with seal pelts, homemade artefacts, and so on, which they bartered for vegetables, oil for the lamps, salt spare ribs, tea, molasses, flour, and other necessities of life that had run out during the long winter. There'd be some rejoicing tonight, for the bartered items would include the demon rum. Yes, today must be the day.

When I went home for my midday dinner, I found Aunt Minnie alone and the table laid for just the two of us. "Where's Lorna?" I asked.

"She's terble busy, Mr. John. She's been racing around all day. She asked me if I would get dinner. Of course I said yes." She put the plates on the table. "I'm not nearly as good a cook as Lorna, but I did my best. We got a nice brace of eggs from nests the lads found, and I made you an omelette."

Well, I was so focussed on my problem of Lorna and asking for her hand, that I paid little attention to the lovely meal and went up to my room to reflect how on earth to propose. On bended knee? I smiled. Rather too old-fashioned. No, just simply, well, were we not such good friends? Just spit it out. But I wanted to be able to handle this whole matter in a way that would both please Lorna, and give me some satisfaction on my own.

As luck would have it, these thoughts were broken by sharp rappings on the front door, which then opened anyway and a voice called, "Mr. John! Mr. John."

More pastoral duties just when I did not need them. Nothing for it, however, but to rise up and shuffle to the head of the stairs. "I'm here. What is it?"

"I been sent to get ya right away. Mr. Sammy John, in Tabacher, they need ya. Gotta go, I'm afraid," the voice said and withdrew, shutting the front door.

I shook my head. What a job! Well, get dressed up and get going.

No question, as I walked up over the hills behind Mutton Bay, Sammy John Robertson was, in all senses, the patriarch. His own grandfather, Samuel Robertson, had been the first settler in Tabacher in the early part of this century. Had it been anyone else I might have begged off, but this man's well-being certainly deserved my attention. His lineage demanded it; the seal factory was also his doing. I hoped he had not met with some serious accident. But like as not, something had come up that would tax my already depleted spirit even more. I quickened my pace.

Such a lovely day, so I tried to absorb it. The songbirds were doing their best to outvoice each other, while high above them the clouds tumbled and romped as they heralded more fine weather. My trail led up hill and down dale to Red Bay inlet. I crossed the isthmus and went smartly on to Tabacher Cove at the end of which lived Sammy John.

The heavy-set bewhiskered patriarch whom I had met before opened the door and ushered me in. I saw at once why I had been called. There, in the flesh, stood the great Wilfred Grenfell. As their clergyman, this meeting was *de rigueur*. Unthinkable for the great man to come and go and not be accorded a visit from their pastor. He was, in the few short years since he had visited the Atlantic Coast of Labrador and raised money to build a hospital in Battle Harbour, already a legend round about.

I recognized him immediately from photos, his dark moustache, high forehead, the bearing of a man used to command, but with it all such warmth and grace, oh yes. He had travelled North America in search of funds to help the Labrador livyers, forgotten not only by the government of Newfoundland, but also, I regret, by Quebec and the rest of Canada. Dr. Grenfell was a walking saint.

I walked over and shook his hand warmly. "Dr. Grenfell, such a pleasure. Wonderful to have you in our little community."

He smiled as he greeted me. "Well, Mr. John, your fame precedes you also, for Mr. Robertson here had been telling me how well you're liked. Delighted to make your acquaintance."

He looked not much older than me, but in that short life he had accomplished so much. How humble I felt in his presence, knowing I had achieved so little. Mrs. Robertson served us the obligatory cups of tea and, as we went to sit down, I offered, "But perhaps I am interrupting?"

"I was just telling Dr. Grenfell 'ere," Sammy John regained

his rocking chair, "how my grandfather, Samuel Robertson, entertained John James Audubon and 'is crew way back in '33."

"Oh yes?" I had no idea who that was.

"You know, the bird fella. He put names on most o' the birds, and he drew 'em too."

"Oh yes." I had heard something about that.

"You know, my ancestor, Old Samuel, 'e told 'im, and 'is son who came with 'im, all about them Basque fellas out there at the tip o' Labrador, who'd came over whaling even long afore Jacques Cartier sailed these 'ere shores. "Parently 'e didn't know about that."

"Fascinating stuff, by George," Dr. Grenfell threw in.

Fascinating or not, I wasn't sure I believed it. No one on the Gaspé ever spoke of it.

"Yep, came on that boat of his, *The Ripley*, July twenty-first, eighteen thirty-three. My grandfather marked it down in the Bible — Audubon was such a famous fella. Didn't like it here much though, hated that we ate birds' eggs every spring."

Well, if it were marked in a Bible, I could be sure it was true. We went on to share more of Sammy John's and Dr. Grenfell's experiences. The good doctor told us that when he'd first arrived from England, he could hardly believe the horrifying conditions. The livyers up the coast to Cartwright, Hopedale, and even beyond, had been all but forgotten by the local government, to whom they paid taxes in the Newfoundland capital of St. John's: no doctors up there, no nurses, no teachers, nothing in the way of services in the many tiny outports strung along that vast coastline, though they faced the rough Atlantic's wrath with its violent storms and harsh winters, which descended even earlier than ours and left a lot later in the spring. So of course, he'd had to act upon that. And off he'd gone to raise the money to help them. And raise it he did. "I heard over and over again,"

Dr. Grenfell went on, "the words of my dear departed mother, quoting the one hundred and forty-third psalm, 'Teach me to do today the thing that pleases Thee.'"

When he went on to say that here, a good ways inland along the gulf, things seemed not so bad, I butted in, "I'm not sure you're right about that, sir. My parishioners are also in real need."

"Hold on. I've seen little here to match anything out on that wild Atlantic coastline, I can tell you." He emphasized his British accent with hand movements, delicate, but forceful.

"Nonetheless, I do presume," I pressed my point home, "that you'll be setting up another of your life-saving hospitals here." Three years ago, he had opened the first one out at Battle Harbour, an island farther north on the Atlantic coast. Word of that travelled everywhere, with fishermen and schooners coming to and fro.

"I'm dreadfully afraid, Reverend," he went on to say, "I shan't be opening any hospitals. I have too much to be done already, out where I have installed myself."

I looked across at Sammy John, sitting in his rocking chair, smoking an enormous pipe and nodding. "Yes sir, 'e's sure got 'is hands full up on that there Atlantic coast, we all knows it."

Don't say they were both against me!

"But Dr. Grenfell," I pressed, "we do most definitely need your help, sir, just as much. We rely only on midwives, and bless my soul if they don't do a splendid job. But they cannot save lives like a doctor might."

He looked at me with warm but piercing eyes. "What about you, Mr. John? You have charge of this parish. Why don't *you* go out and get yourself a hospital?"

Me? How harshly that cut. Right now, I was having a hard time just doing the simple job I had been given; though the remark was, from his point of view, quite justified. "I'm delighted to find your faith in me so very firm, Doctor, but I'm afraid it's not based in any reality. You see, I have only just graduated in Theology, from Bishop's University..." He didn't look impressed by this argument, so I went on, "This parish of St. Clement's stretches four hundred and fifty miles, end to end, so I find it rather full-time." I lifted my hands helplessly. "I wouldn't even know how to start on that enterprise."

"Can't you learn? That's what I had to do."

I shook my head. "One day, perhaps.... But right now, I am convinced my main task is to open your eyes to our poverty here, and our great need that does exist — almost as much as in your own area: nurses, doctors, a hospital with real equipment." I glanced at Sammy John. "I'm sure he agrees we do certainly need a fine medical facility such as the one in Battle Harbour." I hoped I'd made my point.

"That's for sure," Sammy John echoed. Aha, so I had convinced him! "For sure, ya see, we all live 'ere by fishin' cod, huntin' seals in the winter, and that's all we do. Maybe a bit of huntin' of caribou or trapping a few animals for their furs and meat. But like Mr. John here says, we sure do have a demand fer a hospital." He bent and tapped his pipe against the side of his spittoon.

I felt I might be making headway. I got up and began to pace. "You see, Dr. Grenfell, however well we may seem, this parish does have a crying need for good medical attention. If I am the one to bring you this news, so be it." I stopped and looked at him. I could see that he'd been listening with both ears open.

"Well, I'll do what I can," he replied. "Meanwhile, I'm here tomorrow, that is Sunday, and could see people after your service. Monday I hope to sail to Harrington Harbour, where I might do the same. I'll even try to get as far as Natashquan before returning home. I did outfit my little boat with some basic equipment. But this is mainly a trip of familiarization. Nothing can be decided until I get back to Newfoundland."

I know that my face lit up with that news. "Now Dr. Grenfell, may I suggest that tomorrow you visit our beautiful new church over in Mutton Bay? I'd like you to preach, and I shall see that my wardens put it about our village, so that you'll have a packed congregation. Then you can announce your intention to minister to their needs the rest of the afternoon."

He rose from his chair. "Well sir, that's an invitation I can't very well refuse."

We shook hands and turned as Mrs. Robertson announced, "Now, I got 'ere something you fellas'll enjoy for your dinners." She waved us to the table in the next room. "I've asked some relatives because Doctor, it's a real occasion 'aving you 'ere."

No point in recounting our continued conversations over dinner nor indeed how on Sunday, Dr. Grenfell was able to lift everyone's spirit with his glorious and impromptu sermon. In the afternoon, a good many lined up on the dock to receive medical attention.

Chapter Twenty-One

Well, after leaving Sammy John's, I went to check on Owen, to see that everything was right with the boat, before going to find Lorna. He had finished up for the weekend and I bade him goodbye and as I walked up to the house, I went over in my mind what I'd say, joyfully looking forward to what I believed might be the unique moment of my life. And tonight, with the demon rum flowing, might we all not join in a celebration at which I'd announce our decision to wed?

When I arrived, I got the shock of my life. Aunt Minnie sat alone at the table, trying to crochet something, but it was soon clear to me she was only taking her mind off what must've happened.

"Well well, Aunt Minnie, the boat looks to be getting in great shape."

She nodded. Odd she didn't look up and smile as usual. In fact, as I got out of my coat, I glanced at her and saw she looked close to tears.

"Well," I said, "any chance of a cup of tea?"

"Of course, of course." She went to the stove.

"And so where's Lorna?" I asked. "Still working like a demon?"

Aunt Minnie turned and faced me, lips quivering. "No Mr. John, she's left. They took her out to the schooner this afternoon."

I felt as if a bucket of cold water had been dumped on me.

No no, that's much too weak — I felt as if a bolt of lightning had struck. I even felt a bit faint.

She poured the tea and set it down beside me. I was stunned, immobile, my brain trying to come to grips with this horrendous news.

She touched me gently on my shoulder. I leapt up, jammed on my hat and coat, and tore out. I ran all the way down to the dock, not caring in the slightest that I must have looked some fool pursued by the devil.

The place was now mostly deserted, it being the end of the day. One old fisherman, Hollis Mansbridge, Perce's father, was tying up his boat. He saw me standing there, panting, as if I'd seen a ghost. "We all done the bartering we could. She's leaving." He gestured to the schooner. "I reckon it's a good day for us all 'ere, what with all the food and devil's brew she brought. I heard tell of a party over at Willie Reid's, Alice's brother-in-law."

"Uncle Hollis, please, you have to get me out to the schooner. Right away." I looked out: the boat was swinging round; one of her two anchors had already been pulled up.

"No catching her now." He went on coiling his rope

"We've got to try. Please Uncle Hollis. It's so important. I just have to get to the schooner before she leaves. Please!"

He eyed me with an odd look. Certainly no one in Mutton Bay had seen me this frantic before. And then, bless his heart, he shrugged, undid the mooring from the bollard and motioned me down into his boat.

I looked out to the schooner, and then grabbed the second set of oars. "Let's row together. We've got to catch her."

As we started, I realized that he was used to a different pace. "Let's try to row a bit faster," I pleaded.

I kept looking over my shoulders. I saw that the sailors were in the process of weighing the second anchor but they'd seen us coming and one of them had gone to the captain. They gathered at the rail and a couple of the deckhands let down the rope ladder. I reached the ship and clambered up as quickly as I could. I was panting hard from the run down to the wharf and the rowing, to which I was not accustomed. I could hardly spit out the words, "You have a passenger — Lorna Maclean. May I see her, please."

They looked at me in astonishment and the captain appeared. I realized I had better give him some explanation quickly. "I have to give her something," I stuttered. "Very important, she's got to take it with her. Can you get her, please?"

The captain, a much older man, must have had a genuinely good heart. "Don't you worry, good sir," he said, "I'll hold the boat, but I'm afraid, I'll have to ask you to be quick about it. The tide is right, and we must be pulling up anchor as soon as you've done." He spoke to one of the sailors, who went below.

I waited what seemed an eternity. The sailor reappeared, shaking his head. "She won't come." He went to join the others.

Not coming? I stood, not believing. What should I do? Go down myself?

And then, dressed like a princess in her new travelling clothes, Lorna appeared. So very pretty as always, but turning pale when she saw me.

I motioned her to come over so that we could speak in private. We went to the rail and together, we leaned on it, staring out at the village of Mutton Bay.

What should I say? This was my last chance. And I knew it. "You're leaving." How weak! But it was all I could think of.

"Jack, I left you a letter in the house. Didn't you read it?"

"No, the minute I heard you were leaving, I jumped up and ran out. I had to stop you."

"There's no stopping me, Jack. I'm going home. I've had a

wonderful winter here in Mutton Bay. You have been the most important person in my life. I shall never forget you."

"Then why are you leaving?"

"It's all in the letter."

"But Lorna, I love you. Yes, I do."

"And I love you, Jack. More than you ever imagined."

"But I was planning on bringing you home this summer to meet the family. I promise. I've really been thinking about that. I've been thinking about us."

"Jack, you sound desperate."

"I am desperate."

"Yes, but that is not how proposals should be, my love, my Jackie. You are not ready. And that is all."

"But I do want to marry you," I said firmly. "Yes I do."

"Too late. It's too late, Jack. I've gotten to know you pretty well over the last six months. You're not ready. It's as simple as that. I was ready and you were not. What else can I say?"

"But I'm ready now, I am," I pleaded. "Please Lorna, please stay here, be my wife."

She shook her head sadly, turned away and leaned back against the rail looking across the deck toward the gulf. "Those were words I longed to hear for so many weeks. But then, when I saw you weren't ready, I had to prepare myself. I had to go out, work hard, earn my passage. I shall go home, get a job. I'm young, you saved my life, yes, but now, I've got to live it."

With that, she straightened. "I must go. This is hurting me beyond any words that you or I could speak." She left the rail, walked steadily to the companionway and disappeared down into the fo'c'sle.

I watched her go, and then, like one who has been battered by the worst of storms, or struck by lightning, or left adrift on an open boat, utterly stranded and lost, I turned and climbed over the rail and down into the boat, where Uncle Hollis sat waiting for me.

In my room, I found the letter:

Dear Jack,

I know this will come as a shock, but I am leaving on the schooner in an hour. I have been meaning to sit down and talk to you about it, but it just didn't happen. In a way, it's almost better that I write, because I can say things that I'm not sure I could bring myself to utter, looking into your kind brown eyes.

When you rescued me from that schooner, I thought never in my life would I go near another man. I was somehow frozen inside. Deep down, only blackness, and nothing I could ever do would allow me to face normal people again. As you remember, that ice froze my tongue, too.

But little by little, your kindness, your understanding, your warmth, seemed to thaw my frozen heart. And not only thaw it, Jack, but made it leap into flame.

It did take a while, but now I feel almost whole again. I don't know how exactly I shall face the world back in Truro. But your face and your faith will go along with me.

I know you must have asked yourself, why ever did she get on board that ship? Well, the money. No work for a woman in Truro. So I thought I could handle it. Yes, I'd heard rumours about ship's cooks, but the captain welcomed me with open arms, and for the first month I was left quite alone. I even began to cook not badly, and everything went well. It was only those last couple of weeks that those nameless things began to happen. And now frankly, Jack, I can tell you, thanks to you I have almost freed myself from frightening dreams.

What a shame you were not ready. I can't keep on like

this, too hurtful for me, so I have only to leave and to wish you well. You will be, I presume, soon going to another parish. I would have so enjoyed going there at your side. But although I did what I could to encourage you to bring me along, I did not succeed.

I looked down, and saw the letter getting wet. Tears? Oh yes, falling on it. I held it up to read on.

And so farewell, dear Jack. I shall always remember you, always love you. And, I believe, nurture that faith in the Lord which you have given me.

God Bless you, Jackie dear.

Lorna.

Chapter Twenty-Two

What was there left to do?

Should I take the next schooner bound for Nova Scotia and try to find her? Out of the question: I had my responsibility to God and my parish. I could not allow myself to shirk that.

Write to her? What good would that do? Her mind had been made up, slowly but surely over the past weeks. I felt so bereft. As I lay back on my bed, I felt I was plummeting down some everlasting chute into eternal blackness.

I just couldn't see anyone. I stayed in my room, giving Aunt Minnie the excuse that I had a difficult sermon to write, and when the morrow came I took the service without inspiration. Come come, I told myself, here you are, doing God's good work, let that suffice to inspire you as you read aloud the service and preach your sermon. But no, I was lost.

I made myself go back to work on the boat Monday, but I could hardly face Owen. He knew something was pretty wrong but said nothing, and I certainly didn't enlighten him. But then I soon realized that the whole village knew of Lorna's departure. She had been a common sight everywhere, such a striking, willowy, glorious woman with her flashing dark eyes, her black, shiny hair, her red lips and cheeks — oh Lorna, Lorna!

Stop that! I commanded. Every time you think of her, you plunge further into that ridiculous Slough of Despond.

On Monday, after a night of emptiness, knowing I'd never be

happy ever again, I made myself go through desultory preparations to leave with Owen. But these were interrupted by Aunt Minnie. "There's a bunch o' young scoundrels at the door asking for you."

"Schoolchildren?" I forced myself to go right down. "Thank you, Aunt Minnie."

I was greeted by five or six rather excited youngsters. Their ringleader was a thin, blond boy with glasses, probably about eight or nine. I remember Peter as having a grown-up mind, alert and creative, a lad whom I had marked out as my most promising among the smaller students.

"We want to go bird egging," he said. "Can you come?"

"Me? I don't know anything about gathering birds' eggs, Peter," I said. "I'm really occupied. I'm sorry. What about your parents?"

"Our parents is all off working. So my dad said to ask you. He said, he's a clergyman, he don't do nothin' all week, he'll come."

I smiled inwardly. Of course, if you aren't fishing, or hunting, or knitting nets, you're doing nothing. Perhaps to be charitable, he meant now that school was over. So what was I to say? "All right, let me get on a proper pair of boots and a coat."

Off we went. I felt like the Pied Piper with a string of children, heading up into the hills between here and Tabacher where the shag and gulls were nesting. I knew only too well how this community depended upon eggs to supplement their spring nourishment after our long winters. Shag eggs were the largest, but wouldn't fry up, they could only be used for baking with their lighter yokes. Seagulls produced darker yokes, and with any luck the boys sometimes found duck eggs, their biggest treat, for they were larger and tasted closest to hen's eggs. No little murre eggs around Mutton Bay: they nest further north.

I confess the happy chatter of the children did something to take my mind off my own despair; they kept throwing questions at me, for they loved learning. And I kept throwing back the answers. I would tease them, and they'd giggle: a good hour's walk. We came over a crescent and saw, just across the divide, a cliff with seabirds circling, among them a host of gulls called kittiwakes, wingtips dipped in black ink. I loved them, such lovely and hardy birds, small and agile.

"It's over there," Peter cried, and we proceeded to clamber over onto a barren shoulder of rock, back by some woods. The children got even more stimulated, though they kept their voices low as they had been taught. "But now, you've all got to be careful," I cautioned. "I don't want anyone falling."

"Oh no, we never fall, we know how, we've done it before," they chorused. I watched as some began to climb down the sloping cliff to my right, and others gingerly eased over the edge in front of me to find the most accessible nests. I shook my head, my despair returning, and headed back to the woods to sit. But then I heard a flurry of wings and was knocked flat. I lay stunned. The back of my neck hurt badly, and when I felt my head, it seemed wet: blood? Yes, it had been gashed. What had happened?

The children were screaming and scrambling away. A great, brown bird, an eagle, had swooped low, harassing them, protecting its nest. So that's what had whacked me! Then to my horror, I saw it dive at Peter. It attacked the little lad, striking a mighty blow with its claws. He fell senseless. The eagle swooped lower, striking at his head and shoulders with its mighty beak. Then it grasped him in its talons and attempted to drag him off the cliff.

Peter was too heavy, but the eagle persevered: closer and closer to the edge they went.

I rolled onto all fours and scrambled to make a dive at Peter's legs. The eagle took swipes at us. I tried to bat it away. It just rose again, hovered, about to strike. As quickly as possible, I lugged Peter's body toward the woods, but the eagle dove again. I dropped Peter, grabbed a dead branch, swung it wildly, and shouted. As it soared off, I yelled to the others, "Into the woods!"

The children had already run to safety, leaving only Peter and me in the open. Stunned and bleeding myself, I got Peter into the shelter of some spruce, where I laid him down to check his cuts. A lot of gashes. What should I do to staunch the bleeding? He was still out cold.

The children clustered around. As I bent over him, I saw that I was bleeding too, because more blood fell on him. I only hoped the eagle had not broken his neck.

The question was: being an hour's walk from civilization, what should we do?

His bleeding was spurting, meaning that the eagle had severed an artery. I found where to press my thumb and stopped it. My mind raced. I felt my neck to see if I could staunch my own flow. One little girl, Jenny, a bright little thing, came over. "Jenny, feel my wound there, that one, press your fingers, see if you can stop the blood coming." I was already feeling a bit faint.

She did as she was told, and soon let out a whoop. "I got it. I got it, Mr. John! I stopped it."

"Good girl Jenny!" But if I started to carry Peter homeward, he'd bleed again, the main danger right now, and so would I. We had to remain quiet. I hoped he would not come to, and thus remain still. "Now listen everyone! Jenny and I will stay here with Peter and you must run off to Aunt Alice Gallichons', the middah. Tell her what's happened. Get her here as quickly as you can. We'll wait."

The three children looked at each other, very worried, and one of them started to cry.

"Now now, don't worry. Everything's fine. We know how to stop the bleeding. All we need is the middah with bandages and she'll fix everything. So you all must be very clever. You must run as fast as you can for the middah. All right?"

"All right," they chorused and off they went.

Once bandaged up and safely back in my bedroom at Aunt Minnie's, I lapsed again into my former gloom, only worse. Aunt Alice had come after what seemed an age, but in reality was not long, and had brought men who contrived a sling to carry Peter back. I was able to limp home.

That night Peter had revived, and although badly hurt, would live. But myself, knowing that a child had been injured while in my charge, I saw my already shaky self-confidence disappear altogether. Our rescuers had been quick to say they laid absolutely no blame at my doorstep. But I knew in my heart that if I had not been so preoccupied, I would have paid more attention to our surroundings and its dangers. The accident need never have happened.

I felt even worse than in the winter when the dogs had killed that other lad, for this time, I was directly to blame. And what is more, I now had no Lorna to lift me out of my doldrums — none of her understanding, her tenderness, her encouragement. How easily I could reveal my despair to her, back then. In fact, never again would Lorna be at my side, encouraging, making meals, brightening my life with her banter and gay laughter.

How desolate all existence seemed, oh yes! I counted on some form of enlightenment, some way to take away this horrible emptiness, this guilt, and the knowledge it had all been my own doing. I had lost with Lorna; I had failed miserably with the lad in my charge; I was utterly worthless, of no use to anyone, and I wanted to end it all.

And the good Lord, I called out to Him, why are you leaving me to this despair? Why are you not rescuing me? Right now is the time for You to appear in person. Or in a vision. Come now, Lord, all along I have been waiting, waiting for You, all along I have been patient. Where are You?

Chapter Twenty-Three

Nothing for it but the next day, the eagle's wound healing, I journeyed east with Owen to St. Paul's River, calling at various missions on the way — mainly the smaller settlements, for Gene would want us to spend time together at the larger villages. And still my despair continued: every morning I felt as if a ton of lead pressed me onto my bunk: such an effort to get out of it and help around the boat. I did finally confess my problem to Owen, only touching on it briefly. All he said was, "I knew that was it. They all been talking about 'er leavin'."

Eugene and Anna Bell welcomed me to their temporary home in St. Paul's River with great delight. They had been expecting us, and after we got settled, they laid on a grand dinner of stewed murres, seagull eggs, and a fine cake that Anna Bell had baked covered in last year's bakeapple preserve.

I did my best to respond to their high spirits, but I know they saw something was missing in me. On Sunday I assisted Gene at his farewell service. Earlier this winter, he'd been felled by an accident and had to go home to Quebec, but had soon returned to St. Paul's River. He didn't really want to discuss the injury, but obviously, his leaving this community for good now touched him deeply. He assured me that I would be returning myself next year, for that was the pattern that had been laid down over the past few years. Knowing more of these things than I did, he assured me he would prepare a letter of commendation to be signed by him and our church warden in Harrington Harbour, Daniel Bobbitt, to be given to the bishop, one of the prerequisites of my becoming ordained as a full priest. He said he would deliver it to the bishop on his return to Quebec, while I went for my summer break to Shigawake.

The weather held good, and we made it back to Mutton Bay in short order, ministering to the main clusters of parishioners on our way. I asked Gene if he would mind staying for two Sundays, in other words about ten days. Our good people here had finished the Host he had sanctified last autumn, and I had not been able to give them Communion since Easter, when I had unfrozen the last of the bread that he had blessed.

Curiously enough, it was not so much the Bible that helped me through these next harrowing days, but rather, a rereading, several times, of *Pilgrim's Progress*. No doubt about it, I was certainly entrapped in Doubting Castle by the dreadful Giant Despair, and although I searched myself, I could not find the key that I knew must also lie within myself.

And indeed, this whole journey felt perilously close to Mr. Christian struggling through the Valley of the Shadow of Death, as pitch black to me as to him, and equally filled with phantoms, attendant hobgoblins, satyrs, and dragons of the pit. But I drew some consolation from the parallel. It seemed as though the only way to get through the valley was by perseverance.

So yes, the solution: persevere! Keep going, no matter what. After all, once he had passed the Gate of Hell, he did end up seeing a glimmer of light at the end of the Valley. And that was how I came to believe that perhaps I should change my attack.

I went off to be alone all one day, and the next, into the interior, and in the ensuing silence, I made a resolution: commit myself to some form of penance. Physical employment. Atonement.

Yes, unless I started to share fully in the lives and occupations of my parishioners, how could I really return as their full priest? So on Monday morning, endeavouring as always to lift the monstrous weight off me and block the waves of blackness drowning me, I went to enlist myself as a helper on Hollis Mansbridge's stagehead. Though I could not ever bring myself to hope for much, it might just cast aside my ever-present loneliness, this longing for my lost love.

Fishing was in full swing. The day began with their going out before dawn to pull in the nets and empty their cod traps. This year the fish were not being caught in any numbers that would guarantee security this winter, so everyone was worried. Every staple needed to support life was only bought by trading dried cod. In autumn, schooners would pick it up for distribution overseas, either in the Caribbean or Europe. Dried cod from the Canadian Labrador was not up to the quality of Paspébiac fish, due, I believe, to differences in the weather. On the Gaspé, Charles Robin had the advantage of good, clear, drying days, whereas here, fog, rain, and dampness made drying the cod more difficult. But our processed cod still traded for meat, salt pork, spare ribs, flour, oatmeal, dried peas, beans and sugar, and sacks of potatoes and turnips.

This work — I've never seen the like. When I arrived, I was taken around his operation by Hollis who looked so different in his old smelly fishing gear than in the fine suit he wore to church.

I began going out with the boats before dawn and when I returned to shore, the work got even harder: tossing fish with two-pronged forks onto the stage by the splitting table. Hollis's youngest son, Bert, would grab a fish with his left hand, thumb in its eye socket, and slice the cod's throat, give her another slice the length of the belly, then pass it to me. I'd gut it, snap off its head which I'd toss into a barrel, throw its liver into another, and then pass the body on to Clayton, the real expert, who split the fish: in two cuts he'd rid the carcass of its backbone. The resultant flat bodies were then heaped at one side to be salted and kept for a goodly time, after which they were washed, and then taken out by the women to spread flat on the granite rocks and left to dry in whatever sun appeared.

By nightfall, I found it hard to stand upright. My heavy trousers and shirt were laden with sweat and encrusted with salt. But long after dark the work went on, and when I came home, my eyes were red, my hands sore, fingers bleeding.

Those gallant women — I had really no idea how hard they worked until I joined this production line and later became a part of their operation, turning the fish every few hours, covering it at night, uncovering it at sunrise, and when rain came, racing to gather the bodies into neat stacks and covering them, then uncovering them when the rain cleared. Apart from the back-breaking work of bending and turning, the women mixed dough for the bread they baked every couple of days, carried buckets of water from barrel to vegetable plot, weeded the tiny gardens, got meals for the men back from fishing or off the stagehead, carried firewood for the stove, washed the dishes, got scalding water from stove to washtub outside, bent to scrub dirty clothes on washboards. Whew! They even had to make the soap themselves, from ashes and fat, before starting the fishing. And their tiny garden plots, how did they ever build them, I wondered. Well, one bucket of soil at a time over the years.

At the stage, nothing was wasted: barrels of heads were gone through to save the tongues and cheeks for special treats, and then bones, guts and heads went into a puncheon to feed the dogs. What a messy job, as well as being one in which I felt tremendous pressure not to relax, or beg off even for a few minutes. Fish guts slipped off the table so we were always sliding around on slimy footing. Predatory gulls dove at us, screaming for scraps, wheeling around for try after try. Thunderstorms poured down, then strong winds sloughed off their clouds, only to have fog creep in and out. Fishermen came and went, discussing the catch, comparing notes: where the most cod swam this week, off which point or in which cove. But so much seemed a matter of luck.

Of course, everyone working together with mutual understanding, it was all so productive, another reason I found these communities beautifully welded together. So little backbiting, so little ugly gossip, so much cooperation. A unique environment that I felt privileged to have observed by becoming part of their drudgery, though of course, to them, it was good honest toil as commanded by our Lord.

By the end of the first week, nay the first day, I was dropping with exhaustion. But I'd had no time to devote to my own misery, to the fact I'd been brought to this state of desolation by my own misjudgement, botching my life's one great opportunity. The work absorbed me, I almost enjoyed it, though my fingers bled, my hands smarted from the salt, and I was so tired I could hardly think.

After the Sunday services, I asked Gene if he'd mind going to Harrington Harbour by himself to take next week's service there, and ministering also to the fisherfolk who had left for fishing on the various islands around Harrington — Shag, Gull Cliff, and Fox Island — allowing me to spend more time in this tortured atonement. He readily agreed and left his family here at Aunt Minnie's. Minnie seemed pleased to have a baby to care for, leaving Anna Bell time to explore our village properly, which she had not done before.

The second week was just another tumble of torment, arising before dawn, setting off in the chill morning, hauling in traps or nets as the case may be, rowing back to the stage, forking the boatloads of fish up onto it, and then taking my place in the lineup, either at the splitting table, or salting the fish, stacking it, or taking already cured fish out onto the flat rocks, covering and uncovering them, falling into bed at night: all so very good for me, I hoped.

Finally, the next week, I took a fond, almost tearful, leave of my dear hostess Aunt Minnie and sallied forth on Owen's *Evangeline* with Gene, Anna Bell, and their baby to do our duty as missionaries right to the western end of this vast parish.

We touched in and spent time at Whale Head, Wolf Bay, Christian Bay, Kegaska, and Natashquan, giving services, visiting the sick, and doing, I believed, an uncommonly good job of looking after all those homes and settlements left unvisited since midwinter. I did derive some joy from seeing my parishes under such different conditions: no wind now howling about the houses nor snowdrifts covering everything. In summer one could marvel at the lichen blooming and so many tiny flowers and berries covering the islands and the mainland granite.

As we sailed by great wallowing humps of islands asleep in the gulf with the low sun slanting across them, my heart began to soar a little: was not this indeed my home, even if eventually, after another year, I'd be leaving. So curious. The generosity that permeates every human being here somehow reaches out to imbue with warmth the very granite and lichens, the stands of spruce, birch, and alder now putting out their hopeful buds. In the great silence of this North, I could hear the adagios of islands sing out in some prodigal chorus, praising not only the Lord but man's unquenchable will to thrive in this most lovely but also most inhospitable environment imaginable, as my lord bishop had said. How privileged I began to feel in this uplifting beginning to what might be many years of productive ministry!

And to my left, not a boat in sight, not a spouting whale nor lazy seal, nothing to break that deep azure tableland of water. The enormous arc of horizon swept round an ocean so flat I almost felt I could get out and walk upon it, as did our Lord, its hard blue surface seeming capable of sustaining even the greatest host of Hope's messengers. Perhaps, I could even begin to see a gleam of hope that my horrible emptiness might one day leave me in peace and I would be myself again.

In St. Peter's Harbour (*Havre St. Pierre* as it was known) I bade farewell to Gene and Anna Bell and boarded *La Canadienne* for the trip back to the Gaspé Peninsula, where I'd spend a month before returning here next autumn.

Here I was, once again in my favourite spot, at the prow of the schooner — heading south this time instead of north, homeward bound after my first full year as a practising missionary. What a different young man was returning!

And what about my quest, my hope for a personal visitation from the Lord? Well, of course, in my present state of enlightenment, I grew to understand that indeed, He had been with me all along, in each person whom I helped. And that's what I suppose I learned, in all these adventures: to see His face in each person with whom I would ever interact.

I faced bravely into the wind, the scarf my mother had knitted wrapped around, my coat buttoned tight, for even now at the end of July, the gulf winds were nippy. The longer I stayed here in the bow, the more I felt my loneliness lifting.

Lorna would be happy in her home environment where she truly belonged, I could see that now. Perhaps it was right that we had not been joined in Holy Matrimony. Perhaps it was right, and by that I meant God's will, that I should go on alone to fight my battles before I became truly worthy of a fine partner. Now, after my descent into the Underworld, my stint in the Castle, my turn along the Valley of the Shadow fighting the demons and devils that inhabit these dark corners of the mind when all hope disappears, surely I was emerging a better man. Indeed, perhaps even one day, a better husband. And of course, with all that, I should add, a better clergyman.

And now, Shigawake lay ahead. At last I was able to think of home and how much I would enjoy seeing everyone in Shigawake. And after that, my induction into the priesthood in Quebec City. And presumably later, a fine relationship with some woman, happy children, and if I were ever to reach it, a decent old age. But just now, dwell in the present, I told myself. Soon we would dock in Gaspé harbour, and Old Poppa would be there with his next horse, for Lively would surely be out to pasture. I looked forward to the lovely long trot home over the Gaspé hills and dales, along a very different coastline from the one I had traversed this year, one of high, red cliffs, deep forests, and gulls wheeling over lush farmland, on to the Old Homestead with my brothers and sisters, and especially, with my new little brother, Eric.

Glossary

NOTE: The English inhabitants of the Lower North Shore drop their *H*s. And over the years, many French names have become anglicized: La Tabatière has become Tabacher, Baie des Moutons has become Mutton Bay, and so on.

BAKEAPPLE: amber-coloured edible fruit similar to the raspberry or blackberry; rich in vitamin C and widely used for jams, jellies, and pies

BLAINE OAR: a single sculling oar reaching out behind

HOUSE BRIDGE: front veranda

KILLICKS: anchors for nets made of stone and wood

LIVYERS: people who lived year round; from "live 'ere."

MIDDAH: midwife

MISSION BOAT: small sailboat with basic sleeping accommodations for the captain and parson

PACKET BOAT: small boat designed for domestic mail, passenger, and freight transportation on regular, scheduled service

PITTUK DOG: closest dog to the sled

PITTUK LOOP: a shortish loop of rope joining the fronts of the two runners to the dogs' leads

REDBERRIES: a short evergreen shrub in the heath family that bears deep red edible berries delicious in jams, pies, and wines; also called lowbush cranberries

SCULP A SEAL: remove the pelt from the carcass with a skinning knife

STAGEHEAD: that portion of a wharf stretching out over the water from the shed, itself called a stage

Author's Note

My great grandfather fought in 1805 under Admiral Nelson in the Battle of Trafalgar. When his man o'war, the *Bellerophon*, came to the New World, he jumped ship and built his new home in the Gaspé. His youngest son, my grandfather, James, was born in 1835, and my father, Eric, also a youngest son, was born in 1893.

To commemorate these three ancestors, I write this series of largely fictional accounts of a family that helped found a real English community on the shores of the Gaspé Coast, and lived and farmed there for two centuries.

Paul Almond
Shigawake, Gaspé Coast
Summer 2012

Acknowledgements

At the outset, let me say this is a work of fiction (as are others in this series). I have drawn from real surnames who lived on the Lower North Shore (known then as the Canadian Labrador) but none of my characters represent real people, apart from historical figures. If I have inadvertently chosen names of men and women actually alive at that time, I beg their offspring forgiveness. No likeness was intended or implied.

The man after whom I patterned my hero, Rev. John Alford, was in reality my Uncle, Colonel, The Ven. John Macpherson Almond, M.A., D.C.L., C.B.E., C.M.G., V.D. (born 1871, died 1939), the eldest brother of my father, Eric. Although no letters of his survive from that particular time, his story has been recorded in journals. I am grateful to his grandson, Peter Almond, and his wife Emily, for supplying me with some of these documents.

Of all the remarkable help I received, Sharon Ransom, an historian of the region, stands out. She and her husband Jim grew up on these shores, went off for a time, and on returning, used their accumulated savings to beg, borrow, scrounge or otherwise rescue artefacts from early times, as well as developing the only really comprehensive source of how people lived in bygone days. I could not have written this book without their generous help. Sharon answered my daily emails tirelessly and willingly, and even read my drafts to check their accuracy, and added a great wealth of local lore to the text.

I must acknowledge the crew of the Relais Nordic which plies the Coast and bore us along the most picturesque routes imaginable, stopping off first at Anticosti Island, where the deer roam freely about the streets of Port Menier. Especially, with Joan and Ted, I want to thank the chef and also the pretty young waitresses (Maryse, Annette, and Kania) who kindly (and strictly) watched my diet and flung merriment around their tiny mess room.

It makes a difference to how one creates stories when one's reception by strangers is so very generous, as were the wonderful people of Mutton Bay and Tabacher. Randy Jones, the Mayor of Greater M'catna (Mecatina), made sure that Joan and I were welcomed, arranging things with his brother, Lloyd, king of coming and going by air. He also put us in touch with the dynamic Ivan Smith, who not only runs a tour guide service, but also Smitty's Boarding House, Smitty's Car Rentals and even collects the village garbage. Ivan provided us with information and with comfortable living quarters while we waited out the high winds, fog, and rain which marooned us. "Uncle" Russell Robertson (87) kept me on the edge of my seat with tales of his boyhood in the 20s, not so far off in Uncle Jack's time. In Mutton Bay, kindly "Aunt" Minnie Gallichon (now deceased) told me more of the old times, and even found the marriage certificate signed by Uncle Jack when he married her parents, one of whom, Thomas Buffett, was his church warden. I still find it odd that my uncle married the parents of a nonagenarian! Finally, I was also aided by Phil Vatcher, dynamic and friendly long-time church warden of St. Clements.

I also benefited from contact with the lovely Rev. Patricia Peacock's husband, the Flying Clergyman, Archdeacon Bob Bryan, who spent forty-eight years visiting and ministering to the folk along the LNS, and was goldmine. He reassured me that most of these events had also happened to him. Cynthia

Patterson, a wonderful friend and dynamic leader, has been helping me use these books to raise funds for churches along the Gaspe Coast and Lower North Shore.

This story required a lot of delving into archives. Anna Grant, of Bishops University in Lennoxville, searched those cellars for mentions of Uncle Jack. Jim Sweeney, after much urging, sent me a great deal of important information, especially taking trouble to track down Mrs. Bishop's pretty first name: Anna Bell. Contributions from the *Dictionary of Anglican Clergy in Canada born before 1901* in the Archives of the Anglican Diocese of Ottawa were kindly retrieved for me by their archivist, Glenn J Lockwood.

I drew a good deal of material from authors who lived and wrote in the early part of the century: in particular, *Labrador Diary*, the fascinating journals of Rev. Henry Gordon (1915-25) published by Print Atlantic, and his wife Clara who also kept a journal, *Labrador Teacher*, both superbly edited and presented by Archdeacon Frances Buckle (now deceased). The Layton documents, illuminating letters from a missionary in Harringon Harbour 1901-2, were found for me by Sharon Ransom. Anne Carney's delightful *Harrington Harbour*, published in a lovely edition by those invaluable local publishers, Price Patterson, and *Our Lives* (of Labrador's golden oldies) published by the Flanker Press, were both helpful. *Purple Ironweed* by Sylvia Raff, a descendant of one of the old fur traders, illuminated the past. I especially enjoyed *A Woman's Way through Unknown Labrador*, by Mina Benson Hubbard, the first woman to cross that desolate and unknown wilderness and map its northern waterways. Finally, the wonderful photographer, Louise Abbott, fell in love as we did with the LNS and made many trips there back in the 1980s. Her poetic black and white photographs in *The Coast Way* are illuminated by a scholarly text and many verbatim interviews. Our map is based on hers, for which she has graciously given me permission, and amplified by Sharon Ransom. I was lucky enough to have her read and comment on a draft as well. In fact, almost every key event in my recounting of my Uncle's time up there were drawn from real events in these very different books and from my interviews.

An old director friend, Rene Bonnière, with his co-filmmaker Pierre Perrault (now deceased), made a series of three films on the Lower North Shore in the fifties. These were no longer available, so Rene kindly sent me his own cassette. These impressive works recorded vividly the people and their ways of life fifty years ago in beautiful and informative film-making.

Again my old mentor Professor Paul Piehler has come to my rescue with his rather brilliant elucidation of *Pilgrim's Progress*. This important book, read by so many in that era, fits in with his own theories of myth and the hero's journey, the archetype which has inspired my writing and films over the years. I must also acknowledge the snippet from J.B Phillips excellent modern translation in 1958 of St. Paul, published then by Geoffery Bles in Canada.

I am lucky in friendships upon whom I have shamelessly imposed by asking for good criticisms. Nicholas Etheridge, after a distinguished career in the Foreign Service, continues to provide useful insights on all of the books, as do the lovely Diana Roman and Rev. Susan Klein. Joan Dow, a genealogist and founder of the British Heritage Village on the Gaspe Coast, has been a faithful reader of all four, as has her daughter Cynthia. Art P. Campbell, another distant cousin and former teacher at Bishop's College School, (now deceased) made several corrections, according to his knowledge of the lore of the Gaspe region before he passed away; I shall miss our summer visits. And I want to thank Linda Rutenberg for her picture on the cover.

My latest draft was read (and savaged) by many more readers:

especially my old friends from Oxford, film director Peter Duffell and Diana Coleman Webster, both writers and he also a director. Dr. Rex King, who had been in my writing group for years, made helpful edits throughout, and as did playwright Oren Safdie. His father, Moshe, invited Joan and me to his spacious and splendid *palapa* in Puerto Escondido, where I finished this final draft, while Oren wrote his next play. My newfound friend and brilliant Cambridge graduate and novelist, David Stansfield, read the final version and made umpteen wonderful edits, as well as making the map and designing my website with his Quebecoise wife, Denyse. And most important, a special thanks to Miss Whirlwind, Kim McArthur, and her amazing team at McArthur & Company. Kim believed in this series from the beginning and she and her team have done a splendid job of editing and marketing *The Alford Saga*.

Finally, my cousin Ted Wright, my principal researcher and accomplice, came with Joan and me on our Labrador trip, driving our van and hefting our suitcases, and continuing all summer long to be a useful sounding board, giving me great advice and sweeping the Internet for little known facts. He read and commented on all of the drafts.

And of course, the incomparable Joan, my wife and partner of over thirty-five years, a faithful supporter in no matter what predicaments and adventures my writing involves.

Appendix

Most of my material is drawn from imagination, but it is also based upon observations and interviews during my trip to the Lower North Shore, as well as on numerous books and direct accounts published in the Church Society's annual reports and the Quebec Diocesan Gazette. I quote hereunder a few significant passages:

Quebec Diocesan Gazette 1897 No. 1
Mr. Eugene Bishop talks about the work and meeting Mr. Almond. "Here I met our second missionary, Mr. Almond, who had come across from Gaspé on the SS *La Canadienne* on 15 September, having been ordained Deacon on Aug 30th. After walking fifteen miles, when we were within about two miles of our destination, the bad walking led me to say something about the "Slough" in "*Pilgrim's Progress*" whereupon Mr. Almond, who had a copy with him, at once got it out of his grip and read an extract from Goodness and Christian to keep up our courage, and said he preferred such a tramp to "sweating Hebrew."

"In the evening we proceeded to Mingan, whence the Packet will take us to Natashquan where we shall take our own mission boat the Evangeline and visit the places as we go."

Quebec Diocesan Gazette 1897 No. 3
"At length, on November 13th, they embarked once more for St. Paul's River inside Bonne Esperance, where the Reverend C.E. Bishop proposed to winter. After a long trip they reached Old Fort island outside their goal on November 19th an hour after midday, and thence Mr. Bishop sent the Rev. J. Almond and his Pilot at once back on the *Evangeline* to Mutton Bay, while he himself made his way to St. Paul's River that same evening" (p. 46).

Fifty-Fifth Report of the Incorporated Church Society of the Diocese of Quebec for the year ending December 1896
The Rev. C.E. Bishop reports:

"On August 8th, 1896, we became the happy parents of a son..."

"The weather has been very bad and rough this fall, so we have had rather a hard time. Once we nearly lost the 'Evangeline,' also at another time our own lives, but were providentially spared..."

Fifty-Sixth Report (1897)
The Rev. J. Almond reports:
"This autumn we have two lady teachers added to our staff: Miss Lilian Almond [his sister] and Miss Marion Travers [also from Shigawake]...

"I was stationed at Mutton Bay until the 20th of January, and besides my services I taught day school. During the months of February and March I journeyed over 550 miles with my dogs and komatik, down to the Newfoundland district as far as L'Anse aux Loups." Added later: "I have my own dogs and *cometique* and find it very convenient. There is nothing really worthy of the name of hardship, and the work is of a most enjoyable character."[!]

"The months of May and June I spent at Mutton Bay. June and part of July in the mission boat, I visited the Coast line from Natashquan to Bonne Esperance [in the east by Blancs Sablons]... Mr. Bishop, accompanied by his wife, left for the Mission of Hereford on the fifth day of September."

"I was admitted to the priesthood on the 5th of September, and appointed to succeed the Rev. C.E. Bishop as Priest in charge of the Mission of the Labrador. At Mutton Bay, Mr. Organ continues as lay reader, Mr. Thomas Green as our Sunday School Superintendent, and at Harrington, Mr. John Bobbitt acts as Lay Reader, holding service twice every Sunday. Mrs. Dan Bobbitt superintends the Sunday school..."

"The fishing in some harbours has proved a failure the past summer and some of my people will be in sore need of both food and clothing..."

Fifty-Seventh Report (1898)

The Rev. George Pye acknowledges the lord bishop's assistance in getting fifty bags of flour delivered from the government of the day to help the populace through their hard winter. The cod fishery had failed.

WILFRED GRENFELL:

"Dr. Wilfred Grenfell came to Harrington and thus Mutton Bay and la Tabatière before 1900" (ref. *Among the Deep Sea Fishers*). "He came back in 1900 to begin plans for a hospital at Harrington and a nursing station at Mutton Bay in 1905–1906, which in fact opened in 1907."

SOURCE: Sharon Ransom, Curator, Harrington Harbour Museum

JOHN JAMES AUDUBON:
"In the summer of 1833, Audubon, his son, and several friends embarked on the schooner *Ripley* and sailed from Eastport, Maine, to what Audubon called the Labrador.... He was not opposed to hunting for sport food, or commercial gain; he had hunted for pleasure himself.... But he saved his most withering condemnation for 'the Eggers' of Labrador and Newfoundland who caused unbelievable havoc among the nesting colonies."
SOURCE: *Audubon's Wilderness Palette: The Birds of Canada*
by David M. Lank (Toronto: Key Porter Books, 1998)

OTHER BOOKS IN THE BESTSELLING ALFORD SAGA

The Deserter

Imagine you're in a swaying hammock on a British man-o'war around 1800, riding out a harsh spring storm in a deserted estuary of the Gulf of St. Lawrence. Behind those high red cliffs lie a hundred miles of uncharted wilderness, populated only by indigenous peoples. If you jump ship and are caught, you will be branded a deserter – subject to death by one thousand lashes. What can you bring to help you survive? Within minutes, the ice-strewn waters could freeze your body and claim your soul. If this were your one chance for a life in the New World, would you jump?

Thomas Manning did, and his leap into uncertainty begins the epic tale of a pioneer family, one of the many who built our great nation. Through his and his descendants' eyes, we watch one small community's impact on the great events which swirl about them and bring conflicts they must face in their struggles to create homes and families.

Absorbing, touching and full of adventure, THE DESERTER is Book One of the Alford Saga, a series chronicling two hundred years of Canadian history, as seen through the eyes of a settler's family.

ISBN 978-1-55278-977-3
mm paperback $10.99 CAD

OTHER BOOKS IN THE BESTSELLING ALFORD SAGA

THE SURVIVOR

Thomas Manning, branded a deserter from the British Navy, is forced to change his name to James Alford to avoid the death penalty. Determined to forge a new life on the Gaspé Peninsula, he struggles to survive the harsh landscape and win the hand of Catherine Garrett.

After working in harsh sub-zero woods, he saves the life of an orphan working in a sawmill, and so gains crucial lumber to build a homestead out of intractable wilderness. But first he must battle murderous brigands to rescue a starving bull calf he hopes will be the first of the oxen he so desperately needs to clear his land. Finally, heroically surviving Canada's worst famine, he faces down implacable bureaucracies to keep the farm he has been fighting to being under cultivation.

A captivating and fast-paced adventure, THE SURVIVOR is Book Two of the Alford Saga, a series chronicling two hundred years of Canadian history, as seen through the eyes of one settler's family.

ISBN 978-1-55278-967-4
C Paperback $19.95 CAD

OTHER BOOKS IN THE BESTSELLING ALFORD SAGA

The Pioneer

The riveting Alford Saga continues with James Alford, the Deserter, battling old age and ferocious winters, but even more crippling, the departure of his son and only heir, Young Jim, who sets out on snowshoes for Montreal, seven hundred miles away from their home in Shigawake.

Arriving at last in Montreal, Jim is driven by starvation into a back-breaking job constructing the Victoria Bridge. He finds lodgings with an Irish widow in Griffintown, and falls in love. But after a stinging deception, he rejects the bitter realities of urban life and returns to the Old Homestead and its community of pioneers. His ageing father recruits him to rally recalcitrant neighbours to found a school for their children and a church for their worship in Shigawake.

Enthralling and adventurous, THE PIONEER is Book Three in the Alford Saga, a series chronicling two hundred years of Canadian history, as seen through the eyes of a settler's family.

ISBN 978-1-77087-123-6
C Paperback $19.95 CAD